Gooday Nagar

Gooday Nagar

MAITHREYI KARNOOR

First published by Tranquebar, an imprint of Westland Books, a division of Nasadiya Technologies Private Limited, in 2026

No. 269/2B, First Floor, 'Irai Arul', Vimalraj Street, Nethaji Nagar, Alapakkam Main Road, Maduravoyal, Chennai 600095

Westland, the Westland logo, Tranquebar and the Tranquebar logo are the trademarks of Nasadiya Technologies Private Limited, or its affiliates.

'Ringa Ringa Roses' was first published in *The Bombay Literary Magazine*; 'A Writing Competition' was first published as 'Preeti, Prema, Pralaya' in *Mint Lounge*.

Maithreyi Karnoor asserts the moral right to be identified as the author of this work.

ISBN: 9789371970266

10 9 8 7 6 5 4 3 2 1

Typeset by Jojy Philip
Printed at Parksons Graphics Pvt. Ltd

For Rhys Hughes, a more committed writer than me.
He never gets up to clean the house.
'In the middle of writing as a means of procrastination?'
'Sure.'

Contents

1

Return of the Salesman

The town was yet to be called Gooday Nagar. It was a time when the landscape of the hopes and dreams of the townspeople were still just farmland. Their senses weren't dulled by the onslaught of new things. And life was innocently oblivious to a future where it would be labelled charming in hindsight. The town took itself as seriously as it always did.

In this time and space lived people with their possessions. A chronicler might have said they were content with the number of things they had because it was romantic to say so, and the people would have agreed aloud because it was still a time when it was considered virtuous to seek less. Although they did secretly wonder if it would be nicer to have just a little more. And when they couldn't, they held on to what they had.

Gopal Guledgudd was no different. His wife, Hemalatha Guledgudd—who was not Hemalatha Bagewadi Guledgudd, not because her frugality in objects extended to names, but because she wouldn't know about double-barrelling of surnames until her eight-year-old daughter grew up and had her head filled with ideas and cobbled together the extremities of her two identities and emerged as Shruthi Guledgudd Saudatti post holy matrimony—was no different either. Gopal brought home a salary from the local bank. Hemalatha did not. Shruthi went to the only English medium school in town from where she regularly brought home pencil boxes, books of moral stories, water bottles, crayon sets, fountain pens, and plastic vases with plastic flowers and plastic dewdrops that she received as prizes for singing, drawing, essay writing, rangoli, and patriotic speech competitions. Add to it her stellar performance in exams, Shruthi made it clear that she was destined for higher things. Her parents, while secretly proud of her talents, endeavoured to keep her humble by preaching often, if not always, the importance of respect and humility. Completing the picture of the three-generation household, that was the norm, was Gopal's aged father. Gopal's father's thoughts on the possession of objects and wealth were unclear as he had been semi-paralysed for several years and, though mostly functional in other parts of his body, his words came out slurred. So, even if he had known enough words to hold forth on the abstraction of materialism, he was incapable of doing so. Which is just as well, because he hadn't been much of a vocabulary hoarder either. But it is safe to assume his thoughts were no different than Gopal and Hemalatha in this matter.

It is in this still water of homogenous contentment that one day a rock of want was hurled (the last time was a few years ago when an analogue television company decided to use the devil—complete with a triangular cardboard tail and papier-mâché horns on a bald head—as its advocate for the launch of its new colour set. This adversary of an unfamiliar god sold three or four TVs in town and the population was divided between them for the Sunday-viewing of televised epics, which led to a different kind of divide in the future). This rock was shaped like a vacuum-cleaner salesman. Dressed in a smart white shirt tucked neatly into blue-grey trousers with razor-sharp creases, highly polished black leather shoes, and a dark blue necktie; he arrived confidently during business hours to Gopal's office. In a town where the only neckties—stitched knots threaded with strings—were worn by school boys and grooms, the young man, who was neither, drew attention to himself.

Gopal, who had only last evening spoken with gusto before his captivated audience of Shruthi on the mental slavery of Indians in including neckties in their wardrobe—a garment most unsuitable for the sweltering heat of the motherland, despite the cold-country colonisers having left the country politically ('We have independence, but are we truly free?' he repeated several times while Shruthi responded energetically that she would include that in her next Independence Day speech competition before moving on to other topics of equal gravity), put the pen down on the ledger he was filling with numbers and looked up with unabashed admiration at the newcomer. The latter, noticing a ping on his aura, smiled cordially and walked over to Gopal and offered his hand for a shake.

'Good morning, sir. Myself, Arun Sanjay from the Triumph Vacuum Cleaner company. "Why Sweep When You Can Make a Clean Sweep of It," is our motto,' he said in English.

'Nice to meet you, sir,' Gopal said, swallowing twice after recovering from the firmness of the handshake. 'Myself, Gopal Guledgudd, assistant branch manager, Cartel bank. How can I assist you?'

'No sir. You are kindly mistaken. I am not here to seek your assistance. Instead, *I* want to give *you* assistance. Your missus actually, therefore indirectly to you ... haha. I am here in this town, which is a typical specimen of the bandooks ...' he paused at the quizzical look on Gopal's face and all but kicked himself for getting the word for boondocks wrong again (his supervisor had told him a hundred times during training that he should say 'provincial' rather than 'boondocks' as he kept using the word for gun in its place). 'Er … this smalltown surrounded by mother nature …' he quickly corrected himself before going on, 'to introduce the latest technology in home maintenance which will revolutionise domestic cleaning: the vacuum cleaner,' he said and pulled from his leather briefcase a brochure with exhaustive information presented aesthetically, and efficiently, and his business card, and handed them to the gaping Gopal. Gopal studied the documents proffered.

'I thought you must have come from the capital when I heard you speaking in English. Now my doubts are confirmed,' Gopal said and smiled appreciatively at Arun's urbanity.

'Thank you very much, sir. It is for the very purpose of bridging the gap between urban and rural India with cutting-edge technology that my company has sent me here. According to our latest survey, the vacuum cleaner will decrease the working time of a housewife by seventeen per cent and reduce the need for employing a domestic servant, leading to ten per cent saving in your household expenses. That is time and money that can go towards the great cause of nation building.'

Gopal's heart thudded faster to hear mention of his favourite topic—nation building—upon the lips of the stranger who had already made a big impression upon him.

'Today's children are tomorrow's leaders, Mr Arun. And they will write the nation's destiny in golden ink,' he replied with a knowing smile.

After this, Arun had no trouble acquiring approval for his request to demonstrate the magical sucking machine, that made patriots of mere citizens, to as many housewives of

Gopal's neighbourhood as he could accommodate in his two-bedroom, hall-kitchen-pooja-room house.

It was decided that the next day, a Thursday, which was the day of the guru and was auspicious for new beginnings such as learning a new skill (in this case, technology-assisted cleanliness, which, as Gandhi had insisted, was next to godliness) would be when Arun of the Triumph Vacuum Cleaner company would visit Gopal and kindly do the needful.

'You are most welcome, Arun—hope I can call you by your first name because you are much younger than me ... haha. Don't mind. Just one thing, however. When you come, please don't call my missus a housewife. You see, she prefers "home minister" haha ...'

Gopal had no problem acquiring a leave of absence from his office for this purpose. Owing to the temporary absence of the senior manager, who was away attending to the 'family emergency' that was his niece's first moon ceremony, Gopal reported to himself.

> Respected sir,
>
> Greetings! I humbly request to be granted one-day personal leave in order to perform my duties as host to esteemed guest tomorrow (Thursday). Hope you will kindly do the needful.
>
> Thanking you.
>
> Yours Sincerely,
>
> Gopal Guledgudd (BSc, MCom)
> Assistant Branch Manager

He dashed off a quick letter in duplicate, stamped the seal of approval on it, filed it in the manager's folder, carefully folded the carbon copy and put it in his pocket. He looked forward to announcing the news of Arun's forthcoming arrival to his family.

Shruthi, who was sitting watch by the window, ran to tell her parents that the guest had arrived when she saw him getting out of the auto under the large Banyan tree in front of their house. The door did not need to be opened; except for two hours during siesta time, the door remained open all day and visitors simply stood at the threshold and called out to ask if anyone was home in order to be ushered in. Once, inspired by a new neighbour who had moved from the city, Shruthi had tried to shut the door. Hemalatha had told her off for imitating Western ways. 'A shut door turns the goddess away!' she had said.

The Guledgudds smiled warmly at Arun. 'Mister was saying you have come from the capital. Hope you are comfortable in the inspection bungalow. Please come in,' Hemalatha said as greeting.

There were no hotels in this town where the few non-residents were usually just visiting relatives. Although travelling for leisure and pleasure had been invented, not much of either was to be had in this town—or anywhere in the boondocks of which this town was a 'typical specimen'. The rare business visitor usually took one of the four rooms in the government-run inspection bungalow, so named after its original purpose, which was to house inspectors of public works on official tours of the provinces during colonial times. These squat, tiled roof structures surrounded by large yards with gulmohar trees, hemmed in by unpainted stone walls on the wild outskirts of small towns inspired awe in their residents. As the original visitors were high-ranking men, and therefore not without vices, these places were known to serve alcohol and non-vegetarian food. Women and children did not walk past these buildings in the evenings.

'This is our daughter Shruthi,' Gopal said. Introductions were always one-sided.

'Hello,' Arun said.

'Hello, uncle. Nice to meet you.' Shruthi smiled self-importantly.

She was dressed in a pink ghagra-choli of a prickly material with sequin stars strewn all over it and her pin-straight, neck-length hair with bangs was thoroughly combed to form a black helmet around her round face. Nothing in her demeanour disclosed that she had had a heated altercation with her mother only a quarter of an hour ago.

Shruthi's birthday was close to Deepavali. As a result, she only got one new dress a year as opposed to her friends who got two—one for each celebration. She wore last year's dress on every special occasion since the festival, and wasn't too happy about having to wear it again. 'I had worn the same dress when that man who plays the flute was invited home. He called me "Gujarati girl" even though it is a Rajasthani dress! I wore the same thing for the colony's Gokulashtami fancy dress competition where I went as a princess, and they gave me second prize even though I looked nicer than that Poornima only because the judge aunty works in the same office as Poornima's father! Why can't I have two dresses like everyone else?' she had grumbled.

'This dress costs the same as two dresses. And this is the hundredth time you have complained about the fancy dress! It is just a small, neighbourhood competition—not an important school competition. The second prize was a craft box. The first prize was a framed portrait of Krishna and we already have one. Now, let it go. You know we are having a special guest today who will not be interested in your dress but in your achievements. Try and be inspired by him so you can have a bright future!'

Shruthi had perked up at the mention of the future. 'You mean I can also travel from place to place and stay in inspection bungalows when I grow up?'

'Don't be silly. It's no place for girls. Now, before I forget, bring me the notepad. What do you want me to write in your leave of absence note to your teacher? Stomach pain or headache?'

Arun was dressed exactly as he had been the previous day. He was lugging with him a heavy carboard box which he placed on the floor beside the sofa.

'This is the machine I have been telling you about, sir,' he said trying to catch his breath. 'I will demonstrate to you its magic now. Are your neighbours coming?'

'Of course, of course ... we will do all that after lunch. You don't worry about it. First, please have light snacks,' Gopal said. Just then Hemalatha came in from the kitchen with cups of tea and a plate of Parle-G biscuits on a tray. Shruthi followed with a plate of farsaan mixture.

'Bring, bring ... keep it here,' her father instructed, smiling at her fondly.

'No, no ... sir. I cannot. I just had my tiffin,' Arun protested.

'You have come for the first time. We won't let you go like this. Think of it as your own house. Please have,' Hemalatha insisted dutifully.

Arun carefully dunked a biscuit in his tea and munched on it softly, popped a grab of farsaan into his mouth and took a sip of tea. The hosts, satisfied by the reception of their hospitality, did likewise.

'Our Shruthi is studying in the third standard,' Gopal said.

Arun smiled at her politely and said, 'Very good.'

'She is always among the first three in her class …'

'First two,' Shruthi corrected him and her mother glared at her.

'Haha … yes, yes, first two. And we also make her participate in extracurricular activities. We encourage. It is important for all round development. You see studies can be very boring and even though you may score high marks, it is not enough for career. I am sure you were very active as a student, which is why you are in a high-paying job.' Gopal missed the awkward look on Arun's face and went on. 'You see bank job is good. It is safe. But it is not energetic. We have decided that our Shruthi will be a working woman. In this age, we have to treat daughters like sons. In the last exam, she stood first in her class. She is a little bit weak in social studies, but in English and Maths she always gets full marks.'

'Very nice.' Arun nodded.

'Show uncle your certificates,' Hemalatha said to Shruthi who ran in to get them and was back in less than a minute as she had kept them ready for this very purpose.

Arun glanced at the certificates and smiled and muttered, 'Very nice, very nice …' He handed them back to Shruthi and asked, 'What is your favourite subject?'

'English,' she said without missing a beat. 'Maths and science are second favourite.'

'We want her to focus on science. In today's world, if you want to be successful you have to do science,' Hemalatha explained.

'Yes. That is very true.'

'You must be a science student surely?'

'Er ...'

Before Arun could answer, Gopal interjected with another question.

'In your line, do they only appoint gents?'

'Ladies get jobs in the office, sir. In fact, my manager is a lady. But for travelling purposes, they prefer gents because it is too risky.'

Hemalatha nodded approvingly and Shruthi frowned. Arun coughed awkwardly and spoke again.

'Madam, the tea was very nice. If you will permit me, I would now like to show you the vacuum cleaner. When are your neighbours coming?'

'We asked them to come after lunch so you can have some time to relax. There is no hurry. Please think of this as your own house,' Hemalatha said, repeating the cursory offer of home ownership to the guest.

'I have taken full day off actually. There is plenty of time. No hurry,' Gopal added.

'Oh, I see,' Arun said and smiled stiffly.

Just then, the senior Mr Guledgudd shuffled in and fixed Arun with an open-mouthed glassy stare.

'Er ... my father ...' Gopal said, and noticing Arun's confusion over the Picassoesque bearing of his father's physique, explained further. 'He is suffering from paralysis.'

'Oh, I see. Namaste,' Arun said bringing the palms of his hands together.

'Nnnnnstt ... aurgh ... ungh,' the old man grunted and slumped into the armchair by the side of the sofa from where he continued to stare at Arun and was quickly forgotten by everyone.

Lunch was puri, potato curry, coconut chutney, vegetable pulao, cucumber raita, and kheer, of which the guest was force-fed large quantities. He had only just chewed on a digestive mixture of sugared betelnut shaves and menthol crystals and was clapping after Shruthi's speech recital on the topic of 'Science: Boon or Bane?' when a small commotion was heard outside. The neighbours had begun to arrive.

Hemalatha was annoyed that they had come earlier than invited. Shruthi was surprised to see Poornima, her classmate and competitor among the newcomers. What business did she have taking a day off school when it wasn't her home that the guest was visiting? The two girls exchanged sullen looks before proceeding to feign ignorance of each other's presence.

Realising this was his chance to perform the task he had originally come for, Arun jumped up from the sofa and without giving his hosts a chance to stall him further, threw open the box he had brought. The main object inside the box was a dull, red cuboid; it was about sixty centimetres long and had yellow wheels. He called it the 'canister'. He pulled out several pipes of varying lengths, a hose, brushes, and other strange looking contraptions and began assembling them.

'This, ladies and gentlemen, is the future-cleaning equipment. Unlike traditional methods, that involve sweeping, this machine pulls in dust and other dirty things. You can use it for cleaning the floor, carpets, windows, cobwebs from the highest ceilings, sofa sets, under the table, behind furniture, and every corner of your home-sweet-home.'

He showed them how to attach the floor brush to the hose, how to move the canister around as they cleaned the room, and how to throw the switch on and off with their feet. 'See? No bending!'

He held the pipe to his hand and demonstrated the strength of the pull. He asked for volunteers to feel it. Shruthi and Poornima held out their hands and giggled when their palms got stuck to the mouth of the pipe. 'It is very safe, even children can use it and they will enjoy doing housework,' Arun said. He then showed the admiring crowd how to join pipes of different lengths to increase the reach and how to affix the narrowing attachment to suck dust out of tiny nooks.

'It is ninety-nine point nine per cent more efficient than sweeping. You get a sparkling clean home without feeling tired. This is very popular among housewives in America. You can all happily fire your maids,' he said. 'Can it wash dishes also?' asked Rekha Patil whose large family of eight meant piles of dirty dishes that deterred even the most desperate of domestic workers. Arun gave her a condescending look and everyone else joined in belittling her silently. Although the same question had been on the minds of several members of the audience, they hadn't dared ask and it was with the force of relief at not having made fools of themselves that they turned on the one who had.

'It is a dust-sucking machine, Mrs Patil. If you pour water on it means finished! You will be electrocuted!' said another woman in the crowd confidently exhibiting technical knowledge of a contraption she had just seen for the first time in her life.

'I was only joking, Mrs Mathad. You have a bad habit of taking everything seriously,' Rekha shot back and made a face.

'Our vacuum cleaner is a lot more than just a dust-sucking machine, madam,' interjected Arun before the matter could turn into a catfight. 'With this attachment, you can use it to diffuse naphthalene balls and camphor in your clothes and books and other long-term storage material and keep them fresh and free of pests,' he said and gave a short demonstration with a black attachment that looked like the chutney jar of a blender. The whole room was filled with the smell of camphor. 'It feels like a temple in here,' someone remarked and Hemalatha was pleased.

Arun then showed them how to open the canister and replace the dust bag. 'Once replaced, it will be fine for six months. Anything that goes inside will not come out. You don't have to worry about emptying it again and again.'

'How about mopping?' another lady asked cautiously, not wanting Rekha's earlier fate. But she was spared the ridicule as it was a valid and popular question that Arun had answered many times before.

'It doesn't mop, madam. But with it, your floor will be so clean you will only need to mop once every week and not every day ... You can save water,' he said.

'That won't do. Among our people we don't consider things purified unless they are cleaned with water. My mother-in-law will never agree. Anyway, we don't have a municipal water connection. Our water comes from the borewell. There is plenty and we don't pay for it,' she said smugly.

Arun did not want the conversation to veer towards the machine's shortcomings. 'It is the one-stop solution to all your household cleaning needs. One machine, many parts,' he said in the voice of a television advertisement.

'Many parts ... All the world is a stage, and all the men and women merely players. They have their exits and their entrances. And one man in his time plays many parts ... haha.'

All eyes turned to old Ghatge—Professor Ghatge as he liked to remind everyone—the owner of the voice that had made the last observation. Both his son and daughter-in-law were at work as school teachers, and he was the only one who could be spared to represent the family at this important gathering. He had been standing on tiptoes for his turn to add to the conversation.

'*As You Like It*, Act 2, Scene 6,' he explained. 'You see, Mr Arun, as a professor of English, I am a man of the arts.' He waved his hand about at the gathering. 'In the ten years since I retired there is no one for me to speak to in English ... let alone discuss matters of literature in this godforsaken town. I am always eager to have a conversation with a man of learning and refinement such as yourself. Surely, you are a fan of Shakespeare?' he asked importantly.

'Here he goes again,' someone said under their breath.

'Um ...' Arun began when Hemalatha interjected. 'Uncle, this is a high-tech machine. Your literature-giterature is of no use to anybody. Our Arun is an engineer from IIT. Shruthi is also going to study there,' she said authoritatively.

'Barbarians! Barbarians all,' the old professor muttered as he slunk away from the crowd and exited by the front door.

'No one is a barber, here, uncle. We are all upper-caste,' Gopal called after him and everyone giggled.

'Please take no notice of him. He is the headache of our colony. You please continue, Mr Arun,' someone said.

'Ghhhrrrnnn ... trrrrr,' old Mr Guledgudd said from his corner.

'What about guarantee-warranty?' Someone translated for him.

'We have a three-year warranty with free service once every year in that time. But don't worry ... until now, we have not had a single problem,' he said.

He then pulled a video cassette from his briefcase. 'This is complimentary. It contains a short film with the demonstration of the vacuum cleaner. The same as what I showed you just now. In case you have forgotten something, you can watch this. It is in English with local language subtitles. But I see that you are all good in English,' he said, and the audience appreciated the compliment. He held out the cassette for anyone willing to take it. Gopal's home lacked for a video cassette player so he hesitated. Poornima's family had one, and she was quick to put her hand out, but Shruthi pre-empted her and snatched it. 'My uncle is bringing a video cassette player from Dubai coming Deepavali. He said so on the last trunk call,' she said smugly. Hemalatha beamed at her daughter's quick-thinking.

Three orders for the machine came from among the eight gathered families—a high number indeed, as one such appliance had been known to suffice for a whole neighbourhood where people lent and borrowed with ease. Demand drafts would be sent directly to the company in the capital along with the order number, and the goods would be delivered to them by express courier in a month's time. More cups of tea were drunk. Both Shruthi and Poornima sang a song and everyone clapped. Someone made Arun a dinner invitation, which he politely refused. Hemalatha came in from the kitchen with a three-tier tiffin carrier of stainless steel. 'Mr Arun, I have packed dinner for you. Pulao, raita, and kheer. You must be missing home food. They make non-veg and all in that inspection bungalow,' she said making a distasteful face at the last remark. Arun, who was in fact looking forward to the fiery chicken curry on the evening menu, tried refusing the packed food sincerely, but his protestations were brushed aside as modesty.

As the gathering dispersed, Arun also got up to leave.

'Wait, Arun, I will take you back on my scooter,' Gopal said.

'Oh, it's okay, sir. It's only one kilometre. I can easily walk.'

'It is not the distance that is a problem. It is not safe.'

'What? Unsafe in the bandooks? Surely you are joking?'

'Ungh ... ungh ... gow ...gow ...'

Everyone who remained turned to face the old Mr Guledgudd.

'Appaji, do you have to scare our guest like this?' Hemalatha reprimanded him. 'Go wash your hands. I will serve you dinner in your room. You can watch your teleserial afterwards.' The old man gave Arun one last stare and shuffled off.

'Gow? What was he saying?' Arun asked Gopal.

Gopal took a long breath before speaking. 'See Arun, I am telling you because you are like a younger brother to me. It is for your own good. But first, you must promise not to tell anyone.'

Having let slip his morbid curiosity, Arun saw no way out of the forthcoming narration of confidentiality. Gopal spoke in loud whispers. 'My father is an unfortunate victim of an evil spirit. Have you seen that culvert under the tamarind tree near the inspection bungalow? It is haunted by Gowsya—a man called Ghouse. He had been the man in charge of firing the ceremonial canon during the Maiboosaab Urs ...'

'How will he know what Maiboosaab Urs means?' Hemalatha interrupted him. 'There is a dargah to a saint called Mehboob-sahab ... They call him Maiboosaab, these local fellows.'

Hemalatha, whose natal home was a hundred kilometres south of the town yet-to-be-named Gooday Nagar, took every opportunity to distance herself from her uncouth marital home. 'Actually, saint-waint nothing. He was a spy whom our Maharaja caught red-handed and had executed. And not wanting to raise the suspicions of the enemy, he declared him a saint and built a mausoleum for him. They conduct his death anniversary every year,' she explained. Arun was listening with his mouth open.

Gopal took over again. 'This man called Ghouse used to fill the canon with gunpowder and light it to mark the beginning of the celebration every year. Once, he loaded the canon and set the fuse on, but it wouldn't fire. He went to the front to examine it when it suddenly went off. Both his arms were blown off and he died immediately. Since then, he has been haunting the big tamarind tree. My father has been reading too many English books ... this Sidney Sheldon and Jeffrey Archer-Warcher ... I kept telling him not to read ... too much of this Western stuff ... This scientific influence is corrupting ... He did not listen. See what happened now!'

'He stopped believing in ghosts ...' Shruthi tried to intervene at the bewildered look on Arun's face.

'Shhh, Shruthi, you must not interrupt when your elders are speaking,' her mother scolded her.

'But yes, he began insisting that ghosts do not exist and started going for his evening walk there even though we warned him not to. One day, he was sitting on the culvert smoking a cigarette—he was a chain smoker, you see. A man came and sat next to him. The man was wrapped in a shawl. He requested my father for a cigarette. My father is a very giving person and never refuses anyone anything. He opened his packet and held it out to him. But the man asked him to place the cigarette between his lips. It is one thing to be generous but you cannot go touching all and sundry, can you? "Why don't you do it yourself?" my father asked him and that fellow said he had no arms, and he threw off his shawl and started laughing. He really had no arms. It was the ghost of Ghouse! That is when my father had a paralytic attack. Someone saw and notified us, and we took him to the hospital and he was admitted for two weeks. He has recovered somewhat but he cannot speak. That is why I am telling you, don't go alone that side after dark as Gowsya will be there.'

Arun accepted the lift on the scooter. He left for the city by the first bus at the crack of dawn the next day.

The vacuum cleaner arrived a month to the day, as promised, and Gopal and family opened the box with great fanfare. 'It is costly. We must use it sparingly ... Only for spring-cleaning before Deepavali ... or when we are expecting special guests,' Gopal announced to his wife and daughter. It is then that Hemalatha remembered the tiffin carrier she had lent to their last special guest.

Gopal rode his scooter to the inspection bungalow the next day but no one seemed to have recovered a tiffin carrier from Arun's room.

That afternoon, Gopal Guledgudd, Assistant Branch Manager of Cartel bank of the town that was not yet named Gooday Nagar, sat down and wrote a letter to the Triumph Vacuum Cleaner company in the capital city.

> Respected Sir/Madam,
>
> Greetings! Myself, Gopal Guledgudd. I am a customer of your esteemed company as I have purchased your vacuum cleaner. It is a most innovative machine and it has revolutionised cleaning of the country, which is an extension of the home. It is an inspiration to the children of today, who are the leaders of tomorrow.
>
> However, it has come to my notice that a tiffin carrier from my family is in the possession of your competent representative Mr Arun Sanjay. It is made of stainless

steel and has three compartments and has the following engraving: "With best compliments from Shrimati and Shri M.B. Rao". I humbly request that it be sent back immediately to this address via post or courier. Hope you will kindly do the needful.

Thanking you.

Yours sincerely,

Gopal Guledgudd (BSc, MCom)

2

The Bachelor of Artsy Fartsy

'Grandpa, do you want to pee?' she shouted loud enough for the whole bus to hear.

'No.' His response was an embarrassed whisper, but Jayesh could hear it in the neighbouring berth. Although there were no crying babies in the bus, Jayesh knew it would be a sleepless night.

The woman seemed in no mood to give up. 'Go on. Just step out and squat down. I will hold the bus for you.'

'I said no. And don't shout like that,' he said.

'There is no need to be shy about it. Everyone does it. And you are an old man now. You needn't hold on to modesty and such things anymore. Just raise your dhoti and ...'

'Ay! Stop trying to make me pee when I don't need to!' He stood his ground.

'Shhh ... stop pestering the elderly gentleman. We are all trying to sleep,' someone from the other berth intervened.

'You mind your own business. You will know what it is like when you are thrust with the care of your grandfather someday,' she shot back. But she did quiet down and, after a few minutes, all one could hear was the hum of the bus engine on the empty highway at night.

Jayesh lived in Gooday Nagar and worked as a foreman in a chutney pudi factory while pursuing his passion for playwrighting. He was visiting his mother, who lived in a village an overnight bus journey away, during the long Diwali weekend. He didn't miss the village he had grown up in and quite liked the freedom and anonymity of the city. But once in a while, he fell for his friends' romanticisation of his rural background and started believing in the image of his fellow villagers as unassuming people living in harmony with mother nature. That, coupled with his conditioned, filial notion, made him visit twice a year, only to have his bubble burst by his mother's pig-headed refusal to be the picture of serene simplicity. The openminded and large-hearted mother, compassionate and possessing of an intellectual depth that defied the limitedness of her world and education—she was none of that. She was plain annoying and exasperatingly mean-minded.

The last time he had visited her was when she was about to die from sheer stupidity. A diabetic for many years, her theory about food was rooted in none of the available sciences. The body needed all flavours, she argued: salt, sour, sweet, hot and bitter. And if you ate more of one flavour, then you ate more of its opposing flavour to balance it. And if you didn't like something, it meant you didn't need it—and that is how she forewent the bitter part of her dietary plan. Her theory was upheld by the local sweetshop owner that she consulted as the sugar specialist for her sugar disease.

'Sweet things aren't bad for you if they are consumed fresh—hot from the pan—and are made with high quality ingredients,' the sweetshop owner told her. 'In fact, they will make you stronger and help fight every sugar and spice disease on earth.' And he had promised her that his sweetmeats were made with the purest ghee and the best quality sugar. Convinced, she had come up with a more suitable diet plan for her diabetes: a steady ingestion of fresh sweetmeats still warm to the touch. Every time the sweetshop owner made hot laddoos or pedhas or barfis or chandrakalas or jamuns (gulab and kala) or rasgullas, he sent her a kilo of it in a special hotbox. Perhaps her diabetes initially was of a milder kind and that is why she survived the onslaught of sugar on her battered kidneys. But one day, she felt lightheaded in the morning, which she diagnosed as a touch of acid from the extra tamarind in her breakfast bisi bele bhath. Acid is sour and needed to be balanced with sweet. So, she ate extra laddoos to cure her hyperglycaemia. Her neighbour who dropped in to borrow chickpea flour for the jhunka she wanted to cook, found her unconscious on the floor and rushed her to the hospital. Someone called Jayesh in the city and he got there as fast as he could. The doctors had just managed to save her. Jayesh scolded her when she came to and despite her weakened state, she fought back and called him names.

She must have given up sweets since then because she was still alive. And here he was visiting her again. This time it was not an emergency. He was trying to write a play but his ideas had run aground after the first scene of the first act. The woman he was sleeping with who was something of a poet had convinced him to go back to nature to break the block. He had gotten over the unpleasantness of the last episode with his mother and booked himself the last ticket on the last bus to the village. These journeys to the village were mostly uneventful, except when there were crying babies or parents speaking English to their toddlers. But despite the lack of small children on the bus, Jayesh braced himself for a sleepless night, thanks to the presence of the loud woman and her insistence on forced micturition on her elderly charge.

As expected, the disembodied voices from behind the curtain of one of the back berths kept up the banter. It was dinner time and the coach stopped at a dhaba. Jayesh had been practising intermittent fasting and hadn't eaten supper once in the last two months. He stayed in the bus when everyone got down to eat. The woman and her grandfather stayed back as well as they had brought a packed picnic by the sound and smell of it. Jayesh heard the clack of stainless-steel tiffin boxes being opened and food being served on paper plates and passed around. And with dinner came its own chatter.

'Some more bhaji? Here, have another chapati.'

'I suggest you don't overeat the chutney. The bus journey might make you sick and you will throw up all over yourself.'

'Eat the curd rice before it gets too sour.'

'No, no … Not so much fried potato for me. It gives me gas!'

After what seemed like forever, the empty tiffin box was clanged shut. The paper plates were flung out of the window, hands washed with bottled water and long burps let out. Then began the food review. Something was too bland, something else was too spicy, something not quite enough, something else wasn't cooked with the right recipe. It was obvious that the packer of the dinner was not the same as its vociferous consumer and there was certainly no love lost between them.

When the berating of the absent person came to a conclusion, Jayesh fell into a shallow sleep full of strange dreams and voices. The woman from the bus was the heroine of his play. She sat in the middle of the stage delivering a soliloquy about peeing. And then she turned into his mother and began eating laddoos that miraculously appeared before her in a tiffin carrier. She looked at Jayesh through his dream and in the voice of his lover told him to seek nature. Just then, the old man appeared on stage and began singing in a loud voice 'I am a disco dancer! Poojari cycle panchar!' Panchar, panctchurr, puncture! The word repeated like a broken record.

'Granpda, go pee!'

Jayesh woke with a start. The lights had come on and the bus had stopped and there was a bit of a commotion. One of the tyres had a puncture. 'We will replace the tyre with the spare. It will be fifteen minutes. You may go to the toilet in the bushes if you like. But be careful. We are on the highway and there is traffic.'

This time, the grandfather had no excuse. He was made to go out and pee. Jayesh looked out the window. It was pitch dark. He absently played a game on his phone. He couldn't use his phone when the bus was running. It made him nauseous. The woman was on a call now and confirming in precise terms that she indeed had a distaste for another woman—probably the same one as the food packer.

'Exactly! That's what I am saying too. I mean how long must an afternoon nap last? All you need is a lie down and shut-eye for half an hour to digest your meal. Who sleeps for two hours? She is useless, that one. And I have never heard him say a harsh word to her or raise his hand on her. No wonder she acts like a drunk monkey. Yes … yes!'

There was a short pause. And it began again. 'So what if she is pregnant? Has no one been pregnant before? Does that mean you give up on housework?'

By the sound of the curtains being pulled back and forth as people exchanged helpless looks, Jayesh could tell the other passengers seemed to have given up on sleep too. So, rather than struggle, he sat up and listened.

'I have been washing my own clothes. I washed my saree in the shower every day. Not once did that woman offer to do it for me. It is all owing to the slack he has given her. She fears no one in her insolence. And what an awful dinner she packed for us. I am taking grandpa back with me. He has grown reed thin in her neglect. He has to go to the bathroom every so often. I have had to stop the bus for him. Right now there is a panchar ...'

Just then, the conductor called out to see if everyone was aboard. The tyre had been replaced and the bus resumed its journey.

Jayesh sat looking out of the window all night, of which there wasn't much left. A pale halo of diffused light on the horizon—from the day on the other side of the earth lit the landscape just enough for him to pick out the shapes of trees and boulders. The woman, who had taken a break for a snooze, was back on the phone now.

'Ay Sangeetha, we will be home soon. Yes ... yes ... it's a Tuesday. It's water day. Fill up the tank and also an extra drum. Get it from the storehouse. We will be arriving soon and we will want to brush our teeth and go to the latrine and have baths. Yes ... no, the tin drum in the storehouse. Yes, grandpa is with me. We haven't slept a wink in the bus. It's too noisy ...'

'It's Danghypp, sirs .... We are in Danghypp. Who's getting off here please?' The conductor called out.

The woman drew the curtain aside in a hurry and called out. 'We are going to Rottoun, sir!'

'Then why don't you just sit back, eh, my sister? Rottoun isn't for another hour. My call was for those getting off at Danghypp. Must you respond when you aren't spoken to? You have ruined everyone's sleep already,' the conductor shouted back. The woman grumbled something and went back to her phone.

Jayesh grabbed his backpack and got down by the large neem tree, which was the designated bus stop of the village. His house was ten minutes away. As he walked through the dusty lanes of kaccha-pukka houses of a familiar neighbourhood, he was greeted by men and women clutching plastic jugs full of water, on their way to the fields to answer the first call of nature of the day.

'Did you just arrive, my boy?'

'Come to see your mother again, have you? Don't you think it's time you got married and lessened the poor woman's burdens?'

'You have forgotten us after going to Gooday Nagar.'

'Have you had your tea?'

Unabashed by the obviousness of the ignoble task at hand, the people of Danghypp piled their assorted greetings, observations and affectionate admonishments upon the son of the village. But Jayesh, who had been urbanised in recent years, was embarrassed by it. He smiled and mumbled pleasantries and hastened his pace.

While he didn't exactly expect his mother to welcome him with a hug and a blinked-back tear like they did in the films, he wasn't prepared for the scene that met his eyes upon entering the house. His mother was worshipping a goat.

Marigold and mango-leaf festoons adorned the walls. The house reeked of jasmine incense. Bowls of sweet food and plates of coconuts and bananas were placed before a large chair upon which sat a white goat with a garland around its neck and a long vermilion mark upon its forehead. The goat was trying to eat the festoon, but Jayesh's mother kept pulling it back while chanting prayers at it.

Jayesh, stone-faced, stood drinking it all in. His mother noticed his presence and turned around.

'Don't you dare bring your dirty city mouth into my house and berate the purity of my devotion, you whoreson!' she said as way of greeting.

'Have I uttered a single word?' Jayesh said.

While his mother's attention was directed at him, the goat grabbed a marigold and yanked the festoon off.

'Now look what you have done!' she shouted at him and hastened to keep the worshipful goat on the pedestal.

'How is that my fault?'

'Shut up!'

Jayesh sighed and walked into his room and put his backpack down. He drank a glass of water to overcome the dehydration of the previous night. He usually went without water on long journeys to avoid having to pee. He couldn't bring himself to use dirty toilets, and he was paranoid about going to urinate in the bushes and the bus leaving without him.

He lay down on the low bed and shut his eyes. He was tired and thought he would take a long nap before deciding what to do the rest of the day. He had just dozed off when his mother began clanging a bell and singing a hymn offkey. Jayesh woke with a start and rushed out to see the equally agitated goat finally break free of his devotee and run amok in the room knocking into things.

'What in heaven's name is happening?' he shouted over the din.

'I knew your coming was a bad omen. My guru is displeased with me,' his mother said hotly and began sobbing. The goat finally found the main door and bolted.

His mother sat down and wept. 'Don't worry, we will find you another goat,' Jayesh said in consolation. 'But why were you worshipping it anyway? Is it an avatar or something?'

'It was our Guru Maharaj,' his mother said, between sobs. Jayesh remembered she had become a follower of the newest, new-age godman doing the rounds and had been singing the praises of a bearded man she called Guru Maharaj.

'When did he become a goat?'

'The last time I organised a pooja ceremony for him, he had promised to attend. We waited for two hours and he didn't turn up. I asked why he refused me a sighting when I went to his ashram the next time. He smiled and said he had come by but we had failed to recognise him. I then remembered a goat had come to the door and I had shooed it away. Our Guru Maharaj is so pure his spirit may manifest itself in any form. I begged for his forgiveness and promised to be more alert henceforth. This time I recognised him at once,' she said.

'Did it not occur to you that your Guru Maharaj may have chosen a different form for this visit? Or does he always like playing the goat?'

'Don't you take his sacred name with your filthy mouth.'

'How do you know I am not him?'

'He would never take the form of one such as you. Now go brush your teeth and I will make tea. It is the same story every six months. You turn up and make me work. It is not as if you think of your poor widowed mother without reason. When will you get married? You are too old to hope for a bride who hasn't soiled her name already.'

Her grumbling continued as he downed a cup of sugary tea and gobbled the uppit she made him. He knew he wouldn't have much peace at home and decided to spend the day at the farm. The cows would be out grazing and he could catch a snooze in the cowshed that was usually swept clean in the mornings. But first, he had to shower to wash off the pollution of the bus. He had broken from religious ritual a long time ago but this one he maintained in the name of hygiene. He had been eight years old at the time of his thread ceremony. On the days leading up to it, an uncle had told him that the ceremony involved cutting his thigh and inserting a large frog in it before stitching it up. The frog would croak and jump every time he spoke a lie. Little Jayesh nearly fainted with fright. He was relieved to find out that there was no amphibian-insertion surgery and the whole ritual was a rather benign performance of shaving heads and pantomiming begging, among other things. His uncle had giggled mischievously during the ceremony and mimed sharpening knives. Jayesh quickly lost faith in the whole thing. Regular baths and repeated handwashing were all that remained of his brahmin conditioning.

His family owned a couple of acres of land that was handed down to them from a larger parcel that had been divided to shreds over several generations of inheritance among a great number of sons as they were prolific reproducers. His father had overseen its cultivation when he found the time after his job as the headmaster of the village school. After his death, his mother had leased the land to the neighbouring farmer, Saidu, who paid her with a sack or so of corn at every harvest and a basket of vegetables at irregular intervals. It didn't worry his mother as she lived on her late husband's pension. She only went to the land for the Naga Panchami festival, to pour milk over a termite hill known to be the home of a godly cobra. But the family still owned the land, and Saidu didn't mind Jayesh visiting as long as he didn't interfere with the farming. And since all Jayesh ever did there was admire nature, Saidu had written Jayesh off as harmlessly useless.

That day, when Jayesh walked to the farm with a fat volume of modern Indian plays in English translation tucked under his arm, Saidu's son, Milind, fell into step with him.

'When did you come, Jayesh, my brother? Are you well?'

'I'm well, Millya. How are you?' Jayesh felt affectionate, in a patronising sort of way, towards the young people of the village.

'I'm well too, brother. The pure water and air and good food of our village ensure the best of health. We don't eat junk like you do in Gooday Nagar. We may not earn as much as you do, but we live to be a hundred here. Money is not everything you see. Haha ...'

Jayesh noticed that even people who had not left the village had started romanticising it. Such views were quite likely taught to them by television, which had penetrated every home in the country. Perhaps it was the new trend in taking excessive pride in one's own lot that had narrowed down to smaller geographical containments from grander abstractions.

'We don't eat junk either. In fact, there is a greater awareness of healthy lifestyles in the city. It is more scientific. We don't follow superstitions like you do here,' Jayesh said coldly, as his earlier affection for the village bumpkin dropped like a rotten mango from the tree.

'Come now. I was only joking. You took it the wrong way, brother.' Milind smiled good naturedly. 'What is that you are reading?'

'Plays. Natak. They write down what they perform on the stage. It can be read like a story,' Jayesh said more condescending than affectionate this time.

'Oh *natak*! I know natak. We have a committee play here every year. In fact, what a coincidence, this year's play is happening tonight. You should come.'

'What is it?'

'There is a harmonium master who teaches it. The men are from our village. They get girls from town ... real actresses.

The boys practise a few times here. The girls already know their lines and songs. They are so white, so nice …' He blushed at the last mention.

Jayesh and Milind arrived at the community water tank on the outskirts of the village. The poster for the evening's play was stuck on it. It showed about two dozen men, ranging from twenty to thirty years of age, in varying poses of bravado: shirts open at the front, thick gold chains dangling from their necks. Some of them wore dark glasses, one of them sat on an ornate brass throne, another one brandished a machete and tried hard to look menacing. In big red letters of a bizarre, blood-dripping font was the legend 'Corrupt Officer Sucks the Blood of the Very Farmer Who Feeds Him'. Under it an exploding callout screamed 'New Girls!'

'Is that the name of the play?' Jayesh asked, pointing to the bloody letters.

'Yes,' beamed Milind.

'Nothing subtle about it, is there?'

'What?'

Jayesh let it go. He said he would try and make it if he could, patted Milind on his back and sent him on his way.

The cowshed on the farm was empty and clean. Jayesh was pleased to see Saidu had tied a hammock in the corner. He lay down and gently swung himself as he absently thumbed through the first few pages of the book. Nothing registered in his sleep-deprived mind and he used the book to cover his face like an eye mask and fell asleep.

He woke many hours later to the sound of cow bells. He opened his eyes to see a calf staring curiously into his face. He petted it and it licked his face leaving a smear of bovine saliva and freshly chewed grass. He washed his face at the tap and headed back home. He was ravenously hungry.

His mother was watching TV and paid him no attention, which was rather a relief. He went into the kitchen and found three jowar rotis in a round stainless-steel box and some aubergine curry with thick peanut gravy in a pan. Going by the plate in the sink, he realised his mother had eaten her supper, and he served himself the remaining rotis and curry and carried his plate to his room. He shut the door to keep out the noise of the news anchor shouting his lungs out about one inflated non-issue or the other that was supposed to plague the country. The curry was nice. He had missed jowar roti in Gooday Nagar. He mostly bought heat-and-eat chapatis from the supermarket which he ate with either egg bhurji or the chutney powder that his company sold its employees at subsidised rates. Mother may be mad, but at least she cooked, he thought. He warmed to her a little and went out and sat next to her on the cane sofa and tried to speak to her. The channel looked like it had been switched in the meanwhile—or maybe it hadn't, it was hard to tell—and a woman in a bright red pantsuit was explaining how the concept of counting sheep to fall asleep was a Western conspiracy to undermine the scientific Indian philosophy of division of labour. Jayesh reached for the remote but his mother swatted his hand away before turning her full attention back to the TV. Jayesh waited for a couple of minutes before realising his mother was not ignoring him out of some inexplicable spite, but because she was too absorbed in the TV to care.

Just as well, he thought and began shuffling his feet into the sandals by the door.

'Take the torch. There are snakes,' his mother said without tearing her eyes from the screen.

He took the torch that was charging on a power point on the wall and walked out. He headed to Milind's colony. He couldn't watch anything worthwhile on TV. He couldn't read for the noise of the TV, and the internet signal was too weak for him to watch anything on his phone. He decided to see what that village play was all about.

There was great excitement all around and people were gathering in big numbers to witness the year's highlight in terms of local entertainment. There were pushcarts selling pakoras, ice lollies, gobhi manchurian and egg rice. The crowds were made up mostly of people who worked as farmhands and daily wage earners at the nearby brick kilns, broom factories, rice and oil mills. Jayesh recognised some of them and returned their smiles. He suddenly felt awkward and out of place and was thinking he had made a mistake by coming here. He was about to head back when Milind caught sight of him and ran over and grabbed his arm. 'I knew you would come. Let's go in. I will get you a special seat. And don't even think about paying for a ticket.'

Milind took him to an open field that had been readied for the show. Water had been sprinkled on the ground to keep the dust from rising. Soft, sugarcane bagasse was spread out evenly and a tractor had run over it to flatten it for people to sit on. But Milind had a little boy run to the nearest house and bring Jayesh a plastic chair. The chair was placed on the edge of the bagasse carpet. Milind offered to buy Jayesh a bottle of an aerated drink of dubious colour, and Jayesh declined politely. After several rounds of insistent offering and courteous declining, Milind left and headed back to man the ticket booth. Jayesh looked at the stage. It was a cement platform with a painted sheet as the background. The sheet showed a forest scene with brown trunks and green canopies of trees, which housed birds ranging from peacocks to eagles to parrots. A pond in the forest had swans gliding on it and a tiger, a lion, an elephant and a few deer drank from it. From what Jayesh remembered of the poster, it was a contemporary drama about a farmer's plight. The stage setting, not matching the theme, seemed to be of little consequence. He was to discover the same was the case with the lighting.

About three dozen men of ages varying from twenty to seventy-five got on stage and grabbed for themselves the grossly inadequate number of plastic chairs. Some ran into the nearby homes and brought back a chair for themselves. A couple of small fights broke out on the stage, but everyone quietened down once someone grabbed the mic and started calling out names. The person referred to rose to his feet and, without much ado, someone from below the stage ran up and put a marigold garland around his neck. Then it was the turn of the next person. Sometimes, the man reading the list lost count and started from where he thought he had left off causing some overlap. This went on until everyone on stage was sufficiently garlanded. Jayesh sat there watching all this. A woman seated on the ground beside him urged her husband to go up and get garlanded too, but he declined. Then came the speeches. One after the other the garlanded men grabbed the mic and spoke. They mouthed platitudes and such things in bookish language that they never used with each other in real life. Not much of what they said was heard over the din of the audience's chattering anyway. Around eleven at night the speeches concluded and the sea of honoured guests descended from the stage, and the first strains of the harmonium were heard in preparation for the play that had originally been scheduled for eight o'clock. But no one seemed to notice, or mind, the delay. Jayesh had considered walking away in the interlude but had stayed back out of politeness for Milind. As a playwright, he also felt an academic curiosity for this form of theatre.

The lights—probes on pivots—swung into action quite literally. They went from white to red to green to blue and swivelled rhythmically illuminating in turns everything they could: now the stage, now the sky, now the fields on the sides, and occasionally, the giggling audience while throwing the stage into complete darkness. Half a dozen heavily made-up young women came on and danced suggestively. The audience went up in hoots of ecstasy. The men cackled and clapped and whistled and screamed out bawdy propositions and the women in the audience giggled. When the dance concluded everyone but one of the actresses exited the stage. She was joined by a man in a white dhoti and shirt hastily rubbed with handfuls of earth to make it look like he had been hard at work in the fields. Not willing to leave anything to chance, the man launched into a grand speech about being a hardworking farmer who watered the fields with the sweat of his brow to feed the good people of the land. He had just come from the fields and tied his faithful bullocks outside the house. He asked his wife—the one remaining woman on stage—to pour water to wash his hands. She swayed her hips as she walked over to him and pretended to do his bidding. He announced that he was very hungry. And she told him she had cooked his favourite meal. But he said it was her he was hungry for. And then, they danced suggestively. The audience roared.

Jayesh began to grow uncomfortable. He looked around for a way to leave but the excited crowd was thunderously thick and pushing through it seemed less desirable than enduring the play. Just then the villain came on and the audience quietened down. Jayesh knew the actor was playing the villain because with his thick moustache, dark glasses, large mole on his left cheek and the slow way in which he dragged at the cigarette in his hand he could be nothing else. But when he said, 'I may be an officer, but that is just to show the world. What I really am is a bloodsucker of farmers. I take huge bribes from them and don't do anything in return. The harder the farmer works, the more I like tormenting him. Hahahaha ...' it drove home the point in a way only telling, rather than showing, does. 'An honest farmer is like a good meal—hard to come by. But while I wait for one to turn up, I must have a light snack. Hahahaha!' The girls came back on stage and danced suggestively.

Jayesh got up to leave. He could barely find enough ground for a foothold in the milling crowd that was entirely oblivious to the lone dissenter. Try as he may, he couldn't move an inch when the scene changed. This time, it was a young man and a woman constituting the comic relief. They were frolicking in what was supposed to be a park.

'La la la la,' the girl said.

'La la la la,' the man said.

'Hey! How dare you repeat my line back to me!' she said to him hotly.

'Have you signed your name all over this line? It is anyone's to use,' he responded coolly.

She raised her hand to slap him and he grabbed her hand mid-strike.

'Let go! Don't you know who I am?'

'Of course, I do. You are a girl.'

'How do you know that?'

'Because of these two things you have.'

The crowd roared. The duo waited for the roaring to stop before continuing.

'Two things? What two things?'

'Your ...' he took a long pause, 'earrings!'

The audience went mad. It hooted, cackled, whistled, danced and doubled up with laughter at the double entendre.

Jayesh could stand it no longer. Before the actors on stage could break into another suggestive dance, he pushed hard against the people. Help came from unexpected quarters. 'Move aside, you young fellows, I need to pee. I cannot hold it,' announced a senior voice behind him. The hive mind of the crowd that had disregarded a young man's disgust was suddenly fearful of an old man's lack of bladder control. It parted like the sea allowing Jayesh and the speaker of the magic words to slip through. The duo fell to the ground panting as soon as they were out, and the heaving audience closed back into a mass like the flesh of a beast that had expelled a lump.

'Bastards,' gasped the old man. 'Both, the makers and the watchers of this absolute filth are children of incestuous, unwed mothers.' Jayesh turned to look at him closely. He had had no chance to see him properly back there. To his utter astonishment, it was the annoying woman's grandpa from the previous night's bus ride.

'Er … weren't you on your way to Rottoun this morning?' he asked.

'Yes, but I was tired of the constant haranguing by that harridan of a granddaughter of mine. I managed to give her the slip at the Danghypp bus station. I was right behind you in fact,' he said with a chuckle.

'But won't your family worry?'

'Let them. I'm sick of them. They make me feel like an invalid when I'm perfectly fine. Anyway, I am staying with an old friend here in this town. He must have called my granddaughter and told her I am fine. I will go back home after a couple of days. I heard there was a play happening and came to watch it for old times' sake. Hadn't expected it to be such utter rubbish!' he said and blew his nose with his fingers and flung the snot down to the ground.

'Old times' sake?' Jayesh asked curiously.

'I'll tell you all about it. Come join me for a drink,' the old man said as he rubbed his fingers dry on his shirt before pulling out two Tetra Paks of rum with the same hand.

'Er ...' Jayesh hesitated.

'Come now. I'm sure you need something strong to forget the shit you just saw. You would have stayed out for the play all night anyway. You must have told your family you won't be back soon. Spend that time with me. I have many stories to tell.'

Jayesh was convinced by this argument, and they walked along the deserted village street. Anyone in the village who wasn't at the play was fast asleep in their own home and the whole place seemed surreal. Most streetlamps were broken, and the ones that still worked needn't have been switched on as the full moon shone like a Chinese lantern in the sky. The moon's soft glow airbrushed out the plastic and other garbage strewn about the landscape and highlighted the silhouettes of trees and the fields and the hills in the distance. An occasional fruit bat glided gracefully overhead. An owl couple hooted back and forth at each other. The two men found a culvert by the side of the road and sat down.

Jayesh sighed. 'How beautiful it is out here,' he said.

'Don't be fooled by the moon, my boy. There is no bigger liar than him,' said the old man.

Jayesh realised his companion had been drinking for some time now.

'It looks like you have seen many moons in your lifetime,' Jayesh said.

'Too many for my own good,' the old man said and handed one of the Tetra Paks to Jayesh who took it without protest.

He then produced disposable plastic cups from his other pocket.

'No water,' he said and proceeded to pour himself a stiff drink and tossed it back neat.

Jayesh, however, took small sips and tried not to grimace at the taste of the strong alcohol.

'So, did you work in a natak company?' Jayesh asked.

'No company-*gimpanee*. Back in the day, everyone was an artist. We had culture coming out of our pores. We all listened to recitations of our mythical stories and knew all about which gods were married to which goddesses, what penance they performed to beget children, what plots were hatched to conquer kingdoms, what the jealous wives of one man did to the other to gain his attention, who betrayed whom, everything. We assumed roles in the stories and one of our more learned companions taught us dialogues. We practised and we performed during the Dasara festival. Someone played the harmonium and someone played the tabla and we wore anklets on our feet. We put up large gas lights brought on rent from the town for the occasion ... such gaiety, such splendour ...'

'Which plays did y—'

'O mighty Satyabhama, you are as generous as Brahma. Give what Rukmini gave me to further this wonderful drama ...' the old man sang drunkenly.

'Which play is that fr—'

'Three golden baskets brimming with pearls, and shiny silken pyjamas ...' he sang on.

Jayesh took another sip of the rum and sat back as the erstwhile theatre artist delivered the song with more nostalgia than music, not daring to interrupt him again.

'Very nice,' he said finally when the old man stopped and it didn't look like he would continue.

'Yes, very nice were those days. Because of my light skin and slender build, I always played the leading lady.'

'Lady?'

'Of course! Women wouldn't soil their honour by performing in plays, would they? In our times, women were what they ought to be—respectable. Not like these harlots shaking their behinds on stage for everyone to see. Pchah!' he spat before continuing. 'The men with more delicate features played the women characters, and I was always the queen,' he announced proudly.

'What did you wear?'

'Sarees of course. I had this beautiful silk saree—red and green with peacock and mango motifs and a gold border, that was given to me as a gift for my stellar performance by the village headman. I wore that in each play. Until—' He suddenly grew pensive.

'Until what? What happened?' Jayesh was quite light-headed by now.

'My stupid wife wore my prized saree one day without my knowledge and spilled hot sambar on it. I gave her a sound thrashing but my saree was ruined forever. Her bruises healed in a few days but the wound in my heart continues to fester.' He was sniffling now.

'And then?'

'And then what? It went downhill from there. The next season we were playing a grand Mahabharata sequence. I was to play Queen Draupadi. I went to every well-to-do home in the village and begged the women to lend me one of their grander sarees. But none relented. They didn't want their precious clothes to be polluted by the touch of a barber such as me.' He wiped a tear and blew his nose noisily.

'So, did you have to give up your role?'

'No. We had practised for so long and it was the day of the show. No one else could do the role as well as me. We had to go on. I shaved the heads of the others playing women characters and they wore long-haired wigs and dressed in their wives' silken sarees and got ready to perform the roles of servants and such like. As luck would have it, we were one wig short. So I—the great wronged queen whose curse changed the course of the epic, who let her lush tresses flow loose because she had sworn to braid her hair only when it was oiled by enemy blood, who was the wife of five husbands, the epitome of marital auspiciousness—went on stage with a shaven head like a common widow dressed in a drab cotton saree.' He was sobbing openly now.

'We worked with such passion and respect ... we revered the roles we played ... and to think we raised whoresons who make a joke of theatre like these shit-picking mongrels here,' he continued to blabber indecipherable words and lay down on his stomach.

Jayesh was moved by the old man's story but did not know what to say to him. 'It's all right, grandfather,' he said after a long and awkward pause and patted him gently on the back. Jayesh was moved more than he normally would be. He kept mouthing nonsensical words of comfort until the old man's silent sobs turned to snores. Jayesh also stretched out beside him and looked up at the sky. Drunken thoughts, like half-formed dreams, interspersed with theatrical scenes played in his mind. He must write a play, he kept telling himself. A play like no other.

The sun was up when he woke. It took him a minute to realise where he was. There was no sign of the old man but the discarded rum Tetra Paks and plastic cups beside the culvert assured him that it had not all been a dream. There was as much activity around him as one would expect from a community that had sat up to watch a play all night. Drunken stragglers lying around wasn't an uncommon scene in the village, so no one had given him a second thought—if they had given him a first one to begin with. Jayesh felt a crushing hammering in his head. His mouth was dry as cotton and his stomach churned like a semi-automatic washing machine with an imbalanced load. He rose to his feet and steadied himself on an electric pole before slowly walking back home.

He was relieved to see that his mother was on an oath of silence that day. She only glared at him when he entered the house and let him be. He drank as much water as he could without getting sick and went straight to bed. He slept all day and, sufficiently recovered from his hangover, left for Gooday Nagar by the night bus.

He wanted to have nothing to do with theatre or plays or writing or nostalgia or romanticising rurality or anything artsy-fartsy henceforth. He decided he would go to the chutney-pudi factory every day and focus on his work and let his soul mingle with the roasted peanuts, lentils, garlic, chilli powder and salt being pound into delicious condiment and packed in plastic pouches bearing the brand name. He would turn his labour into passion and gain spiritual freedom and transcend from all things worldly, not by moving away from, but by being one with his work.

But as it happened, his hope for emancipation by acceptance was dashed the very day he returned to the factory. Someone had noticed that one of the languages used for the ingredient section on the chutney pudi label was of a ropey, squiggly script leading to a rumour that spread like wildfire on WhatsApp: they were producing the chutney pudi for consumption in a strange country and hence were (in all likeliness) mixing the bones of dead animals into the chutney powder! How could they dupe the vegetarians like this! Production was suspended for official investigations. The factory workers were given an unpaid holiday until further notice. Jayesh, with time on his hands, was forced to brood over his play through no fault of his own.

But his recent experiences had left him somewhat cynical. Plots, he felt, were superfluous, dialogues were redundant, costumes and makeup were pointless, and all messaging was farcical. He had to write a play that transcended all this. The chutney pudi factory remained closed for several months and gave him enough time to agonise over his self-imposed constraints before finally coming up with what he decided was the most ingenious play ever known in the history of theatre. The uselessness of costumes would not be challenged but reinforced—the actors would wear exaggerated, unergonomic and impractical things such as accordion pants made of tinfoil, blouses in the shape of giant tennis balls, skirts made of straw brooms, and even other actors as apparel. Makeup would similarly be rendered ridiculous by overstatement. And the dialogues would be in an invented language that no one spoke. It would sound vaguely similar to real words but it was open to interpretation; the idea that language worked on consensus of meaning was reinforced by the actors pretending to understand one another's gibberish and responding to it with their own. But most importantly, he would pre-empt heckling by philistines by having his own hecklers—actors dressed in regular clothes seated among the audience who would get up and protest at pre-planned intervals.

This play would mean little as literature. It was a play for the stage and he would direct it himself. Jayesh knew he couldn't find sponsors to stage it the traditional way, which is to be rich or plead with someone who was. He wrote grant proposal after grant proposal and finally struck gold with one organisation. He also found some eager college students to act in it.

By then, the chutney-pudi company was back in action after having absolved itself of all accusations, it was employing an aggressive marketing strategy to make up for the losses and was going overboard to recreate its image as a development-minded, culturally-inclined, pro-youth company that contributed heavily to—if not singlehandedly led—the development of the country. So, when one of its employees said he wanted to stage a play, the company entirely supported him by making it compulsory for all employees to watch the show. *Flippin' Hecklers* opened to a full house.

A bulb, with fluttering red paper strips (powered by a small fan) that signifies fire, burns silently in one corner of the room. Some green props that resemble bushes are strewn about the stage. Wind whistles in the woods and the shadows of trees dance on the screen. Two actors dressed in haute couture absurdity sit warming themselves over the fire. The action follows the following script:

Character One: joots hen dudu sink dish manesh ill umm tuyan enn?

Character Two (looks up and raising his hands heavenwards): Knotiny ime choo n'm renn, baid uhl ukks offy. Knotiny ime choo'n.

Character One: ummin uiya gizro eed byo nyep?

Character Two nodded sadly.

There is a rustling sound and a loud bang is heard. Another character steps out of the bushes with a long pipe in his hand. One of the first characters lays prostrate and still. The other one lets out a scream.

Character Three: Goh uttyoot raichars tud anay chunn! Spu wwee n'gnaygay tu-whit-tu-whoo. Eegyumeeg rayt spezzut cheey ood ayd.

Character One stops crying, stands up and puffs his chest out. He gives Character Three a look of scorn and spits at him. He pulls out a pen from his pocket and brandishes it at Character Three.

Character Three throws his head back and guffaws. He pulls a carboard sword from his shirt which he has worn as lower body clothing, and proceeds to hack Character One, who falls to the ground, writhes for a moment or two, raises his fisted hand as if to shout out a slogan but drops dead.

Lights go off and the stage goes dark. Silhouettes of the fallen characters get up furtively and leave the stage. The scene changes. A yellowish, paper lamp with dark spots on it to signify moon craters comes on overhead. Soft flute music is heard. A bald woman, dressed in a leopard print straw cone for a dress, comes on stage and sings a melancholic tune to the moon. When the song ends, men dressed in cardboard boxes with buckets over their heads jump in and push the woman away. They throw ink at the moon and dance vigorously to fast-paced drumbeats.

Scene after strange scene, interspersed with songs, came and went and the audience sat rivetted to their chairs, not daring to blink. The meaning teased them; when they thought they had grasped it, and the jigsaw of the story was forming a picture in their minds, it drew just out of reach and broke the image in their heads into nebulous abstracts. Their hands rose in sudden involuntary claps during moments of epiphany, which was gratifying when others also reacted at the same moment and disappointing when no one else experienced it at the same time.

And then, on cue one of the actors in the audience rose to his feet and shouted, 'Stop this nonsense at once! It hurts my rebellious sentiments.' Then another actor joined in, 'Stop it! Stop it. Down with the writer of this play!' The actors on stage froze and looked at the audience acting scared and confused. Another actor in the audience rose up and shouted, 'Do you take us for fools?'

Jayesh was smugly enjoying all this in the wings. The next thing that was supposed to happen was that the 'hecklers' would rush on stage and pick an argument with the actors. More and more people would join them and everyone who landed on the stage would start speaking in the strange I-think-I-understand gibberish of the play. And before the real audience could react, everyone would break into song. The audience would relax, there would be exhalations of relief and sheepish laughter, and the play would continue.

But a director can only direct the actors. Jayesh's expectation from the audience turned out to be a miscalculation. The audience had been spellbound by the performance and did not appreciate the disturbance by the planted hecklers. They reacted with the rage of an animal interrupted and beat up the hecklers without stopping to ask questions. Along with the planned fourth wall, the entire facade came crashing down in the violence of the incensed audience. Jayesh rushed out and tried to reason with them. But the audience would have none of it. He had to finally let on that it was intentional, and then the audience fell on him for destroying their meditation-like attention. Security had to be brought in to break up the fight and the play came to an unholy end.

The next morning, following complaints by the parents of the beaten actors, Jayesh was arrested for rioting and inciting violence. He had to wait until Diwali to get bail. And when he returned to work at the chutney-pudi factory, he found out that he had been fired according to company policy that considered guilty anyone arrested, even if later proven innocent. That's also when his girlfriend left him for another man whose poem was published in a paid literary magazine.

He would have slipped into depression and drink, and lived the life and died the death of a failed artist had it not been for soan papdi. The flaky confectionary, neither reviled nor loved, hides in plain sight. No one knows its taste because its function is purely representational. Like money, it lacks intrinsic value and its arbitrary worth is artificially created through exchange as it changes hands during Diwali. Someone gave him a box of soan papdi as a Diwali gift and instead of passing it on to the next beneficiary in the chain of the Diwali-greeted, Jayesh, caught up in the melancholia of his situation, carelessly opened the box and ate one. The inertia of a sweet in motion was broken, causing a small seismological phenomenon in his soul. As the first person to have stopped and consumed the formidable soan papdi in its innumerable revolutions around the earth, he shone with the aura of unique revelation. That's when he received news that his uncle, who had terrified him with descriptions of frogs in thighs, had died. And since he had no legitimate children of his own, Jayesh would inherit his share of the land and a not too trivial sum of money.

'So much for theatre and all that culture-vulture' Jayesh thought. He would start a soan papdi factory on his new land with the money he had inherited. It was a self-marketing product. As long as there were festivals in the country, there would be great demand for soan papdi. And if he felt like its steady circulation was prohibiting production, he would bring out new flavours such as jackfruit or cola rendering the old ones, like cardamon or saffron, unfashionable and making the public fall over itself to acquire boxes of the new variant. It was all about the graphics on the wrapper and the PR.

The scales of artistic aspiration fell from Jayesh's eyes. He gave away all his books, sold what little furniture he had, packed his clothes, and left Gooday Nagar for good to return to the village whose bucolic peace no longer fooled him. It would be a place to get cheap labour, and he would ensure his workers never performed plays.

He boarded the night bus to the village with a smile on his face. He fell instantly asleep.

3

Mapmaker, Mapmaker Make Me a Map

The onion juice in her hair had begun to drip and Rani reeked of stale salad as she hurried on with her chores. Parlour Bobby would not allow her to wash it off for another hour. And all of Rani's grumbling about the cold and how the juice was leaving sticky streaks on the sides of her face and neck, and making the lapels of her dress uncomfortably wet, wouldn't budge Parlour Bobby from her resolve in disallowing Rani a shower anytime soon. Although root vegetables were taboo in her kitchen, Parlour Bobby made an exception for onions and potatoes as cosmetics: onion juice mixed with lime to soften hair and improve its growth and potato juice to brighten skin and reduce the dark circles under eyes. Twelve-year-old Rani, although technically a servant, was not spared these beauty treatments.

It was the day of Parlour Bobby's get-together with the other bobbies. The women of Gooday Nagar who wore their sari pallu right shoulder down and not left shoulder up like everyone else, were addressed as 'bobby'. Although they spoke the language of the land fluently—albeit with a strange, stretchy accent—they spoke another language among themselves.

They met every month in the house of one or the other of the bobbies where they drank glasses of Rasna and Coke, ate the potluck fried snacks they brought—which they called 'snakes'—played cards, and made known their opinion on everything. There was no element of surprise in their potluck really as each woman almost always brought the one recipe she had mastered. In fact, Rani remembered them by the food they carried. The one who covered her head with her sari even as she rode her scooty was 'Khakra Bobby'. The modern lady who wore dark purple lipstick was 'Dhokla Bobby'. The fat one was 'Gulab Jamun Bobby'. The one with the 'boy-cut' was 'Samosa Bobby'. Samosa Bobby also wore salwar kameez sometimes showing that the clothes did not make the bobby, and that there was something deeper, more innate, to this esoteric identity. Rani wasn't quite sure what it was. Her own 'Parlour Bobby' made eggless cake. And then there was 'Hobby Bobby' whose house was filled with art of her own making—oil paintings of sceneries and gods, stained glass butterflies, framed knitting, organdie flowers, crochet, papier-mâché masks, and models of houses. She also conducted craft classes for teenage girls during their summer vacations. She was too busy to cook for these get-togethers and always got store-bought chakli or shankarpali but compensated for their poor quality by presenting everyone with a paper flower or party hat.

It was Parlour Bobby's turn to host the bobbies that day and she wanted the house spotless. She was finishing up her last client before getting ready to receive her guests. Rani was on the other side of the door sweeping the floor. But bending over the broom made the onion juice drip more, and she decided to put the broom away and sit down to listen to the conversation between the two women in the parlour.

The floor was as clean as it got and she could get away with claiming she had cleaned it. This was a new client who came to Parlour Bobby upon the recommendation of her colleague. She was in her thirties and had wanted the whole deal—full arms and under arms, full legs, bikini waxing, tan removal facial, eyebrow threading, and hair henna. She had just come back from a holiday with her husband in the Maldives, she was saying. She had eaten and drunk too much and had put on a ton of weight, and she needed to join the swimming pool to get back into shape. For that, she had to have smooth skin to look good in her swimsuit. She would be leaving for the USA in a month's time on important business and she couldn't expect to be taken seriously by her company seniors if she looked dowdy. Parlour Bobby, while nodding along, was in turn sharing details of her foreign connections. She had relatives in England, America, Canada and Australia and they were all wealthy and successful and several of them had come close to claiming high ranking political positions in the countries that were their homes. They had all called her to join them there, but she had refused. Everyone there is light-skinned. Who would have use for her beauty parlour?

Rani loved to hear the names of all these countries. Her geography teacher back in the village school had one day brought a large map of the world and hung it on a nail over the blackboard and with a long stick pointed to the continents and important countries. He also gave them a list of capital cities of these countries, the languages they spoke in them, and their main imports and exports, and asked the students to memorise the information for the exams.

Rani sat behind the door lost in reveries of her time in school. The client looked at herself in the mirror carefully and was satisfied with the achievement of her hairless and lightened body aesthetic. After she had paid and left, Parlour Bobby opened the door suddenly and knocked Rani over.

'Listening to grown up talk, again? How many times must I tell you these things are not for your ears?' Parlour Bobby asked trying to look angry.

Rani laughed. She had been scared and shy the first few days when she was sent to Parlour Bobby to be her live-in maid after her father lost his smartphone and her education was stalled. But upon realising the older lady with the funny sari was kindly, the girl let her guard down and even teased Parlour Bobby once in a while.

'Bobby, do you really have relatives in all these foreign countries?'

'Why is it any of your business?'

'Tell no, Bobby.'

Parlour Bobby looked at Rani for a long moment trying to assess how much of a threat the girl would be to her fib foliage. Everyone in Parlour Bobby's circle carried a mutually balanced aura of perfumed half-truths and carefully woven untruths. It was sacrilege to openly question the other's claim or ask to prove it—what they did behind each other's backs was inconsequential. Parlour Bobby was obliged by this unspoken 'Bobby Code' to indignantly reject such a probe. But Rani was not of her circle. Plus it was unlikely that she would disclose it to anyone. So, Parlour Bobby decided to tell her. It was a bit of a relief to be honest—like changing out of a prickly sari and heavy jewellery into a loose cotton nighty at the end of a wedding reception.

'What foreign relatives? Most of them are here only. In this Gooday Nagar or that Gooday Nagar. You think all that my client was telling was true? I'm sure there is no husband. She probably has an older, married boyfriend who pays for her fancy holidays. It could be her boss even. I don't want to ask her why she is getting a bikini wax—but she feels the need to make up some story, so I let her. It is awkward for both of us when I am touching her in intimate places, and we have to drown it in constant conversation. But at the same time, we don't want the other to know more about ourselves. So, we make up stories.'

Rani giggled at the mention of intimate parts.

'Hush! Naughty girl. Who asked you to poke your nose in matters that don't concern you? Now, go have a bath. It's time for my friends to arrive.'

But Rani wasn't ready to quit the gossip just yet. 'But is it true that people in foreign countries have light skin?'

'Yes'

'Completely? All over and not in patches?'

Parlour Bobby was saddened by Rani's question.

'Yes, beta, they do. But it is very cold there. You don't need a fridge for water to turn to ice. You will be cold even if you wear three or four sweaters. A family from my village tried to go there, but they all perished in the cold—father, mother, son, daughter. They all froze to death at the border of that country even before they could enter it.'

Rani was horrified. She imagined the unnamed country to be like a giant refrigerator. It had a marked border and it was warm immediately outside of it. And whoever went in had to have light skin to resist the cold within.

Looking at Rani's horrified expression, Parlour Bobby tried to change the subject. She couldn't stand there feeding the young girl's fantasies all day.

'They don't wash their bums in those countries. They don't even bathe every day. Do you want to be like them? Go take your bath. I know you haven't swept the house, kaamchor!

Wash up and get dressed. Wear the green frock I bought you last week.'

Rani came from a village a few hours bus ride away. Her parents worked as farmhands and she used to attend the local government school. Her father was illiterate and her mother, who had studied up to the fifth standard, could sign her name and follow the newspapers to ensure she did not miss a single government scheme in order for their daughter to better her lot. They made sure Rani had the books and the equipment to attend school every day. No festival nor illness allowed her to take a day off, and she slapped Rani harder than the teacher if she missed her homework.

Her parents' faith in education hit the ceiling when about three years ago Rani, with no forewarning, developed 'whiteness'. A small, uneven white patch appeared on her chin and her mother thought the wayward child had not been spreading the 'fairness' cream properly on her face before going to school. She told her to rub it in with a circular motion and to ensure that it was absorbed properly everywhere on her face so fairness could come 'from within' like the advertisement claimed. Rani protested that she had been meticulous—as she was with everything else. But not only had the patch of lighter-hued skin not faded, it had grown bigger and the edges of its amorphous shape had turned more defined, making the skin around it look darker than it was. Despite what their friends and neighbours told them, they chose to take Rani to the village doctor rather than to the temple. And there, their worst fears were confirmed. It was vitiligo.

On their way out of the clinic, Mohan, the doctor's assistant who was lovingly known as Compounder Monu, called them aside.

'Don't go by what this doctor says. He knows nothing,' he whispered. 'He is of the,' he looked about him before lowering his voice further '... *special* category ... just pass case.'

Rani's parents didn't know what to say to that.

'Bring her to me on Sunday. I have handled many such cases. If I don't cure her, you can have your money back. I will give it to you in writing.'

The countryside was dotted with the 'clinics' of compounders—men who had worked as doctor's assistants and had picked up a working knowledge of patients if not medicines. They knew how to look thoughtful while reading the pulse; how to take blood pressure and tell if it was high or low and to increase or decrease salt intake based on the reading; they knew the dosage of antipyretics for fevers based on age, gender, and weight and menthol balms for colds; they knew how to find a vein and insert the needle to administer intravenous fluids; and how to dress minor wounds. Since they were not exactly allopathic doctors, they combined their practice with grandmother's cures of poultices and herbs and fashioned themselves as 'ayurvedic doctors'. Compounder Monu was one such ayurvedic doctor who, with his powers of persuasion and placebo, was very successful in this field. He only took on skin-deep illnesses and referred bigger ailments to the various private hospitals in the nearest big town from where he earned a small commission. He employed a midwife to handle the natural births of the village. Caesarean and other complicated births were also shunted off to big town clinics and there had not been a single death under his supervision owing to which he had gained a reputation as a healer.

Rani's parents consulted their neighbours who assured them that he gave good medicine, so they took her to him. Compounder Monu lifted her chin to the light and touched the white spot on her face with his finger a few times to assure himself. He also listened to her heartbeat with a stethoscope and took her blood pressure and temperature. He asked her about her dietary habits. She claimed she ate like normal people, which was upma or poha in the mornings, two jowar rotis, a vegetable curry, a dry dal, rice and curd in the afternoons, biscuits and tea in the evening, and a chapati or two at night. Her mother used the opportunity to admonish her chigali eating.

'She is always sneaking things out of the house. She and her friends take turns bringing salt and chilli powder and jaggery and garlic. They hurl rocks at tamarind trees on the side of the road to fell the fruit. Then they all run off to the woods and crush to a pulp the sour fruit with the sugar and spices to make chigali and eat it by the kilo. I have told her it causes pitta. It is not good for a growing girl. She won't listen. Sometimes the rocks they hurl fall on passing vehicles and the drivers chase after them. If they catch you, they will skin you alive. Why don't you scold her, doctor?'

Rani sat with a downcast, sullen look.

Compounder Monu's eyes widened at this revelation. 'This is what I suspected from the beginning,' he said smugly. 'I was going to say it myself but wanted you to volunteer the information. That is the root cause of your problem.'

Rani's mother looked relieved even as she shot Rani a triumphant look. Now that her daughter's condition was diagnosed to be minor, she wanted to celebrate being proven right. She could go back to being a good mother, which meant admonishing her daughter for everything.

Rani's doting father tried to take her side. 'It's not all that bad, is it? Just a little chigali. Girls her age cannot help being playful. It's the boys that are real rasca—'

'You be quiet! It is your extra love that has spoilt the girl. Will you go to her in-laws' house to plead her case for her travesties when she grows up?' The superior mother cut him short. 'Let me catch you eating chigali again! I will flay you!' Her last retort was directed at the deviant daughter and then, turning to Compounder Monu, she said 'Doctor, please give her an injection on her buttocks. No, give two—one on each cheek.'

Compounder Monu did not give her an injection, however. He gave her a prescription for tablets—to be taken twice a day after meals for a fortnight, a syrup to improve digestion and sleep, a medicated soap, an ointment to be used before bed, and a hefty bill.

Rani's father brought out a wad of notes from his pocket to pay, but his wife pushed his hand back and asked Compounder Monu to reduce his fee. Compounder Monu held his ground.

'The diagnosis was not easy ...'

'What diagnosis? You wouldn't have known what it was unless I told you she ate chigali!'

'Aren't you glad it is nothing serious? The other doctor told you it is vitiligo!'

'And you want to charge us the Earth for this chigali disease? I would have cured her myself with two slaps for eating the sour pulp. Anyway, you are not even a real doctor. You are only a country quack.'

'Then why did you come to me? You should have gone to the city hospital where they would make you pledge your home and hearth for the same diagnosis and prescription.'

'Don't insult us. We may be poor, but we have our dignity.'

Rani's father was embarrassed by this exchange. He pulled out a couple of banknotes equivalent of one fourth of what Compounder Monu had demanded, placed it on his table and got up to leave.

'That's enough now. Let's go,' he said to his family.

Compounder Monu played his indignance further. 'I don't want your money. Learn to control your woman first. Henpecked rascal,' he said hotly and pushed the money back.

'You don't teach my husband what to do. We are hardworking people. We don't live off other people's sweat!' shot back the woman who could not be controlled.

'It's okay, it's okay … leave it be now,' said her husband, and he pushed his family out of the clinic door.

'I'm letting you go because it is you. If it was someone else, I'd teach him a lesson.' He heard Compounder Monu mutter after him. As soon as the family left, Compounder Monu looked at the notes on the table and stuffed them into his pocket with a satisfied smile. He had not received even half of this from his last patient—only threats of exposing him.

Rani and her parents, who had walked a couple of hundred meters from the clinic, were also in a self-congratulatory mood.

'I think you gave him too much,' her mother said to her father.

'Let it go. He has a belly to fill too,' he replied.

'Anyway, I'm relieved it is nothing big,' said Rani's mother. 'He is known to give good medicine though.'

But she had spoken too soon. Although Rani diligently took the prescribed medicine, and used the products on time and gave up chigali, the white spot did not reduce. In a month's time it had grown bigger and another tiny spot had appeared on her stomach.

Her parents took Rani to the bigger hospital in town where the doctors ran some tests and gave her the straight-faced diagnosis: vitiligo. This time no apo-quackery could prove it otherwise. A kindly nurse in the hospital spotted the bewildered couple fighting back their tears as they wiped the eyes of their little girl and uttered what words of consolation came to their heads.

'Shhh … the doctors are wrong. We will take you to a bigger hospital in Gooday Nagar … be quiet now,' father said.

'I will make a pledge at the temple and the dargah … I will fast for twenty-one Tuesdays and offer a coconut each week … it cannot fail. Wipe your tears …' mother said.

'All you need to do is eat well and sleep well. Stop going out in the sun … it will go away on its own. Stop crying,' father said.

'You must have unwittingly stepped on a cursed lemon cast on a crossroad the day after a new moon night … we will go to the guru and have him exorcise the curse … shhh now … it's enough. Stop crying or I will slap you!' mother said.

And so on were their loving words of encouragement to Rani, who sat shocked and overwhelmed by the prospect of having her life shattered by a grotesque skin disease.

The nurse came up to them and counselled them. She told them that the skin condition was not life-threatening or contagious and that it would not affect their daughter's growth in any way. But most importantly, she assured the parents that this affliction that had no known cause was most certainly not a result of lack of care or poor parenting. That consoled the parents somewhat. The nurse then pulled out her smartphone and showed them a photo of a young woman with an advanced case of vitiligo, dressed in a doctor's blue scrubs and a cap beaming at the camera. 'That is my niece doing an internship in medicine,' she said smiling proudly. 'Vitiligo did not stand in her way of becoming a doctor. Now she has got a seat at a foreign university for her master's degree. She is going next month. You can also become like her,' she told Rani.

'Is that true?' Rani stopped crying to ask.

'Indeed, it is. You must study hard and not waste your time worrying about your looks. Looks are not here to stay—we all grow old and grey and wrinkly. But the knowledge you gain remains with your forever,' the nurse said conducting an impromptu TED-talk for the depressed, but impressionable, young girl's benefit.

Rani and her parents went back to the village comforted and encouraged. The only reason it did not turn into a Chicken Soup for the Vitiligo Soul story was the family's traditionally ardent vegetarianism.

Rani's parents put their heads together and decided that they would take their daughter out of the village government school—which was all very well for children with even skin tones and poor ambitions—and send her to the English medium school in the neighbouring town from where her hopes could take wing. They spoke to the landlord of the farm where they worked and he spoke to a relative who had a friend in the school's administrative body who agreed to admit Rani to the school. Another social-worker friend managed to secure Rani a scholarship that covered half her tuition. Rani would have to wake up before the crack of dawn to get dressed and catch the bus for the one-hour journey to school. And rather than race her friends through the fields after school and fling her bag down before rushing back to play until dark, she would now have to hurry to get a seat on the last bus home and hope to return before she was too tired for dinner. But Rani agreed eagerly, despite the big shift in lifestyle, because it meant she could learn English and become a doctor.

But excitement about new experiences does not diminish the sense of fear they bring with them when one is poised at the cusp of the unknown. The night before she was to go to her new school, Rani couldn't sleep. To ease her churning stomach, she drank glass after glass of water from the earthen pot—uncovering and replacing the steel lid ever so gently, so as not to wake her sleeping parents. And all that water made her want to pee. She grabbed the torch her father had got her to check for snakes when she went out to pee at night. The toilet was in the backyard a short distance away from the main house, but Rani simply peed in the open at night. As she squatted down, she held the flashlight in her mouth and the beam fell on her inner thigh and caught another small patch that was forming there unnoticed. But rather than sadden her, it added to her excitement. After she peed, she sat down on a stone and examined her white patches. The amoeba-like patches on her body made the skin around them look darker in contrast. What did this mean? Why did it happen to her? Wasn't there enough colour in her body for all of her skin? And if it had indeed lessened, could it not make her lighter as a whole rather than bit by bit? People who tried to lose weight did not cut off their limbs to weigh less, did they? But this unseemly skin condition was what was going to give her a bright future. Nobody would marry her, she'd heard some of her neighbours whisper. Now, she could have a career and not have to balance it with domestic responsibilities.

'What are you doing out here like this?' Her mother's sudden whisper made her jump out of her skin. Her mother's normal reaction at catching Rani doing something she was not supposed to was to whack her on the head. But tonight, her mother refrained because she was overcome by deep emotion as her tender-aged child was to start on an ordeal for a new life the following morning.

'Yavva! You frightened me,' Rani complained. 'I came out for number one. Then sat down to look at the patches on my skin. Don't tell father.'

While it was Rani's mother who was the stricter parent, and the father wouldn't so much as raise his voice at her transgressions, threatening a truant child with telling on her to the father was traditional admonishment.

Rather than grab Rani's arm and lead her back indoors, her mother sat down next to her, and they looked up together at the night sky. Clouds were a rarity in the rain-shadow plains where they lived, even during the monsoons. And the land made up for its dry hotness by offering spectacular night skies. The mere sliver of a moon did not outshine the stars.

The expansiveness of the vision mellowed Rani's mother's heart. 'Promise me you will study hard,' she said.

Rani wiggled her head to mean yes.

After a long moment, her mother said, 'So, you will learn to speak English now. You will be too smart for your yokel of a mother.'

'Hi, hello, thank you, sorry,' Rani said and they both giggled.

'Let's get out of the chill. You don't want to catch a cold on the first day of your new school,' her mother said and they got up and went inside.

If she found the new school regimen hard, Rani wasn't unprepared for it. She threw herself into her studies. She gave up playing and the tomfoolery and banter she enjoyed with her parents and neighbours at home. She memorised her lessons late into the night and woke up earlier than everybody, made herself a cup of sugary tea, and sat down to memorise some more before leaving for school.

The biggest change, however, was the toilet. Back in her old village school, the girls and boys had divided the wilderness—of which there was plenty—to 'do recess' during the recesses. The girls got the side with the bigger bushes and more shelter. And whenever a girl had to pee, other girls protected her honour by standing watch against predatory eyes: they grabbed their own school uniform skirts on the sides and spread them to form a fan of sorts. With two or three girls standing side-by-side they formed a veritable curtain for the squatting girl who would later stand up and take her turn in the curtain formation for the next girl to do her business. The boys were happy to relieve themselves in the open, as they did it standing up anyway, and all they had to do was face the other way. If an unduly curious girl looked in their direction, all she would see was the tail end of a jet.

Rani's new school was in a busy part of town and there was no wilderness around it—no thicket, no shelter, not even a tree. Although there were two short, and one long, recesses during school hours, no one seemed to want to 'do recess' and Rani felt too self-conscious to ask her new schoolmates about it. After struggling through the first day, she decided to not drink water during school hours in order to do away with the urge to pee. And that proved to be a fairly fool-proof method. Whenever she felt terribly thirsty, she wet her lips with no more than a couple of spoons of water from her bottle. She drank the rest of her bottle on the bus home taking care not to do so too early into the commute.

But learning English did not prove to be as frightening for Rani as her parents had thought it would be. She had been taught the alphabet and small words at the previous school, and she just picked up from there. She had good teachers who explained things thoroughly, and she was not afraid of asking questions. One day, the teacher was reading aloud a story by O. Henry, called 'The Gift of the Magi', from the textbook. He had reached a point where the poverty of the protagonists was being described when Rani shot her hand up and asked, 'Sir, what is meaning of, "In the *vegetable* below was a letter-box into which no letter would go, and an electric button from which no mortal finger could coax a ring"?' The teacher gave her an encouraging nod. 'It is not vegetable. It is vestibule! It is like a corridor from room to room.'

But Rani was not satisfied. It was not the word she was unsure about but the entire sentence. 'Yes, sir. Sorry, sir. But what is full meaning, sir?'

The teacher took this opportunity to enlighten the students about the process of meaning-making. 'A letter-box in which no letter would go means they did not receive any letters. They were so poor that their relatives and friends did not write letters to them because they thought they would ask them for money. In the next part, there is a big word, "mortal". What is meaning? To die. So, what we understand from this is that if you pressed electric button, you would get shock and die! So, nobody went to their house. They were so poor. I am glad you ask this question. You must always clear doubts to understand better. Without understanding, you will not learn anything. Well done.'

Rani beamed at this verbal pat on the back. And that is how she learned how to latch onto the definition of the main words in a complex sentence to form an abstract image that would give her the whole picture. Before long, not only had she come up to par with the other children who had been learning the language much before her, but she was coaching her new friends on the nuances of it.

She explained to them things they had accepted without question. The morning school prayer, for instance, addressed to the father in heaven, was not asking that their father go to heaven, but it was a plea against orphanhood, Rani told her new friends. But for those who had already lost their fathers, well … their fathers were already there, so they addressed their fathers in heaven and sought favours that earthly fathers couldn't grant. Rani also taught them that they had been pronouncing the last word all wrong. It was not 'a men'. That was grammatically incorrect. It had to be 'a man'. What was the phrase doing there? One hoped to remain a man for ever and ever, didn't they? As girls, they were supposed to say 'woman' but to avoid being caned by the teachers, they had to say the 'wo' under their breaths.

The evening prayer was a much shorter one. It was a three-line verse that sounded like a collective murmur of strange phrases, which is what it was as no one quite knew the words. The prayers may have been taught to the first batch of students who took admission in the school and the following classes were expected to pick it up from them. As batch after batch of students graduated from high school and left in search of pastures of various hues, the following students inherited little more than a collection of sounds and intonations. And as there was safety in numbers, everyone shirked the responsibility of knowing the words and decided to lend voice, but not meaning, to the hasty recitation before running home. The prayer, therefore, went 'ee ew ee ax, ol-my-tee-go, froll d ice, froll d enchy wee chew sewed rom die ountee'!

Dextrous Rani dwelled on the prayer long and hard and gathered all her friends around her to explain the real words: 'We give the tax, for all my tea God, for all the nice, for all the benches which we received from that donkey'! And the explanation went thus: The school fees were akin to taxes, were they not? The last school she attended was exempt from fees, as it was government run, whereas this one charged a big fee and it was taxing to the parents. And rushing to school in the mornings meant forgoing a proper breakfast. Most children barely managed to eat a few biscuits with their morning cup of tea while others did not get even that. So, you asked God for tea. And it was nice here, wasn't it? Hence the word nice. Also, they had benches unlike the students of other schools who sat cross-legged on the floor for their lessons. The donkey bit was harder to explain and the process was rather convoluted, but she succeeded anyway: the donkey was unjustly derided as a stupid animal. It was, in fact, a most peaceable and hardworking one (hadn't they seen the hundreds of donkeys employed in the brick kiln between the bus stop and the school? They carried terrible loads on their backs without complaint). It ought to be a role model for the children in the school who were being told to emulate the animal in their strife for education.

Thus, meaning was given with confidence and received in good faith, and the students began reciting the prayer more loudly and clearly than they had dared in the past. Disconcerted by the new zeal in the evening prayers, a teacher pulled one of the students aside and made her repeat what she was saying. The student did so with great self-assurance and received a sound thrashing. When the punished student told the teacher that it was Rani who taught the prayer to her, the student was beaten again. 'She told you and you listened, eh? Haven't you got a head of your own?' The other teachers approved of his actions, but when they nominated him to give the erring students the correct version and take the problem of prayer to its logical conclusion, the teacher found his bravado wavering. 'Er ... um ... it's late and they might miss their bus back home. I will teach it to them tomorrow.'

The teacher took a leave of absence from school the next day to dig deep in his files and papers to find the words of the prayer. When he returned to school, he wrote the prayer on the blackboard and asked the students to copy the words down in their notebooks: 'We give thee thanks, O almighty God, for all the grace, for all the benefits which we have received from thy bounty'.

'Memorise it and say it properly. Anyone who messes with it will receive a skinning!'

Rani lost many friends that day. The one who had received the punishment turned out to be extra bitter and became head of the group that was formed for the express purpose of taunting Rani for her vitiligo.

But rather than be morose, the friendless Rani grew more defiant and determined in her goal for academic excellence in the newfound language. She sat alone in a corner of the playground as the other girls played lagori and hopscotch and the boys cricket, and did her sums or memorised her lessons. Soon she began doing better in her exams than her belligerent classmates and that made them hate her more.

While her dream education happened in this manner, her vitiligo continued to steadily develop. White patches appeared and expanded—too slow for the naked eye but fast enough for Rani to feel that her skin was a changing landscape. The patterns of this week were not the patterns of the past week. Vitiligo gave ten-year-old Rani a crash course in flux and impermanence that birth, growth, aging, and death took a lifetime to teach. Her joy and pride in education was balanced by a sense of gravity that her skin condition imposed on her young mind, and this gave her a dignity far beyond her years.

Her parents kept up their encouragement and faith in learning, and they did not give up on their quest for a solution for her vitiligo. Every doctor they consulted told them there was no cure; however, it was impossible to silence the voices of well-meaning friends, neighbours and countrymen who kept up a constant stream of testimonials of miracle cures that they had heard about far and wide and insisted Rani try them. Although Rani's parents relented out of politeness, they did harbour a secret hope that the next treatment or ritual would be the right one. Thus, Rani came to wear amulets with special spells cast on them and rings blessed by holy men of every description. She was rubbed with ashes, anointed with oils, made to drink herbal concoctions, and forced to give up this food, moderate that food, and load up on another food. She went through all of this without comment.

One day, her geography teacher brought a large, rolled-up print to class and hung it over the blackboard. 'This is the map of the world. The Earth is spherical, but imagine you could cut it open with a knife and spread out the top surface on a large sheet. This is how it would look. This is the North Pole.' He tapped the topmost part of the scroll with his long stick. 'And this is the South Pole. And this is the equator that divides the world into the northern and southern hemispheres,' he said. 'And this is our beloved motherland India, the best country in the world,' he said pointing to the green peninsula jutting into the blue sea with the drop-shaped Sri Lanka beneath. It was a geographical map and political borders were faint and all the land on Earth looked like one solid, interconnected mass with varying shades of colour for different types of terrain. The bottom part had an amorphous white patch like a spill of whitener. The islands looked like parts cut off from the nearest mainland floating in the sea. The students had a colour map of the world in their textbook but this large one was more fascinating.

The teacher divided the class into six groups of nine students and assigned them each a continent. He instructed each group to come up to the board and study their respective regions for five minutes. Their project for the next week was to learn the names of the major countries in their assigned continent, their capital cities, the languages they spoke, and other primary data, and make a presentation on it.

'What about Antarctica, sir?' a student asked.

After soundly insulting that student for not knowing what wasn't taught, the teacher went on to explain why they were not studying Antarctica just yet. 'There are no countries there. It is only ice. That is why it is white. You can study it in higher classes. In your syllabus for this year you are only required to study the other six continents,' he said.

Rani's group was given North America. Since there were nineteen girls in a class of fifty-four students, the other eighteen girls formed two groups and left Rani out. And that was a huge relief as the girls weren't her friends and would have put her down had they been in the same group as her. The boys she was teamed with were friendly, in a guarded sort of way, and they gave her a wide berth. She went home reeling with excitement at the forthcoming project.

After a hasty supper, she went to the corner of the room where the family slept and sat down with her geography textbook. She gazed at the world map under the solar-powered reading lamp and traced the outline of the continents with her finger. Then, as if remembering something, she got up and grabbed her torch to head to the backyard when her father, having downed a well-deserved drink or two after a long day's work, staggered in and beamed at her.

'My little Rani … issh learning Inglees … one day you will become beeg … offisher … and everyone will shtand to ash … asshenshun and shlute you. Only yeshterday she was thish high,' he said and held his hand about half a foot from the ground grossly underestimating her height as a baby.

'Shh … appa, go to sleep. It's late,' said Rani. Her mother was doing the dishes outside and had no patience for her husband's shenanigans. He sat on the common mattress on the floor, glassily smiling at his daughter, and persisted with his maudlin monologue. 'They will have to call you "madam" …. "Rani madam … " they will shay with bowed heads, and my head will go high for being your father … you won't forget your poor old father then, will you?' At that his voice cracked and he began sobbing.

'That's enough now. Go to sleep,' she said and gently pushed him back on the bed and covered him with a blanket. He continued to mutter and sob with his eyes closed.

'What shins did I commit for my darling baby to be afflicted with this horrible disheesh? Tish not your fault, my child … sniff sniff … But itsh all for the good. You are born in a poor mansh housh with the dark shkin of people who live and work under the shun. But God hash better plansh for you. He wantsh that you have white shk- shk- shkin … like the foren … forennersh … and have good life of eash and plenty … Only, he ish giving it a little at a time … You will be completely … completely white one day, jushyouwait … Rani madam … just … yuuu …. rrrmff …' He had fallen into a drunken sleep.

Rani sat there frowning thoughtfully at her father's last words when her mother walked in.

'Your father is such a cry-baby. I might as well have married a woman,' she snorted. 'Turn off the light and come to bed. I'm so tired, my arms might fall off.'

Rani snuggled in next to her mother, but couldn't fall asleep. As soon as she heard her mother's first snore, she slowly pushed her arm away, crept up, and grabbed her torch and tiptoed out to the backyard. There, she sat on a rock and lifted her dress up. She shone the beam of the torch on her belly. What had been shapeless blotches of whiteness forming on her naturally dusky skin now seemed like the contrast between water and land on the map she had just been studying. She looked at her skin with fascination and thought of her father's recent inebriated words. Was she actually going to become a foreigner? A white woman who lived in a country that was forming on her skin? She would have to work hard to polish and perfect her English. Would she actually be addressed as 'madam' when that happened?

She sat spellbound by these strange new reveries. The pain of loneliness covered up with proud defiance, the meanness of schoolmates, fear of ugliness, everything fell away as she looked into the darkness around her and sensed hope and joy of a new kind. She sat there until her eyes grew heavy with sleep and she rose to head to bed and her mother's arms.

Rani prepared for her presentation with great zeal. Finding the information in her textbook inadequate, she took her father's smartphone, which he used mainly to take photos and to listen to music while he worked, to research more about the countries of the North American continent. She prepared a list of data and facts far longer than the others in her class: since there weren't too many countries in the continent she was given, unlike the group studying Europe, she also memorised and recited the names of the states of the USA. Either owing to sympathy for Rani's skin condition or because he was himself fascinated by all the new information, for once, the teacher did not take offence at a student being 'over smart' and his praise was not laced with admonishment for insubordination. 'Very good, Rani. It is a best presentation. You have shown that hard work and dedication is the path to success. One day you may even go to these countries. Look at her and feel some shame,' he said. His conclusion was directed at the other students who had merely copied large portions from the textbook and quoted it verbatim. This brought Rani grudging respect from members of her own group, which had scored higher marks than the rest thanks to her Columbus-like exploratory fervour, and greater hatred from the girls. But Rani was beyond caring. She had discovered a most fascinating secret: her own skin as the map of her destiny.

Every night she waited for her parents to fall asleep to sneak out and gaze at the skin on her belly and on her thighs under the beam of the torch. The vitiligo's changing contours were like secret messages from a big-hearted sender with a mischievous smile who watched over her. The patches resembled landmasses contrasting with the water: peninsulas, gulfs, lakes, and isthmuses that slowly disintegrated and stretched until islands broke away and turned into archipelagos. These were the countries of the world, places she would go to. And soon, she would transform into a white person.

But unlike the continental shift happening on her skin, an event that would change their lives happened with the suddenness of an asteroid impact. A disease that had started as a mere rumour in a distant part of the world came to town like a crashing plane. At first everyone teased the group that had spoken about China in the geography class presentation and called them 'corona' and 'chinki' and 'hakka noodles'. Then, the strange new disease claimed its first victim in the village. She was an eighty-year-old asthma-patient, so that didn't alarm them. The next one was a thirty-year-old flour mill owner who had been full of life and health until the day before the infection struck. A strict lockdown was announced by the government within a week of his death. All schools, offices, and public places were shut down with immediate effect. Public transport was suspended and people were confined to their homes. Rani and her parents were better off than most, as they lived away from the village and their need for human contact was minimum. They were given rationed supplies by the authorities, they grew their own vegetables and their employer helped them with other needs.

No one knew what was going on or how long the carnage would last, and the suspension of Rani's education and her dreams were the least of anyone's problems. Rani stayed home and read and reread her school books, helped her mother with her chores and tried not to think too much about her future. If she was depressed, it was but a little drop in the ocean of depression that the world was battling and, hence, got little attention.

A couple of months after the chaos and uncertainty settled into a more familiar rhythm, they received a message from her school that classes would resume 'online' and students and their parents were required to attend a short, in-person training session on the use of smartphones to attend classes. Rani's family was given a time and a date to attend the session and they were warned that they were to adhere to the time strictly—a minute late and they would be refused admission. 'Everyone must wear a mask and carry a bottle of hand sanitiser, maintain social distance and avoid contact at all costs. And don't forget to bring your smartphone,' the message read.

Rani was to attend the session at 2 p.m. Her father borrowed his neighbour's motorcycle for that purpose. The town was deserted. Even the school grounds seemed ghostly when they entered. An attender, seated near the gate, gestured to them to wait at a distance and instructed them on the behaviour during the session. Then they entered a classroom, sat at the last desk, and a teacher who sat far away from them used a projector on the blackboard to show them how to use video-conferencing software for online classes. The teacher then asked Rani to approach the table and leave her father's phone on it. After thoroughly cleaning the phone with a spray, the teacher installed the free software and again thoroughly cleaned the phone before handing it back to Rani. Classes would be for four hours a day, five days a week and the schedule would be shared on a messaging group.

Rani went home with renewed hope. Once again, her loving parents set up a corner of the house for her home-based school. Her father fashioned a desk out of a carton where Rani sat cross-legged on a mat, her textbooks strewn around her as she made notes on her notebook, which she balanced on her lap. The phone, connected to a charging point, was propped up on the box. The video was grainy and the sound cracked and rasped, but that was what everyone else was getting, and she didn't feel she was being denied opportunities available to others. She liked the lack of physical proximity to her vicious classmates, moreover.

News of death and sickness began to come too frequently for it to seem like something that happened to other people. While this strangeness drove some people inward, others gave loud vent to their anxieties and annoyed everyone else who were just holding it in. Rani's father was of the latter disposition. And he missed his drink most of all. Sale of all liquor was banned and shops were shut indefinitely. His desperation was driven higher at the sight of Motya, the village drunk, who lived in a hovel by the edge of the village; Motya did not miss his inebriation. Although one was not to touch or visit Motya's hovel and acquire its pollution, Rani's father made his stealthy way there after dark and stood by the hedge and called to Motya.

'Psst … Motya … psst … over here.'

'Uuunngh? Who?'

'Motya! Where are you getting your alcohol from? Get some for me too, please? I will buy you a round.'

It took Motya several shakes of the head to understand what was being said to him.

'Alcohol? You think I am rich like you to buy alcohol?' He let out a sardonic laugh.

'Shhh … quiet … someone might hear me here. So, what have you been drinking?'

'Desi. I make it myself.'

'Will you give me some …?' he asked before realising he could not drink something prepared by a hovel-man and instead asked, 'Will you tell me how to make it?'

'Simple. Grind some cashew fruits, put them in an earthen pot and add a banana and some jaggery. Secure its lid tightly. Leave it untouched for a week. Strain it and drink.'

That sounded too easy. 'Just like that? What about distilling it?' he asked Motya.

'No need for all that. These are dire times.'

Rani's father could not argue with that.

The next day when his wife and daughter were busy, he set to work in the cowshed. He prepared the concoction according to the recipe and dug a hole in the ground and hid the pot in it. A week later he strained it with his wife's old sari and gulped it down without ceremony.

They found him slumbering peacefully in a ditch outside the village oblivious to the panic of his frantic family. He was unhurt, his clothes only lightly soiled and his phone was missing. He sat shame-faced with his head in his hands as his wife berated him, and Rani cried quietly in the corner. He tried to promise her he would buy another phone, but with all shops shut they knew it was impossible.

Rani's education came to a sudden halt. She cried for a few days and then just moped about with a vacant expression. The pandemic raged all around. News of deaths near and far kept coming. People were just grateful to be alive. But Rani wasn't. In the war for survival, dreams—especially mad, untenable ones—were the first casualties. For the first time since it had struck, her skin condition looked to her like a horrible disease and the patches grotesque and ugly.

Rani's father lived under a heavy burden of guilt. Sometimes he raged with self-pity and threatened his family with suicide. But rather than forgiveness or a kind word, he only received indignant silence from Rani and goading to follow through on his threat from his wife.

More months passed heaving under the constantness of things that was the only change. Even more months passed. Vaccines were invented, bought and sold, injected, resisted, registered, chests pumped up and thumped. The dead were brought out, counted, buried or burnt, and life turned to business as usual in a permanently changed world. The doors of schools creaked open, and school administrations scratched their heads about how to restart classes without risking the lives of teachers and children. What they chose to do did not bother Rani as she resolutely refused to return to school. The others in her class had been promoted virtually to a higher grade and she would have had to repeat a year and attend classes with children younger than her. Wouldn't her former classmates relish her humiliation? And Rani wouldn't go back to her former government-run school. Having dreamt of a new life in an English-speaking world with skin to match, she couldn't demote herself to her old reality now. No entreaties or cajoling by her mother would change her mind. She had stopped beating Rani when she started attending English school, and she couldn't bring herself to resume traditional mothering methods. The girl had attained puberty in the meanwhile. It wouldn't be many years before she would reach the legally marriageable age, but they would have trouble finding her a groom with her vitiligo. What was to happen of her now?

It was then that one day Parlour Bobby came with two other bobbies in a car for a picnic at the farm of the people where Rani's parents worked. Parlour Bobby had gone to school with the landlady and they had recently found each other on social media. Parlour Bobby was bored and bothered by the lockdown where everything from groceries to medicines to pizza were delivered to the home. She had not stepped out of the house for three months and Parlour Bobby needed to air herself and had turned up at her old friend's house in the lap of nature.

Upon seeing the shy girl with patchy skin slinking in shady corners, shelling peanuts, Parlour Bobby inquired about her. She needed a maidservant to help in her beauty parlour. Work was light. In fact, work was just an excuse as what she really wanted was a companion. Parlour Bobby had been widowed a few years ago, and her only child had not survived infancy. Her jeweller husband had left her enough property and wealth to keep her comfortable for life. The beauty parlour she ran was more to keep herself busy and interested in life than a source of income. She would feed and clothe Rani, pay her a modest monthly fee and take care of her needs. It wouldn't be seen as employment—mostly because it was illegal to employ a minor and also because there was barely any work to be done—but as a young woman assisting an older lady and being rewarded for her good deeds.

Rani, who had given up on dreams at a tender age, saw novelty and discovery and the possibility of a renewed hope in this offer and begged and pleaded with her mother to send her with Parlour Bobby. But who sends a young girl to live with strangers? When her mother refused, Rani went on a hunger strike. Her mother troubled and weakened by everything animal, vegetable and mineral since Rani's vitiligo diagnosis relented with a heavy heart. Her father tried to intervene, but his authority had slipped away with the phone he had lost and no one took notice of him. The landlady vouched for the good intentions of her former schoolmate, and Rani's mother accompanied her to Parlour Bobby's house in Gooday Nagar.

Parlour Bobby had a spacious three-bedroom apartment—one room was her beauty parlour—on the third floor of a nice, tree-lined neighbourhood. There was a large TV in the living room that came on in the mornings to play sermons led by bearded or bald men about the modern science behind the ancient practices that baffled Indians who failed to take pride in their heritage. That was followed by serial dramas about mothers and daughters-in-law and the nuances of their quotidian shenanigans that left one uncertain about which of them was good and which bad. A film or two about love and marriage or patriotism came on in the late afternoons, and various talent shows played in the evenings. The TV was switched off only at night before bed.

Although shy and nervous at first, Rani loved it there and wanted to stay. After assuring herself that Rani would be safe and cared for, her mother left her there and returned to the village.

Parlour Bobby promised to treat Rani like her own daughter and so she did. She cooked and fed her choice dishes with chickpeas, paneer, capsicum and cauliflower. Syrupy sweets and fried things were always handy for elevenses, twelveses, thirteenses and so on. She let Rani watch TV with her and they took long naps in the afternoons. Rani was given herbal beauty treatments whenever it pleased Parlour Bobby to do so. Rani's chores included cleaning the house, watering the potted plants and chopping vegetables, which she was very happy to do. Although she was allowed to interact with Parlour Bobby's guests, Rani was discouraged from meeting her customers. The customers came to Parlour Bobby to make their hair and skin beautiful. Having a vitiligo-afflicted girl in the house would affect that image. She only went in the beauty parlour to sweep up the hair that was cut or to collect used wax strips and put them in the rubbish bin. But she didn't seem to mind this in the slightest.

Rani slept in the room that would have belonged to Parlour Bobby's daughter had she lived past infancy. The room was filled with things that were unwanted but considered too precious to be thrown away. The room had a small bed with fresh sheets, a soft pillow and a warm blanket. For Rani, who had always slept on a mattress on the floor, this was a big luxury. She also got a steel cupboard to keep her things in. Although she had been showing no interest in them of late, her mother had packed her school books for her. They went into the cupboard. But the greatest surprise awaited her at bedtime. When the lights were turned off, the ceiling lit up like a shining night sky: stars, planets, the moon, spaceships, and comets glowed in hues of green, blue, yellow, and red. The little girl for whom the painted sky was meant had not lived long enough to see it. But Rani lay mesmerized under it, her eyes sparkling with wonderment.

Night after night, she rushed through her work and left TV shows midway to run back to her room. She took extra-long naps in the afternoons so she wouldn't fall asleep too quickly at night. And there, under the phosphorescence of celestial shapes that contrasted with the surroundings, she regained her lost marvel for the shapes on her skin.

That day Gulab Jamun Bobby arrived earlier than everyone else. Her husband had come to drop her and was about to head back after greeting Parlour Bobby when she dutifully insisted he stay for a light repast.

'What will I do in ladies party? It will be awkward. I know you have your own matters to discuss …' he tried protesting when Parlour Bobby asked him if he would have walked away from his own sister's house without so much as partaking in a cup of tea. Overcome at the mention of the second most virtuous of relationships—the first being that of a mother and son—that formed the theme of half the produce of the Gooday Nagar film industry, he agreed to stay back to chew the fatty snacks.

Powdered and perfumed and dressed in pretty clothes—with the onion juice thoroughly washed off, despite a lingering smell that remained—Rani ran around fetching glasses of water and cups of tea and asking after the guests' well-being. She liked Gulab Jamun uncle. He was kind to her and greeted her in English and gave her sweets for responding correctly to his hellos and 'how-are-yous'.

The Gulab Jamun couple belonged to the Four Corner Club, which was a group that invited people from other countries who liked to talk about how they had dug wells in Africa or given first-aid kits or blankets to children in Bangladesh and elsewhere. And they had food and drinks afterwards. Parlour Bobby had told them that the club aspired to cover all four corners of the world with the things they gave. Once, upon Parlour Bobby's request, the Gulab Jamun couple had taken Rani along to one such party where she saw the first real white woman. She was dressed in a shiny blue sari and although she held it up rather awkwardly, she seemed pleased to be draped in it. She had a garland of marigold flowers around her neck and the bangs of her long blonde hair had rubbed and smudged the bindi drawn on her forehead. She smiled a lot and spoke loudly, slowly pronouncing each word with exaggerated lip movements. The men fawned on her and joked with her as she sipped the whisky in her glass, and the women smiled and exchanged looks with each other. Rani had been fascinated by this exotic creature. The patches on her face were growing wider and she thought it was only a matter of time before they would even out and she would transform into a white woman herself.

'Bobby,' Gulab Jamun uncle said to Parlour Bobby, 'by the way, we are looking for a groom for our Unnati ... let us know if you know someone suitable.'

'What? Already? Isn't she still in the final year of engineering?'

'Yes. Which is why we are looking now so we can get her engaged before she completes college. What if later she gets a job and then starts insisting on not marrying for two or three years? Better to get her settled right away. We will find a guy who will allow her to work.'

'That is a good idea,' Parlour Bobby agreed. She brought out a note pad and a pen and asked for details.

Gulab Jamun Bobby was delighted that her husband's casual remark was being taken seriously.

'I told you, your rakhi sister is one in a thousand. If anyone will find us a good son-in-law, it will be her,' she said approvingly to her husband. There was more laughter.

'We are not very particular about America. Too many shootings happening there these days. Our Unnati is our youngest as you know. We are rather possessive about her. We don't want to risk it. Somewhere here only ... like Singapore. Hong Kong would be better—it is only a five-hour flight. We are not particular about the groom being a software engineer either. He can work for a bank such as HSBC ... they are earning the same as engineers these days ...'

'More than them,' his wife chimed in.

'Yes. More. We just want a boy from a good family, with a good salary and preferably fair. No non-veg.'

Parlour Bobby was writing all this down. 'I have a couple of options in mind,' she mumbled.

'Oh, but please make sure they are a broad-minded family. Our Unnu is five feet, seven inches.

'She takes after my brother,' Gulab Jamun Bobby said.

'Yes, yes ... you need a tall boy. That should not be a problem.'

Just then, the bell rang. The other bobbies had started to arrive. Gulab Jamun uncle got up and took his leave.

The women came in, took off their masks, cleaned their hands with the sanitiser on the table and sat down to party. They ate the snacks, drank the soft drinks and giggled and guffawed about this and that. Rani ran around looking busy.

A couple of days later, Parlour Bobby walked into Rani's room expecting her to be asleep. She wasn't. She was lying in bed alternating between gazing at the ceiling and the patches on her arms.

'Not tired? I don't give you enough work,' Parlour Bobby teased her.

Rani sat up and held her arms out to her. 'Look bobby, there is Australia on my right arm.'

'It is your obsession about foreign countries that I came to talk to you about. I just spoke to your Gulab Jamun uncle on the phone. I had called them about a prospective groom for their daughter. He told me that their Four Corners Club is doing a cultural exchange program with America for a girl child from a low-income background. They will select one girl between the ages of ten and fourteen and send her to America for six months. And they will take care of everything—flights, stay, food. The only condition is she must know enough English to memorise and recite speeches at their events. Since you have this whiteness condition, they will feel sorry for you and Gulab Jamun uncle has promised to nominate you. Nobody will refuse him. Are you interested?'

No words came to Rani. She looked at her in disbelief for a second and then started crying.

The next morning, Parlour Bobby spoke to Rani's mother and she came over with the documents to apply for a passport for Rani. Rani's mother knew the bureaucracy of government schemes like the back of her hand. She brought with her a big bundle of ration cards, unique identification cards with biometric information of the whole family, election cards, her husband's two-wheeler license card, Rani's birth certificate, proof of school admission, girl child welfare scholarship certificate, etcetera, etcetera. With Gulab Jamun uncle's help they filled out the forms and made the application in the fast-track category. Parlour Bobby bought Rani new clothes. Her departure for Chicago was a fortnight away. Rani, who had stubbornly refused to visit her family in the village since she had come to stay in Gooday Nagar, agreed to go stay with her parents for a few days before leaving for America.

Back in the village, she was engulfed in a strange nostalgia. It was the only home she had known until she went to live in Gooday Nagar. Yet, it seemed more distant now that she was going to the other side of the globe. It almost felt like she had already gone and was looking at her village in a grainy documentary film. She even spoke kindly to her father. 'All that happened was for the good, wasn't it?' he said. He was redeemed by her sudden weepy hug.

'When you return, you can go back to the school. You will have to repeat the year you missed. But you can tell them that is because you went to America in between. You will have all the paperwork, your ticket and photos to prove it,' he suggested and Rani couldn't have agreed more.

Her mother took her to the local temple and had the priest perform rituals to protect her from the evil eye. The priest praised her for her cleverness and told her that the burden of bringing a good name to her parents and her village lay upon her young shoulders. 'Come back and clear the IAS,' he blessed her. He warned her to stay away from boys and tamarind trees in the foreign land.

The night before she was to head back to Gooday Nagar and then on to America two days later, Rani sneaked out to the backyard to sit under the stars as she used to when she went to school. She looked at her vitiligo and felt reassured. Her mother, who had found it equally impossible to fall asleep, knew exactly where her daughter was and followed her there. They sat together wordlessly looking at the night sky.

'Are there tamarind trees in that country?' she asked Rani.

'I don't think so.'

'Then what do ghosts swing from?'

'I don't know. Apple trees?'

'Well then you don't walk under them. It won't do if you come back possessed by an English-speaking ghost and start to say "thank you" and "sorry" like it costs nothing.'

'I already speak the language,' Rani said hotly.

'You're right. It will be hard to tell whether you are possessed by a foreign ghost,' her mother said. They went back to gazing at the stars silently.

4

Uncity

You said: I'll go to another country, go to another shore,
find another city better than this one.
Whatever I try to do is fated to turn out wrong
and my heart lies buried like something dead.

The City, C.P. Cavafy

I. This Way and That

They boarded an airconditioned bus at Cultural Capital that was headed to Fiscal Capital in Gooday Nagar because they lacked a home and place to quarrel. She had been at work all day and he had been drinking in a seedy bar, waiting for her to punch out. They had very specific bones to pick with each other. But the minute the bus wound its way onto the hilly highway they fell into an exhausted sleep in each other's arms. She woke before him when they were high up in the ghats and, seeing he looked peaceful, didn't wake him up. But he had in fact woken up before her and had let her sleep for the same reason. This confusion in chronology came to an end when she began singing along to a muffled *Kabhi Neem Neem Kabhi Shehad Shehad* that was playing on FM in the driver's cabin.

He remarked that she knew the most obscure songs. 'What's that to you, you tone-deaf bastard?' she responded cordially and they were back in action. They fought furtively in the darkened bus throughout the journey, taking care to keep their voices low in order not to wake their fellow passengers who were heading to real homes. They paused only when the destination was announced as the last stop.

They got down and walked through dark alleys where a male prostitute offered her his services rather aggressively and the lover-quarrellers clung to each other in fright. The disappointed venereal vendor cursed them with eternal dryness.

'See what you got us into!' the man said as soon as he regained his composure.

'*I* got us into it? You go oinking up the wrong tree all the time!' she exclaimed.

'The expression is *barking* up the wrong—' he began correcting her but stopped. She smirked. All they had in common was that both their immediate families had perished in the Covid pandemic—and the fact that they did not wonder what they were doing together. Even their perceptions of their predicaments were different: he suffered from survivor's guilt and she thanked the heavens for the freedom.

It had been a warm day and she had not worn her jacket over her rather low-cut, sleeveless blouse and a passing policeman had to be convinced by her broken attempts at the local language to let them go for only a hundred-rupee 'fine' for being young and big-breasted at that hour. They drank sweet milky tea in a tapri. 'It's handy to know the language of Gooday Nagar,' she said as she blew into her tea with flared nostrils. 'Fucking stooge,' he said taking a sip. 'Sanctimonious arse!' she whispered back.

They couldn't find shelter quick enough when the rain came down unannounced, and they were soaking wet when they boarded the same bus back to Cultural Capital. The AC in the bus gave him a cold and she tried warming him with her body. They slept fitfully and ate omelettes with bleached white bread at the station in the morning.

She headed to her women-only, paying guest accommodation for a shower and clean clothes before going back to work, and he stumbled his way towards the old college where he had topped the class and received a degree in economics many years ago, hoping to run into someone who might recognise him and buy him a drink. She hadn't sung on the way back.

II. Colour, Colour, What Colour?

How long can I let my mind moulder in this place?
Wherever I turn, wherever I look,
I see the black ruins of my life, here,
where I've spent so many years, wasted them, destroyed them totally.

– *The City*, C.P. Cavafy

His shirt was missing. Blood dripped on to his shoulders and chest and even his trousers and dried blood was caked on his closely cropped hair. There were bruises and scratches on his bare chest. She all but screamed when she opened the door for him.

'Wha ... What ...?' she stuttered. He only looked at her sadly.

'Were you robbed? In the day? Where's your shirt?' the questions tumbled out of her. 'We have to go to the hospital,' she said when he gave no answer. She grabbed her purse and, seeing that he stood rooted to the spot, tried to get him to turn around and head out of the door. He didn't budge.

'I'm fine,' he said finally. He sounded more fatigued than injured. 'There was a scene on the new highway.' She drew him close and examined his wounds. They were unpleasant but not serious. There were a couple of cuts on his head from which most of the blood had oozed. But while they were deep, they didn't look like they needed stitches. The green and purple bruises on his pale torso looked more dangerous than the cuts. She examined him for broken bones and was satisfied at finding everything intact. She dipped a towel in water and cleaned the clots on his skull.

'The network of blood vessels is thick and intricate on the scalp. The smallest of cuts draws a lot of blood. It looks worse than it is,' he said as she mopped his head with the wet towel. She did not respond. She dabbed disinfectant on his wounds with a ball of cotton, and he flinched at the sting.

After dressing his wounds, she went to the kitchen and made coffee for both of them. When she came out, he was changing channels on the television. She took the remote from him and muted the TV.

'Why do you get into fights?' she asked him as she handed him his coffee.

'It wasn't a fight. They were beating up a woman. A young African woman. They tore her clothes off—'

'Who were they? And who was she?'

'A mob of onlookers. People on the road. She was from Tanzania—or so she said. There had been an accident. A hit and run. A woman had died.'

'The African woman?'

'No ... no ... listen!' He was irritated by her interruptions. She realised her mistake and waited for him to explain.

'Some African men—students presumably, from Nigeria or one of those places—had run over a woman crossing the road and sped away. She died instantly. There was a lot of blood on the road. I didn't see the body. A mob gathered and blocked all oncoming traffic. I was held up by it. And then, an African woman arrived on her scooter and the mob fell upon her and beat her up before she even knew what was happening to her. When she realised she was being accused of murder, she pleaded with joined palms and insisted she knew nothing about it. But her screams were drowned by the baying of the angry mob. They ripped off her clothes. I don't even want to remember some of the things they called her. Some of the onlookers were laughing while others hit her with whatever they had. That's when I pushed through the crowd and gave her my shirt. I tried to shield her and the blows fell on me. But a few people who were looking on helplessly felt encouraged by my intervention and formed a circle around her even as the others accused us of protecting a criminal and attacked us. I have never seen anyone so terrified before. She was shaking like a leaf. The police arrived then. But they were not helpful either. As soon as they were abreast of the situation, they tried to arrest the woman instead of helping her. They wanted her to hand over her "accomplices". The policemen speaking to her in broken English as the poor woman responded in her heavily accented English would have been comical if it wasn't such a terrible, violent situation. "Bring and give friends. Hand over ... Hand over ... Africans! Drug dealers," the policemen were saying in their gruff voices. She kept telling them that she was a pharmacy student from Tanzania and she didn't know what they were talking about. But all her pleading fell on deaf ears. It was gut-wrenching. Some of us tried to intervene on her behalf but the policemen threatened to arrest us too. It's only when the car of the actual culprits was apprehended further down the road when they tried to jump a signal that they let the woman go. But not without first noting down her details and checking her identity papers. The woman was too traumatised to go on her own. Some of us managed to calm her down enough to get the number of one of her friends. We called her and left only when she arrived to take her away.'

She was listening with a horrified look. 'So, this woman did not know the guys who ran over the victim?'

'No. They were from different countries, studying in different colleges in the city. It was simply coincidence that she happened to be travelling on the same road a little after them. But all our people saw was that they were Africans. Some of them probably think of it as one country rather than a continent.'

She looked at him intently. 'I'm proud of what you did. But I wish you wouldn't take such risks. What if the police hadn't arrived on time and what if the mob had hurt you?'

'What if you were in her place?' he asked.

She didn't reply. She gathered the empty mugs and took them into the kitchen. When she came back, he had turned the TV sound on again and a newsroom debate was in full furore. 'African drug peddlers run over Gooday Nagar woman,' read the ticker below. 'Does our motto of atithi devo bhava—guest is God—make us soft targets for these ungrateful countries???' A news host was shouting as he thumped the table with his open palm.

She grabbed the remote from his hands once again and turned the TV off. 'Go shower. I have turned on the geyser. You need rest,' she said. He went in without protest.

Ten minutes later, he came out showered and changed. He refused offers of food and went straight to bed. It was still early afternoon and she got busy with the housework while he slept. She went into the bedroom an hour later and found him asleep. She opened the cupboard quietly looking over her shoulder to make sure he was still asleep and pulled out a packet of cigarettes from under a stack of clothes. She tiptoed onto the adjoining balcony and closed the bedroom door behind her.

She had quit smoking during the pandemic. But she still kept a packet handy for stressful occasions. He pretended not to know, and she feigned ignorance of his knowledge in return. Their marriage was content by consensus.

Their flat was on the first floor in one of the hundreds of apartments in a large, middle-class housing complex. The apartments adjacent to theirs were unoccupied and she felt freer in blowing smoke out of her nostrils without worrying about neighbours complaining—or worse still, morally judging her.

She finished her cigarette and tried to open the door to go back inside when she realised she had locked herself out. She didn't panic. He was right behind that door. All she needed to do was to wait for him to wake up and let her in. The first time this had happened, it was agonising. They had had a fight just before he left for work in the morning and she had headed to the balcony for a smoke and managed to lock herself out. She hadn't carried her phone and couldn't call for help. She had to wait all day on the small balcony before he returned in the evening. If he had stopped for a beer with his friends after work, he would have been even more late. She had shot the bolt of the main door, moreover, and he would have to break the door to let himself in. But who would tell him that? He would ring and ring the bell for a long time, imagining the worst while she was stuck out of earshot on the other side of the bedroom. Since it was only one floor above the ground, she thought of jumping down. With one leg dangling over the balcony wall, she realised she would not die from the impact but could hurt herself badly. She gave up thoughts of jumping and sat back on her haunches crying. It was a long time before the security guard passed under her flat, on his way to the toilet. She shouted to get his attention and he promised to convey her message to her husband so he would know what had happened. That took care of his panic. Now, she had to wait all day for him to return. It was the fear of being hungry and thirsty and needing to pee that wore her out more than actual hunger, thirst and the need to pee. When he finally arrived and pushed the door in—the screws of the bolt were weak and gave in with a powerful kick—and released her from her self-imposed prison, she was near hysterical. He had hugged her close and comforted her. But that was years ago.

This time, locking herself out wasn't a big concern. She sat on the chair and lit another cigarette and thought of the poor African woman. How horrible it must have been to be nearly lynched by a mob. And to think it was all because she had the same skin colour as some people who had committed a crime! She would probably leave her education incomplete and return to her country now. She had to be traumatised after all that.

Back when she was at university, she had shared a course with an Ethiopian girl called Hannah. She had the smoothest skin and the most chiselled features she had ever seen and her clothes were expensive and chic. Hannah also had a quiet, proud demeanour and hardly spoke in class, but when she did it was to make a counter point to some liberal idea being discussed. One day, a photograph had fallen out of Hannah's wallet and she had picked it up for her. She had glanced at it before handing it to her. It showed a smiling woman in a beautifully cut pantsuit, elegantly made-up and coiffured.

'Your mother?' she had asked. Hannah smiled and nodded as she took the photo from her. 'She is very beautiful,' she had added, and to her surprise, Hannah's smile had vanished. She replaced the photo in her wallet and had left without saying goodbye. She had wondered what she had said wrong. Was it wrong to compliment women for their looks in Africa? She was only being nice. Had she sounded patronising? Perhaps she ought to have asked Hannah what her mother did and said something complimentary about her profession or education. Perhaps she was someone famous. Had Hannah been irritated that she had not recognised her? How could she have known? She remembered thinking it was hard to understand the wealthy from hungry countries!

Just then the door to the bedroom opened.

'Locked yourself out again? How long were you waiting?' he asked.

'Not long. How are you feeling?'

'Fine. Some of the cuts sting a bit but the pain is dull.' He smiled and leaned in to kiss her but recoiled at the smell of the cigarette. She stepped back but said nothing. That would mean acknowledging the lie between them. She began taking her bra off. He watched her. She was so used to removing it from under her shirt that she didn't need to think about it anymore. She reached inside her shirt and unclasped the hook at the back. Pulled the strap over her arms from under each sleeve and then pulled the undone bra out from under the front of her shirt. She flung it on the bed and went in to brush her teeth.

He was holding her bra and looking at it contemplatively when she came back.

'These little lacy flowers they put between the breasts. Is it to ensure only women wear them?' he asked. 'Yes,' she said simply. He looked silly.

'Want coffee?' she asked.

'Yes please!'

'Which mug do you want it in? The solid blue one or the pretty pink one with butterflies on it?' she asked, her mocking smile intact.

'Oh fuck it! Fuck you!'

'Okay.'

'Huh?' He looked up to see a twinkle in her eyes. 'Come here, naughty you ...' They began kissing. He unbuttoned her shirt. They had reached a place in their marriage where sex was almost entirely a tactile experience. They did not talk like they used to. His mouth was on her breast when she spoke.

'Ummm ... today ...'

'Hmmm?'

'What are black breasts like? Are they beautiful?'

It took him a couple of seconds to understand what she was saying.

'What??? What is fucking wrong with you???' He got off her so quickly she was unable to grab him to try and keep him back. She realised it was off now. For several days—perhaps even weeks.

She chided herself silently for her grotesquely misplaced jealousy. They lay back staring at the ceiling, neither wanting to utter the next word. They must have fallen asleep because when she opened her eyes, it was dark outside. She could see his outline beside her in the diffused streetlight coming through the thin curtains. She was glad he hadn't walked away like he usually did when he was angry. She suddenly longed for the mountains—somewhere she had never been before; a cold place that demanded several layers of clothing; conifers, mist, the glow of yellow lights on mountain slopes in blue-coloured nights. She could almost breathe the crisp, thin air. She could feel it crumble in her mouth like high altitude wafers. A song came to her out of nowhere. It was as if she had known it all her life although she could not remember where she had heard it.

'Barfili sardiyon mein kisee bhi pahaad par vaadi mein gunjati hui khaamoshiyaan sune aankhon mein bheege-bheege se lamhe liye huay,' she hummed softly.

'Where did you learn that song?' he asked. He hadn't been asleep after all.

'Not sure. I don't remember,' she said.

III. A Higher Sky

You won't find a new country, won't find another shore.
This city will always pursue you.
You'll walk the same streets, grow old
in the same neighborhoods, turn gray in these same houses.

—*The City*, C.P. Cavafy

The names of most localities in Gooday Nagar had a history to them. Abyssinianguda, for instance, had been the settlement of Abyssinian slaves who worked in the royal stables back in the day. But whatever Custardapple-mandi's history may have held, no traces of its fruity past remain. It is a lower middleclass—tending to poor—neighbourhood with few relics of the colonial grandeur that the rest of the city boasted. It is 'bustly', as the class that inhabits it must bustle to survive. The constructions are 'jostly', as horizontal spaces are owned, while the nothingness of vertical length is everyone's for the taking, and everyone takes them. Adjacent buildings co-own walls and the comings and goings of the people within them. Time is kept by the azaan of the local mosque and the arrival and departure of the local trains. People mind businesses—their own and that of others. They believe in moving, on and about, and are resolute in their ability to unmind heaps of rubbish. The voices are shrill, quick and jagged. To be heard over the din of trains, and each other, is an important instinctual development and anyone who joins the milieu gains it. Vegetables are sold in open bazaars; vendors shoo away thieving goats while haggling with shoppers. The goats grab mouthfuls of greens or a carrot or a tomato before heading off to dive into biryani or haleem pots. The newly-built flyover that goes over the railway station and connects Custardapple-mandi with the more commercial Secondtonone area provides respite to animals and humans alike during the harsh summer months when death by sunstroke is as natural as death by time. Tangled telephone and electric cables dominate the skyscape. If one manages to look beyond them, one will find some of the most brilliant sunrises and sunsets. The dry air that used to be heated by the famous historic rocks of Gooday Nagar, but is now warmed mostly by concrete, refracts light beautifully.

One would assume that nothing would stick out as odd in this moving collage of a locality. But monkeys are rare in Custardapple-mandi. They have too many goats and cows to contend with for food, too many dogs to escape, and the higher planes they might inhabit are too gnarled. And that is why, when a lone adolescent rhesus monkey strayed in, it made such big news.

Everyone was agog with stories of its destructive ways. It had made off with someone's mobile phone and dropped it from the second floor of a building after realising it could not be eaten. It had peed on the poppadums drying in the sun on someone's roof. It had made off with a packet of biscuits from a child's hands. It pulled down the washing hung out to dry on someone's balcony and pooped on it. The dogs were going off on barking frenzies. People hurled stones at it which fell in each other's houses, sometimes hitting them.

The boy was supposed to be studying when he heard the commotion outside. Nothing out of the ordinary there. He sat on a mat on the floor with his books strewn around him in the only room in the house that had a door. His mother had insisted he sit there to study for his tenth standard exams as the rest of the house was noisy and people walked in and out all the time. They had a single-storey house with a walled-in backyard, which was something of a luxury in a jam-packed neighbourhood. His mother ran a small grocery store out of the outer room. It had been their primary means of sustenance since his father died a few years ago soon after the pandemic.

People had been dying all around them. Even the boy and his mother had been infected only to survive by the skin of their teeth. So, when the dipsomaniac father was entirely untouched by the virus, they thought he would live forever. But he surprised them by dying just as soon as death finally eased its frenzied reaping. He was a low-ranking railway employee, and they had lived in the quarters across the tracks while they rented out their Custardapple-mandi house, which his wife had inherited from her parents. The alcohol shops had only just opened after being shut for months on end during the pandemic. He quenched and quenched his mighty thirst and passed out on the tracks without realising the local train service had resumed.

Mother and son moved to their Custardapple-mandi house after that. She did not waste too much time mourning and opened the store in her house with their savings and ran it well. She also had her husband's pension and not paying rent was a big financial relief. Many people suggested she sell the house to a builder who would build four legal and two illegal floors with two flats per floor on it in no time. She could own half the flats and make a comfortable living on the rent. But she had refused. Space was as important as subsistence for her idea of comfort. Which is why she insisted her son study hard and create more space for himself.

'Don't be like your father' was as much a warning as a blessing. The boy was bored, however. School didn't interest him. He wanted to help his mother in the store but she wouldn't let him.

He was flipping unseeingly through his class notes when the cat came in through the window. The cat was a stray, but it walked in and out of several houses in the neighbourhood and established ownership of the ones where it wasn't shooed away. This time it had brought in a praying mantis. He watched the cat quietly. It played with the insect for some time before pulling off its limbs. When the mantis stopped moving, the cat lost interest in it and walked away. It then sat cleaning itself in a corner. The boy saw that the mantis was still alive. He uttered an expletive under his breath at the cat and lifted up his slipper. The blow was so hard that the rrrrrrrrup brought his mother running. The crushed mantis looked like a green chilli being pounded for chutney in a stone mortar, its white entrails the mangled seeds.

'Why did you hit it so hard?' she exclaimed after she had taken in the scene.

'I had to make sure it died in one go. It would have been sheer agony for it otherwise. What is that noise outside?'

'The municipal corporation guys have been called to catch the monkey.'

'Why don't they just let it be?'

'It's stealing things and breaking things. It even bit some people.'

He sighed and closed his books and went to look out the window.

'It's nothing to you. Get back to your studies. Do you want to end up like your f—' Her nagging was interrupted by someone asking to buy a packet of detergent, and she left him alone to attend to the customer.

He looked out of the window. Two khaki-clad municipal workers were walking about with large nets tied to poles. Children and adults were milling around the streets calling to the monkey and holding out foods to lure it. The monkey was nowhere to be seen, however.

The boy got bored of the scene and walked to the backyard. He was bouncing a ball on the compound wall when he spotted the monkey on the papaya tree. He whistled at it, and it scrunched up its pink face at him. He laughed and it bared its teeth. He ran in to the kitchen and brought a banana and held it out to the monkey. It looked askance at him for some time. He didn't go closer or make any sudden movements. The monkey leaned over cautiously and grabbed the banana and rushed back up the tree. It stuffed the banana in its cheek pouch. The boy went in and brought another banana. This time, the monkey approached him more boldly. His mother came out to see why he was not studying and was surprised by the scene.

'Be careful! It will bite!' she shouted.

But the monkey didn't bite. It took his hand and shook it like a person.

'It has been a pet. They have taught it tricks. It must be either lost or abandoned,' she said.

'Can we keep it? Please?'

'I don't know ...' she mumbled.

He noticed she had hesitated rather than say a decisive no.

'Please! It will starve to death. They will poison it! Dogs will rip it apart! They will throw stones at—'

'Okay! Okay. But you must look after it.'

'I will!' He promised.

They kept it in the balcony adjoining his 'study' that overlooked the backyard. The balcony had metal grills on one side and the other was enclosed by the window of his room. The gate leading to the backyard was kept locked at all times to keep the monkey from going out. It slept on a warm pile of rags on the floor in the enclosure and ventured into the boy's room through the window when he was home from school. The boy was only too happy to have the monkey there as it gave him an excuse to not study. For all its reputation of being destructive, it was surprisingly docile and well-behaved with him. It did not pee on his bed or try the edibility of his books. It sat on his lap and fidgeted with his shirt buttons and sometimes got on his shoulders and looked for lice in his hair. The boy fed it bananas and peanuts and vegetable scraps and scooped out its poop with old newspapers. They kept the monkey hidden from prying eyes lest someone insist on having it caught and taken away.

Custardapple-mandi soon forgot about the monkey and went back to haggling and shouting over itself, interspersed with the azaan and the train's whistle. The monkey had been with them six months now but the novelty hadn't worn out. The boy rushed home from school as usual that evening. His mother was sitting at the cash counter in the store, but she didn't mock or chide him for throwing his education away over a monkey like she normally did. He reached into the sack of peanuts that she sold by weight.

'You won't need it.' She sounded very sad.

'Why?' He was worried by her expression.

She took him inside before telling him that the monkey was dead. She had forgotten to close the gate to the backyard when she went there to pluck some chillies. It had escaped, gone out into the streets, been chased by a pack of dogs, jumped up and caught an overhanging live wire.

He sobbed all afternoon until the crowd arrived at their door. The unemployed youths of Custardapple-mandi who spent their days standing in the street corner chewing gutka, playing loud songs on their smartphones, and whistling at any girl who dared pass their way, had seen the dead monkey hung out like washing on the wire and knocked it down with a stick, tied it to a metal chair, put some vermilion on its forehead, and strung a marigold garland around its neck. They were taking the monkey from house to house to collect funds for a Hanuman shrine they planned to build for it.

'Minimum 500 rupees!' they demanded. The boy gaped at them and his mother did the talking.

'Our monkey. Give it back,' she said in a quiet, menacing manner that punctured their bravado.

'How? How?' One of them began demanding when she unleashed a volley of curses on them.

'Aye Srinivasulu! Do you know how many men your mother sleeps with every day to feed your filthy mouth? Every morsel you eat is a knife in her heart! Split your chest and we will not find so much as a trace of the alphabet there. And you, Kotesh! Why aren't you helping out at your father's Curry Point? The old man works so hard he salts the chapattis with his sweat. I'll ask him to take away your mobile the next time he comes to buy dal from me. Yakub! Didn't those Sudanese boys give you a job in their shawarma shop? Why are you not at work then? See how they come from other countries and work hard to pay for their education? And you have no shame eating your poor mother and father out of house and home! Venkatesh, wait till your uncle hears about how you were caught peddling ganja. You told everyone at home that you are visiting your friend in the village when in fact you were in jail. You will get the hiding you deserve. Wastrels all! Girls from the university have been complaining of molestation. It is louts like you who bring a bad rep to our locality. I will set the police upon you. You must die of shame trying to make money out of a poor monkey's death! Hanuman will curse you to be bitten to death by fleas! *Haulepana nakko karo.* Put our monkey down and go away!'

The young men who inspired fear and loathing among students of the nearby university were near tears when this slightly built woman began picking individuals out of the gathering for a tongue lashing. The crowd began dispersing until only the man who held the corpse of the monkey remained. He put it down and muttered, 'I'll come back for the chair later, aunty,' and slunk away.

They buried the monkey in the backyard and planted a custard apple tree on it. The boy pressed its leaves in his notebooks for good luck. He went to the local university and got himself a completely useless degree. He dated a Columbian exchange student who left behind a book of Cavafy's poems when she returned to her country.

By now, he was spending more time in the grocery shop and had ideas about expanding the business. His mother let him take over. She had started colouring her hair with henna to cover the first signs of greying.

'The sun sizzles down into the Arabian Sea dragging behind it threads of silken orange through the inky brine swirling and swooping like neon ribbons of a burning kite on a new moon night,' he said of the orange strands in her hair one day. She gave him one long look and arranged his marriage.

The daughter of her old schoolmate was a sweet young thing. Her son fell in love with the girl the moment he saw her because he believed in love at first sight. Some neighbours told her it was wrong to bring her son a bride from a different religion while others boycotted the wedding. His mother responded to the former with unfazed silence and to the latter by calculating the savings on *double ka meetha*.

They added another floor to their house, converted the entire ground floor into a supermarket, planted more trees in the backyard and bought a car—although parking in the narrow alleyway was not without its share of problems. He spent his days at the store's cash counter and the evenings courting his wife to make up for the lost romance of marriage by arrangement. He took her for strolls around the lake, to the cinema, to restaurants, and to teashops where he fed her butter biscuits and thick sweet Irani chai. He took her for *mushairas* and *mehefils* in the old city. Although she understood nothing of the latter, she went along enthusiastically to please him. He stuck black vinyl stickers on the walls of their bedroom in patterns of butterflies of diminishing sizes and silhouettes of trees from which hundreds of birds were flying away, strung fairy lights and made gentle love to her on a spring mattress of Chinese make. He wrote her poems and she smiled at him. For the soft idlis and two kinds of chutney—coconut-chilli and ginger-tamarind—she had served him so demurely on the day of the bride-viewing, he titled all his poems *Serenade on the Grinding Stone*. He took her on holidays to the mountains and the seas where after days of revelry they returned to Gooday Nagar with nostalgic eagerness.

IV. Serenade on the Grinding Stone

You'll always end up in this city. Don't hope for things elsewhere:
there's no ship for you, there's no road.
Now that you've wasted your life here, in this small corner,
you've destroyed it everywhere in the world.
– *The City*, C.P. Cavafy

The heart's ball and chain is a smooth granite
rhythmically crushing rice
of the daily grind of my people:
a people in ferment.
I joyfully partake of their food—our food
of fluffy dreams made of memory and desire
fire and water, monks and monkeys
left to rise overnight in the City.

This city, that city, and the other
are mine for mining meanings
and honing tones in the tongues of brothers
made over cosmopolitical trades of love and language
that are coloured in earthy and earthen hues;
every man and woman an intimate unfamiliarity,
every sight, smell, touch, taste exciting an impossible nostalgia.

I journey for return
to cities set in grids of longitudes and latitudes:
geographic amoebas heaving with concrete,
longing for skies, defined by platitudes.

From mirth to mirth and lust to lust I return
made, unmade mad for air and airing
chests dampened in rains of happy tears.

I return as a journey
wise and wisened by suns of many slants,
hair moonspun, voice drunk on songs of farewell.
My return written on your bosom and your womb;
you as my home, make worlds of every small corner,
and render cartographical spaces uncities.

5

Ringa Ringa Roses

Vighna harta sign the Magna Carta
separate the church from the state
of our minds—give us this day our daily roti
with peanut chutney and baingan bharta

'Maria, *go,* Maria!' Aruna called to her neighbour from across the short laterite wall that marked the boundary between their houses. She hadn't learnt the language despite spending more than a dozen years in this village that was a short drive from Gooday Nagar, but she knew how to pepper her English with stray words and the occasional address of familiarity or respect to make it sound like she wasn't an outsider.

'Maria! Are you there, *m'go?*'

After being away for two months, Aruna had returned to the village a fortnight ago. But she had spent nearly all her time indoors, sitting in silence. The house alternately comforted and haunted her.

This is the house she had lived in with her husband since the early days of their marriage. They had met at design school as twenty-somethings with big dreams—hers articulated aloud and his held silently like a colourful nebula behind his brown eyes. She was sociable and chatty, and he was the quiet brooder. He had been a gifted child but found praise unnerving despite having had it all his life; she worked hard and aimed to please. They had made an unlikely pair. It all started with that nickname he had given her. She was the resident animal-lover on campus and fed and cared for the stray dogs there. When she wasn't in class or in the studio she would be seen walking around with a varying number of dogs following her with wagging tails. 'Dogma!' someone had shouted at her, and she had caught the hapless guy by his collar and shaken him so hard he had apologised profusely. She had let him go only after he had disclosed the name of the person who had coined the term. Sameer? Soft-spoken, contemplative Sameer who painted like a god? He had smiled shyly from under thick eyebrows when she confronted him and did not deny the charge. Romance had blossomed between them like it did in a typical Hindi film.

They were inseparable: they sat together in class, ate their erratic meals together, and drew and painted the rest of the time. They lived in a place where sisters and daughters were safe on the streets at night—but not if they were found with a lover. But the duo threw caution to the wind and roamed the streets hand-in-hand; she talking away nineteen to the dozen and he listening keenly until exhaustion caught up with them and they returned to catch a few winks of sleep in their respective hostel rooms before beginning another day of the exact same routine. Two years of this and their love was a legend at the university. Their graduation party doubled as their wedding and the whole university joined in the revelry.

After spending the first five years of their marriage in corporate careers, it was her idea that they move to a village on the outskirts of Gooday Nagar and live in an old bungalow like a power couple of the art world. There would be pastoral quaintness in the shades of green surrounding them and urban comforts an arm's reach away.

He painted and drank endless cups of tea that she made for him. He did art for art's sake and exhibited in galleries all over the world while she worked for money. She did book cover designs, took landscape commissions from big hotels and portraits from the rich and the made-up. She brought in cash, he the accolades. There was bread and brain, heart and hearth, pleasantness and plenty in their lives.

'What would you say to youngsters wanting to pursue art?' an interviewer from a national newspaper had once asked Sameer to which he had replied, 'I would ask them to leave me alone.'

There was laughter and cleverness too. They lived happily ever after. But unlike what fairytales suggest, ever after is a finite period. Princes grow bald, glass shoes break, princesses are emancipated, castles grow mould, plumbing needs maintenance, and kings are no longer born to kings.

For Aruna and Sameer ever after ended with the arrival of twenty-two-year-old Rituparna. She had just finished studying at their old art school and her teacher, who had been their classmate, had spoken endlessly about Sameer's genius to her. She came with her portfolio—large sketchbooks covered in watercolours, tubes of oils on canvasses, acrylics, pencil sketches, a hard disk full of graphic designs—and wondered with great earnestness if she might intern with him. 'Please, sir, I really, really want to learn from you. Please ma'am, would you convince sir?'

Sameer wasn't sure, but Aruna thought it a good idea. They had decided not to have children and this could be a way of giving back to the world. Since public transport to Gooday Nagar was unreliable, and getting anywhere was impossible during the monsoons, Aruna invited the young woman to stay with them. It was a big house and they had a spare room she could use. Rituparna accepted with such a show of gratitude that Sameer was too awkward to talk with her for days afterwards.

Rituparna turned out to be an ideal student. She hung on to Sameer's every word and spent long hours with him in the studio. She was also a good guest—she not only helped with the chores but took on some of the household responsibilities and was always thanking Aruna for allowing her to stay. 'This is not an internship, this is the continuation of the guru-shishya tradition,' she would say and jokingly call Aruna her 'guru-ma.'

It was no wonder, therefore, that Aruna was not threatened by the proximity of her husband to this sultry, curly-haired woman nearly fifteen years their junior. Moreover, Aruna was herself every bit 'the shade of monsoon clouds with a cascade of ringlets like the falling of nights that held the promise of laughter in them,' in Sameer's words that she had pretended to brush aside while secretly committing to memory in the early days of their relationship. She had turned many a head in her time and though slightly heavier under the chin now, and with some grey peeking out at the temples, she was aware of her charm. That's why she noticed nothing when a month later, stylishly unkempt Sameer began paying special attention to his grooming. And that's why she noticed nothing when guru and disciple began going on long walks into the hills to discuss art history—she was just happy to have the house to herself and enjoy the peace of solitude. And that's why she noticed nothing when something furtive crept into Sameer's behaviour and Rituparna began avoiding eye contact. That's why she did not think anything was amiss when one day, she came home from shopping for supplies to find them both missing and his car gone. It is only when she sat down to work, she saw she had an email from him.

> I'm sorry we left like this. This was the only way we could do it without unnecessary drama. You know I hate scenes and cannot handle confrontations. I'm in love with Ritu. It's not about you. I still have great respect for you. Hope you can forgive me.

She sat in stunned silence for a long time. Then she walked like a zombie over to the table on which sat a small wooden idol of Ganesh. It had been left behind by the previous occupants of their house and, as ardent atheists, Aruna and Sameer had no use for it. She wanted to throw it away, but he had stopped her and made up a funny verse about the Vighnaharta, the remover of obstacles.

'Where would art be without idolatry?' he had said in his usual quiet way, and she had kept it.

But now she picked it up and tossed it out of the window. She went on as if nothing had happened. Her income and savings were sufficient. She saw that he had not touched their joint account. She lacked for no material comfort. Weeks went by before her neighbour, Maria, casually asked her if Sameer was travelling.

'No. He left me,' Aruna said simply.

'Wha— with that girl? What a little whore! Aruna why you allowed her in your house, man?' Maria's passionate outburst was in deep contrast with Aruna's lack of outward emotion.

'It's ok, *go*. You cannot force someone to love you.'

'You should have had a child, ya. Then he would think twice before doing like this. Men are bastards only but as fathers they think little more, no?'

Maria herself had four children with her sailor husband who was away on the ship six months in every year. Maria stitched dresses for the village women to keep herself busy, although she didn't lack for money—her husband's pay was ample owing to the risks his job involved. Her children were born a year apart; each conceived on her husband's annual visit. 'She's a tailor on chore leave,' Sameer had remarked one day when they heard rhythmic creaking and heavy grunting from their neighbour's house—regular music whenever Maria's sailor husband was home.

Aruna refused to change anything in her life simply because her husband had run away with a younger woman. But two years after they left, there was a phone call from an unknown number. It rang twice then stopped. It rang again after a minute.

'Hello?'

There was a moment's hesitation on the other end.

'Er ... ma'am, this is Rituparna.'

Aruna felt like she had been punched in the solar plexus.

'What do you want?' she asked through gritted teeth after she recovered her breath. The coldness in her voice could freeze blood.

'Ma'am ... please don't hang up. I know you are very angry with me. You have every right to be. This is not about me, ma'am. It is ... er ... Sameer. He has Covid. It looks bad. In his feverish deliriums he keeps asking for you. Would you please come see him once? I beg you. He may not make it. Just once ... please ma'am ...' Rituparna's voice cracked.

Aruna sat in silence.

'Hello? Ma'am? Are you there?'

'Go to hell. Both of you.'

Aruna cried for the first time in two years. Her body convulsed with sobs. She sat on the floor until the tremors receded. Then she packed and went to visit her mother. Her mother knew that time must be allowed a free hand to heal. She never offered solutions or hope. Instead, she gave the comfort of routine. Cook, eat, clean, water the plants, go for walks, read, sleep. There had never been a TV in her house and there never would be.

'Don't you want to find out if he made it?' Her mother once asked.

'Dead men don't die,' Aruna said and that was that.

Aruna returned a fortnight later to a silent house and got back to her old routine as if she had never been away. She kept to herself and barely went out. One day, she was looking out of the window at a pair of racket-tailed drongos frolicking in her bougainvillea when she spotted Maria's pigs eating the parboiled rice laid out to dry by the little chapel. She tried chasing them away herself but the large sow was rather aggressive and, taking her for a threat to her brood, grunted menacingly at her. So, Aruna went to fetch Maria instead.

'Maria, go, Maria! Your pigs are eating your rice, man!'

Maria came running out. 'Ayyyyy when you came? Heeeeeeeeey!' The second scream was aimed at her pigs, but she continued her neighbourly prattle in the same breath. 'You went to mummy's house-huh? Mummy is well, m'go?'

'She's fine ... Maria, your rice!'

'Heyyyyyyyy!' Maria hurled a rock at the sow, and it fell off its back like water off a duck's. 'She is very sad or what? Hard at her age to see her daughter's life destroyed like this, no?'

'She is fine, Maria. And so is my life.'

'What you are fine? Don't pretend to be so strong huh. It's okay to cry m'go. I'm here for you.'

'Thanks, Maria. But I'm okay, really. Look, your pigs have eaten almost half your rice.'

In their village—as in all of Southern Gooday Nagar—they drained the lakes and grew one crop of paddy in its bed every monsoon. And after the harvest, the lake was filled again and fish were spawned. Its maintenance and profits were by rotation for each family in the community. It was Maria's family's responsibility that year, but with four children to raise and a husband at sea, she was too drained of energy and will to do much. The paddy had been soaked and steamed in its husk. Drying it was the last step in the process but Maria's patience had only lasted that long and she wanted to stop and gossip rather than salvage her flora from her fauna.

'It's ok ya. The sorpotel will be more,' she giggled. 'Both also I will only eat, no?'

Aruna couldn't help laughing too. It was the first time in ages that she had expressed any joy or mirth—even if thinly.

'So sad to see you like this, dear.' Maria smiled kindly at Aruna before dropping her voice: 'Listen ... you want to give it to that bitch? I know a man near Sonarvaddo. ... He's very secret ... full secret, but most effective. Only 1,000 rupees, one chicken, one bottle—' Maria's enthusiastic attempt to convince Aruna to destroy her nemesis with sorcery was interrupted by the honking of a car. A shiny blue hatchback with chrome fittings drew up on the dirt track under the ridge, where they stood talking. The registration plate was unpainted and a temporary number was stencilled on with a black marker. The windows lowered and Rency stuck her head out, pushed her aviators back on her head and flashed Maria a toothy smile.

'Hey Maria! Come, look at Docky's new car!'

Maria rushed to her and examined the nail varnish-like shine of the brand-new car.

'Haaaaaaa! So nice, m'go!' Maria expressed her admiration loudly. 'Must be costly, no? Your Docky is a rich man, girl!'

'Hop in. Let's go for a drive.'

Maria didn't need any convincing. She got in on the passenger side all the while complimenting Rency for her fine boyfriend with a fine car. She looked at Aruna who stood taking the whole sight in with no comment.

'Aruna, you take care. I will talk to you later. I have perfect idea. Just look in on the kids, huh? My older girl will look after younger ones, but they may fight … I'll be back soon.' They zoomed off leaving a cloud of dust behind.

Aruna bent down and picked up a rock and threw it half-heartedly at the pigs. The piglets scattered but their mother grunted and gathered them back and they continued to convert rice into ham. Aruna walked back to her house.

Rency Varghese was a nurse at the big multi-specialty hospital in Gooday Nagar. She was also Docky's girlfriend. Docky was the head of the department of obstetrics and gynaecology. Rency had met Maria in Docky's office when Maria had gone to consult him for a contraceptive procedure. Maria wanted to stop having babies, but the doctor had advised her to discuss it with her husband first and come back with him the next time.

'The process is simple enough but I don't want any trouble on my hands later if the husband rejects your decision,' he had said.

'Nonsense!' Rency, who had stood listening to the exchange, cut in. 'Why does she need her husband's permission to decide what she wants to do with her own body? She has had four children already! How many more would he want anyway?'

Maria looked up at Rency gratefully from the examining table where she lay splayed as Rency's boyfriend stretched her cervix with an instrument that looked like a duck's head. They exchanged a smile that laid the foundation for their friendship.

'He says children are God's gift and we don't have right to stop it,' Maria explained.

'Rubbish! Give her a tubectomy, Docky. She can blame her infertility on Covid. She says he goes on a ship. It's unlikely he'll be back for many months. Enough time for her to get fixed and healed and "recover" from Covid. A laparoscopic procedure will be quick and the scars will barely show. Just dim the lights when he wants to get on top of you the next time.' She winked at Maria.

'I always do that,' Maria said and blushed.

Docky gave Rency a fond smile and agreed to tie Maria's tubes.

It was evident that cheerful, gregarious Rency had the male gynaecologist wrapped firmly around her little finger.

'Your boyfriend is looking at other ladies' … er … privates. You don't feel strange, m'go?' Maria asked her one day as they sat with a by-two cup of coffee in the hospital cafeteria. Their friendship had developed quickly and guilelessly. Both were the same age, and although they came from very different backgrounds, they were happy with their respective lot. Where there is no envy, goodwill sets in easily.

'No! On the contrary, I am glad I can keep an eye on him when he pokes around the genitals of other women.' Rency laughed so loudly that the people at other tables turned to stare at them.

'Shhh ... You have no shame only ya!' Maria giggled covering her mouth.

'What? I am serious! Think of how bored he must be of what he sees all day. After that, he cannot help but be faithful. It's like a professional hazard.' Rency continued laughing.

The hospital's code of conduct required that a male doctor have a female assistant present when he examined a female patient. Rency was young and beautiful and an efficient nurse. Many a time she reminded the doctor of medical nuances that he had forgotten as trivialities owing to the great demand his profession put on his memory. And she did it in a way that made it appear as if she was only assisting him in his intellectual labour by holding up a trayful of shiny and sharp pieces of information for him to pick from—a familiar transaction. Her general demeanour was jovial and he found her irresistible. They had become lovers within weeks of working together. Affairs between doctors and nurses weren't uncommon but theirs acquired special status. Rumour had it that Docky—as her nickname for him had caught on—was devoted to her and had cared for her lovingly when she came down with a bout of Covid.

'This car is very smooth, ya. My husband keeps saying learn driving, learn driving, but I'm very afraid. He tried to teach me last time he came ... I was so scared I confused break and accelerator. Almost had accident with scooty fellow. Afterwards he also stopped asking me to learn. Now car is sitting in garage. I wash it every week otherwise it will look like scrap metal when he comes home,' Maria narrated her driving woes as Rency smoothly eased the car into top gear after hitting the highway.

'The only way to get over your fear of driving is to drive. You mustn't let friends teach you—they will transfer all their mistakes to you. Join a driving school. They will train you on a simulator first. That will get you used to the controls and you will be more confident when you get on the road.' Rency didn't take her eyes off the road as she spoke.

'Hmmm ... I can try. But where I will go in car anyways? Dropping children to school, going to fish market, going to shop—everything I am doing on scooter. And church is here only ... walking distance.'

Rency drove in silence for a while before turning onto a side road that led to the river.

'It was so muddy during the rains. It must be nice now. Let's go make rocks bounce in the backwater ... How is your stomach? Scars reduced?'

'It's fine. Very light ... my husband will not notice. Thank God no more babies.' Maria giggled. 'But what about you? When you will have babies m'go? When you will marry your Docky?'

Rency turned to look at Maria. 'Don't be such an aunty now! I don't like children.'

'Arre now you will say like this. Later when it is too late, you will regret see ...'

Rency screeched the car to a halt. 'Get out of my car!' she said.

'Oh my God, you are mad! I was only making observation—'

'Well then observe in silence or I'll observe a minute's silence for you.'

'Okay, okay ... baba ... you scared me only.'

Rency flashed Maria a bright smile to show that she had only been feigning anger. Maria laughed in relief.

'See the bakulas are in full bloom. Such a lovely fragrance,' Maria said, changing the subject.

'Who's that walking ahead of us ... is that Imambaunty? Hi, Imambaunty!'

The lady walking briskly with the loose end of her sari covering her head stopped and turned upon hearing her name. She peered into the car and smiled when she recognised Rency.

'Where are you going in this heat, Imambaunty? Can I give you a lift?'

'Oh me? I was going to jump in the river and die.'

'Die? Why?'

'My daughter-in-law, our Latif's wife, is bad.' Imambu stopped to catch her breath. 'She is not good,' she explained.

'Oh come on, Imambaunty. You must not let these small things affect you. You are a mother. Mothers have big stomachs so they can swallow the mistakes of their children. Come, get in. I'll take you home.'

Imambu wiped a tear from her eye and got into the backseat without the need for coaxing. Once inside, she cheered up quickly enough.

'Let's stop for chai somewhere,' she said.

Imambu—Imambaunty to most people—was in her fifties. She had been widowed in her twenties when one day her porter husband, having finished the palm toddy in his pot and with no money to buy more, had decided to climb the tree to tap some himself and fallen to his death from a height of three feet. He had suffered a heart attack as he was scampering up the teak tree. Imambu had raised the two sons he had left her—with a combination of her cleaning others' homes and the general tendency of children to grow up in spite of deprivation.

Asif had remained in the same town and become a porter like his father while Latif moved a hundred or so kilometres to the north and a little to the right (as all that was left of there was the sea). In Gooday Nagar, he had found work as a ward boy at the big, multi-specialty hospital. Imambu had remained with Asif until a year ago when he died of Covid, after which she had moved in with Latif whose wife was unhappy about the extra mouth to feed. Rency had met her at the hospital when Imambu brought her son his lunch in the afternoons and with her usual sociable nature, she had befriended the older woman. And now, having abandoned her plans to end it all, Imambu was looking forward to a cup of sugary, ginger tea.

A gentle drizzle came down, rendering the greenery around them a shade darker. The grey tar of the road before them turned black and everything suddenly felt more defined and enhanced like a photo with a filter on. The three women felt lighter and happier. They found a small teashop with a coconut-frond roof by the side of the road. They got down and, despite the shop owner's insistence that they sit inside as there were no men in there, chose to stand outside and enjoy the gentle rain. Although Rency was a common friend, Maria and Imambu were mutual strangers and hence shy in each other's presence. But a sip of the cutting chai brought smiles to their faces.

'Nice colour,' Maria pointed to Imambu's sari as she blew into her tea.

'Haan ... our Asif bought it for me two years ago. Your dress is also nice.'

'I only stitched it.'

'You stitch sari blouse also?'

'No aunty. Only dresses I know.'

The easy banter and the jolly ride elevated everyone's moods and soon it was time to go back. Imambu insisted that Rency not drive her all the way to her house in the shantytown that had developed as migrant labourers thronged together on the little hill just outside the city. She didn't want her daughter-in-law seeing her getting out of a car and hurl some snide remark at her.

'Don't worry about your daughter-in-law. If she is mean to you, tell her you will tell me. I will have Docky talk to your son,' Rency assured Imambu.

'Come home sometime when you are feeling bored, aunty. I am alone only. Children are also there. Rency knows where I live. Ask her ...' Maria called out to Imambu as she waved goodbye. As she neared her house, Imambu didn't feel like going in just yet. She walked over to one of the pakka houses on the hill set apart from the shantytown and knocked on the door.

'Savitrakka ... It's me Imambu!'

The door was opened by a smiling woman.

'Ay ... Imambu come, come ...'

'What were you doing?'

'Oh me? What would I do? Simply sitting. As passive as a stone used to break a lump of sugar,' Savitri said with a laugh.

'You are no sugar-breaking stone. You are a stone used to pound tamarind chutney—with extra spice,' Imambu laughed.

'Haha ... I wish my husband would hear you say that. He's at work now. Come, sit. You are right in time for tea.' Savitri smiled as she ushered her in. Although older than Savitri by a few years, Imambu addressed Savitri as akka—elder sister—as a mark of respect owing to their unequal stations in life.

When Imambu first arrived in Gooday Nagar, she ran into Savitri Naik at the fish market and heard her speak their language on the phone. For Imambu who had never ventured out of her own state before, this reminded her of home and she had gone up to her and introduced herself in the regular way.

'Which town, ri?' she asked when she caught the younger woman's attention.

Savitri too was happy to have someone address her in her language. They had found out that they both came from neighbouring coastal towns of the southern state. Savitri had been a teacher of literature back home before marrying her bank manager husband who plucked her out of her small town and took her around the country with his transferrable job, in states that had no use for her knowledge of the written word in her language. They settled in Gooday Nagar a few years ago for their daughter Shweta's education and decided to stay for the bracing breeze and lower price of fuel even after Shweta graduated from college and left Gooday Nagar for a job in a big city.

After exchanging basic information, Savitri had invited Imambu home. Since then, Imambu had been visiting her regularly for a cup of tea and nostalgic gossip about their home state—and how everything here was not as good as it was there.

Savitri brought out two cups of tea and a plate of samosas.

'Oh … there's no need for this. I just had some in a teashop when I was out for a walk,' Imambu modestly refused the tea as per tradition.

'One more cup won't kill you,' Savitri pressed it on her as per the same tradition.

Imambu took a sip and nodded appreciatively. 'Very nice. Only your home has good cardamom tea in all of Gooday Nagar.'

'Have another samosa. Shweta doesn't want any. She is visiting for her wedding shopping. She wants to lose weight. I said why bother since it's only a registration but you know girls these days want to look good all the time ...'

'Ah, little Shweta is getting married? Where are you giving her?'

'She is giving herself. She met her fiancé at work. Debashish Mitra.'

'Mitra? What kind of name is that?'

'They are Bengali.'

'Bengali? I thought Bengalis are called Chatterjee.'

'Not all of them, Imambu! Haha ... Anyway now she will have to cook river fish for him. I simply cannot stand it. Too many thorns and they smell of mud!'

'I know. I cannot eat anything but bangdi ...'

Just then Shweta came out dressed in a rather low-necked, red evening gown and paraded it for the benefit of the older women.

'Oh, hi, Imambaunty. When did you come? How is my dress?'

'It's so nice,' she said to Shweta and turned to Savitri, 'You are book-read people. You can allow love marriage and such things. If we do it, we will be ostracised from our community.'

'It was different in my generation. These days who listens to their parents? It's better to go along with the children's wishes if one wants to remain relevant. They will go ahead and do as they please anyway. Shweta, isn't that neckline a little too low?'

'No, it isn't,' Shweta said, marching back inside.

'She is wearing a dress at the wedding? No sari?' Imambu asked.

'There will only be a reception in the evening following a registration in the morning. We decided not to have a religious ceremony as the groom's mother has boycotted the wedding.'

'What? Why?'

'God only knows. She's mad. Shweta tells me she has been very rude to her since the time Debashish took her to meet her. At first, she told Shweta that she was very modern and would not demand a dowry of her to which our Shweta replied that we, her parents, weren't offering one anyway. Since then, she has been acting like a cat with a burnt tail. She told Shweta that girls had lined up for her precious boy and that Shweta was lucky to have his attention—'

'Our Shweta? She is so beautiful! So light skinned! Anyone would be lucky to have her for a daughter-in-law. Look at mine! She is my own brother's daughter and see how she—'

'She even blames Shweta for Debashish's father's death last year of Covid. She thinks it's her jinxed aura that brought misfortune upon their house. The man had been a heavy smoker. Covid was just the excuse he needed to die,' Savitri didn't want to let Imambu take over the conversation and make it a never-ending rant about her own daughter-in-law.

'What? No, no! Our girl is too good for this fiend. You must forbid this marriage,' Imambu said with hot indignation at a woman she had never met.

'I cannot. Shweta does exactly as she pleases. But I have told her that we are always there for her if that crazy woman tries to make trouble in her marriage—which she will. She's already going around telling everyone within earshot that Shweta is after her son's money. Haha ... she earns much more than him. But I have great experience handling a difficult mother-in-law myself.'

'Oh yes. Mine was a chudail. She beat me until welts stood on my back—and all for that drunk lout of a son of hers. In the end, I was the one who bathed and fed her in her old age. Mothers-in-law are monsters,' Imambu chimed in forgetting that she had since rolled into the same role she was deriding.

'Apparently Debashish has a sister who ran off with a man much older than her, a couple of years ago. A married man too. She has been estranged from the family since then. Apparently, her own mother won't talk to her—but the mother doesn't admit to it. She has been telling Shweta she is no patch on her daughter when in fact she herself won't talk to her daughter. Imagine? It's all so complicated ... I worry what kind of family my girl is getting mixed up with ...'

Shweta walked out again holding two earrings—a pearl chandelier and an American diamond stud.

'Which one?' she asked her mother holding them up to her ears.

'The stud. Listen, Shweta, I'm going to invite your grandmother. She is the most senior person in the family. You must have her blessings.' Savitri grinned mischievously.

'That old hag? But she treated you so badly! Besides, she is on her deathbed now,' Shweta said of her paternal grandmother who lived with her uncle back in the village.

'Oh, I'll have her brought one way or the other. I'll put her in an ambulance and tell the driver *maduvego masanako bekenda kadegodu ...*' She laughed quoting the famous lines by her favourite poet.

'What?' For Shweta the mother tongue had been no more than a medium for tongue lashing by her mother.

'Life is a carriage/ destiny, its driver/ whether a wedding or a funeral/ you, the horse must go where he takes you/ slip, the earth will hold you,' Savitri translated the verse into English for her daughter's benefit. 'We'll load the old witch onto an ambulance and let the driver decide where he ferries her,' she continued savouring the implication of her words. Shweta rolled her eyes.

'Imambaunty, come for my wedding,' she said knowing very well that she wouldn't.

'Of course! Would I miss our little girl's special day?' Imambu said knowing equally well that she wasn't really wanted there.

'Oh, but we are going to our town the day after tomorrow for the bangle ceremony. Just when you think she is too modern, Shweta springs this demand on us. She wants a dozen green glass bangles put on her wrist by Ilahi the bangle-seller back home. Ever since I told her that he had adorned the wrists of women of three generations in our family, she wants it for herself. Before that, it was his father who sent off our brides to their matrimonial homes, tinkling with auspiciousness. Ilahi is a decrepit old man now. His son does most of the work while he just sits in his shop looking out of the window, smiling at passersby. Imagine a bangle ceremony before a court wedding ... haha! We are leaving in the morning and hope to be back by nightfall the same day. We don't plan to stay. There's room in the car. Come with us?' Savitri said to Imambu.

This, unlike the last one, was a real invitation, and Imambu perked up at the prospect of travel.

'I will ... I will ... Hope it is not too much trouble for you?'

Just then Shweta's phone rang.

'Who is it?' Savitri asked her.

'A friend,' Shweta said simply and walked inside with her phone. 'Hey! All okay?'

'I don't know man. But I called to see how your preparations are coming along. Done shopping?'

'Almost. Need to hem in the gown a little. My mother is going to do it herself. We are going to our home town for the bangle ceremony.'

'I cannot believe you are doing all that jazz. What does Debashish say about it?'

'He laughed and called me mad. But he thinks it's cute. Listen, you better come. I'm not taking no for an answer.'

'I'm not sure re. Ma will make it worse for you … and I don't know how Debashish will react.'

'Your mother is not coming. And even if she finds out later, she won't hurt me. She can rave and rant all she likes behind my back. She is already doing it. And don't worry about your little brother. I am not going to let him be a mama's boy for long. Remember, you and I are on the same team.'

'That's sweet of you. I want to come, but everything is so strange.'

'You said your boyfriend recovered from Covid …?'

'He has. But he has been acting weird since then. He has stopped painting. He doesn't talk to me, hardly even acknowledges my presence. He has brought home a small wooden Ganesh from God knows where. I caught him standing before it with folded hands—'

'Ganesh? But isn't he—'

'Yes,' she pre-empted her friend's reference to the uncouth matter of religion. 'It's like I don't know him anymore. I feel like I am living with a stranger. I'm beginning to think it was all a mistake. I did a terrible thing falling for a married man …'

'Ritu, stop the self-flagellation. You did nothing wrong. It was his responsibility to stay faithful to his wife. He must have his reasons for not doing so. Love has no rules. You can't help developing feelings for someone.'

'He couldn't be true to his wife and I want him to be true to me now. I'm being punished.'

'Shut up ya! Umm … but … do you think he wants to go back to her?'

'She won't take him back. She's too proud.'

'Er … Ritu … You think it's over between you?'

There was silence on the other end.

'Ritu …?'

'I don't know.'

6

The Man Who Dreamt He Was Gobhi Manchurian

'Philistine Dental Clinic.' Puppy Kicker read aloud the writing on the board across the street from the café where he was sharing a cup of masala chai with his friend.

'It's "Pristine". You judge everyone, don't you?' His friend gave him a bored look.

'Of course not. I just forgot my glasses today.'

'You judge everyone,' his friend said matter-of-factly and drained his cup and asked for the bill.

Puppy went home for his music practice. The vuvuzela isn't the best instrument on which to practise the *Malgudi Days* theme song. Or any song. But Puppy Kicker's eccentricities were ignored and tolerated in equal proportions by his friends and neighbours. And he blasted the horn for nearly an hour as images of the fictitious, colonial-quaint town played in his mind.

Called Pushpendra Kirloskar on his birth certificate, high school certificate, university certificate, master's degree—and almost a PhD that was abandoned midway—and passport, his nickname was an unfortunate and misleading coinage since the only way he touched puppies was gently and lovingly whilst uttering coos, gurgles and endearments. He belonged to a generation whose parents were wedded to the strains of *Baharon Phool Barsao* played by brass bands clad in red uniforms with gold aiguillettes and tassels in varying states of wear. A generation where insult comedy was not yet discarded as bullying behaviour by a burgeoning number of mental health professionals and people crushed each other's souls for a few good laughs. Thus, quiet, inward-looking Pushpendra Kirloskar was saddled with a nickname that was contrary to his nature, purely owing to the accident of the permutation of his initials.

Puppy Kicker was about to head to Gooday Nagar when he was thoroughly disillusioned with the idea of the revolution he had failed to bring about in his village. That's when he had found the garish yellow and green plastic vuvuzela lying discarded in the garage behind a pile of old tyres. One of his brothers had brought it back from the FIFA World Cup in South Africa many years ago. The cacophonic souvenir was unwelcome in a household that prided itself in its classical tastes. The horn had gone from corner to corner before finding its way to the garage where even the family Doberman had not so much as peed on it. Puppy Kicker had picked it up absently and put it in his jute backpack as the driver pulled up the car to take him to the bus station from where he would board the bus to Gooday Nagar.

Puppy Kicker was the youngest of three brothers. The older two were good and made their parents proud. They had high IQs and focussed on objective disciplines in the most prestigious institutions in India before going on to study at even more prestigious colleges in the West and getting high-paying jobs and accents and settling down into lives of comfort, freedoms and opinions.

Puppy Kicker, on the other hand, after finishing high school with top grades had worried his parents by going into the arts. But they were optimistic people. Perhaps he would become a writer—a thinker-aristocrat—who would handle the vast family lands but also sit in an elegant study overlooking the fields and write big, fat books that would be discussed in genteel circles over expensive wines. After all, wealth was no problem and the old-moneyed were starting to come around to the idea of earning a living. Perhaps he could get a BA at a good college with Edwardian buildings and lawns in India and then head to Oxbridge for higher studies, they thought. He did get that BA, but no one knew what turned his head because instead of packing up and flying to Europe or the US for an MA in philosophy or literature, he chose to study sociology at a rather notorious university in India.

The first sign of his stupidity was seen in the abandonment of grooming. He came home during his vacations with a scruffy beard and hair that hung down his neck. His mother's sniffles and his father's thunderous admonishments did nothing to change his mind. His grandmother, the shaven, widowed matriarch of the family whose soft-spoken demeanour commanded a power that seemed contrary to her slight build, bade his parents to let him be. 'He must seek his own answers. He takes after his grandfather. He is in a brittle phase at the moment. Pushing him will only break him.'

But Puppy Kicker's nonsense continued resolutely rather than abate over time, as his doting grandmother had predicted. He started visiting the hovels of the farmhands, wanting to eat with them and asking to be served meat. The terrified servants respectfully refused before complaining about the young master's aberrations to his grandmother. His brothers, who were visiting at that time, tried reasoning with him. 'It's different here. You cannot overturn a system with hundreds of years of history with your cosmetic efforts. Upending the structure is not the solution, moreover,' his oldest brother said while his other brother merely asked him to stop being a dick.

His brothers had become non-vegetarian while living in the city, but when visiting the village, they were respectful of the family's gastronomic traditions. They sat on the ground for banana leaf meals on festive days without a hint of urban conceit. They took water into their cupped right palm and poured it in a circle twice around the leaf in which rice and kheer were served with a pinch of salt, a lemon wedge, a spoon of chutney, and a small helping of cucumber salad lining the top of the leaf. They took a few grains of the soft rice and placed it outside the watermark they had just made and symbolically put two pinches of rice in their mouths before their mother spooned ghee and dal on top of their mounds of rice and poured piping hot aamti into their leaf bowls, and the meal officially began. 'Hypocrites,' Puppy called them out of his grandmother's earshot and refused to follow suit with the eating rituals.

Puppy's shenanigans of revolt continued throughout his MA. Although inwardly glowering, his parents continued to tolerate him as per the dowager's command. He was a year into his PhD when one of his friends vanished and three more went to jail. He quit his studies and returned shaken and silenced to the village. He spent a year deep in thought. He didn't read anymore. He clacked away on his laptop and dispatched opinion pieces over the high-speed internet, which one of his brothers had recently installed, to his friends working at independent media houses who were barely evading jail themselves. Most of the pieces were rejected as too rhetorical but the few that were run were ridiculed for their saviour complex. After that, he stopped writing and simply moped around for a year.

His grandmother was less alarmed than his parents. Her akimbo god—the brick-stander, the verisimilitude of patience who waits without fanfare for his devotees to attend to their daily grind before seeking their acts of faith—gave her quietude. 'Wait,' she said, 'not long now.'

Vithu—Vitthal—her oldest grandson, was blessed with a white wife and she was with child. He needed his parents to move to his country to help and to guide him in the tender ways of life. The second brother lived only a short drive away in the same country. That is where the future was. The parents were eager to don the pride of immigration as choice and not compulsion. But the grandmother resolutely refused to cross the seven seas. 'My elements will return to the land I came from,' she said. 'Your father awaits me here. Besides, Puppy is going nowhere. He needs me.'

With his parents gone, the large ancestral manor felt like a happy place. While earlier Puppy had frowned at the injustice of inheritance, he had to now admit that he liked the comfort and freedom it afforded. Built as an imposing three-storey stone structure by the father of his great-grandfather, the house had been renovated and modernised by every generation, most recently by his brothers. It was now a proud possession that combined the aesthetics of heritage and elegance of ease: high ceilings with chandeliers and skylights, antique furniture, carpets, mirrors, expensive artwork and installations, air conditioning, modern bathrooms, every kind of kitchen appliance needed to cook and serve international cuisines, a washing machine, and a dishwasher that his mother worried would spoil the servants. Now, with only his doting grandmother and himself in charge of all this splendour, Puppy felt more hopeful than he had in years.

The family lived on the returns of their investments in modern commerce, and the farms were more for indulgence than income. Puppy decided to change that and take over the administration of the farms. If not revolution, he would bring reforms.

He said they would go completely organic—no more chemical fertilizers, pesticides or herbicides. They would buy cow dung and poultry manure and compost it. Insects would be rid with pheromone traps. Rodents would be kept in check by encouraging snakes to thrive, which meant no more killing snakes at sight and allowing weeds to form a thick undergrowth. They would rally all the neighbouring farm owners to start a cooperative and market their own produce. He would invite experts on agriculture, horticulture, permaculture, vermiculture and even sericulture to hold lectures and discussions for the benefit of the farmhands. And most importantly, he would facilitate a slow but certain transition from the old feudal system they followed to sustainable, collective farming by allowing the tillers to share ownership over the produce. Puppy asked the farmhands to gather in the manor's courtyard every evening, showered and refreshed after the day's labours where Puppy would read aloud and translate for their benefit, from *Das Kapital, One-Straw Revolution* and *Anna Karenina*. The farmhands were not to while away their time watching pointless reels on their China-made smartphones anymore. They were to cultivate their minds with insights into worlds beyond their own.

The farmhands heard him out with bafflement then video-called the senior master in America once the young master started demanding that they call him by his first name and use the informal 'tu' rather than the more respectful 'tumi' to address him. The older master called Puppy and put an end to his wild schemes. 'We left you there because you are not good enough to be anywhere else. That doesn't mean you have the run of the place. The property belongs equally to your brothers. And I am still alive! Don't you dare go thinking you have poured water over your head to cleanse yourself of the pollution of your father's death yet. It was a mistake sending you to that godforsaken university. Now, keep out of matters that do not concern you or get out of there. Get a job and be a man!' yelled the absentee landlord at the disappointing last run of his loins.

Puppy Kicker went back to moping. The servants, though still respectful to his face, sniggered behind his back and their laughter followed him everywhere he went. His grandmother, the picture of rectitude, continued to allow him to find his own answers. A month into the ignominy, the answer came to him in the form of his grandfather. Dead the past twenty years, he asked Puppy to sneak out and buy him a packet of cigarettes.

'But didn't you quit before I was born?' Puppy asked his late forefather.

'Yes. But I feel like a puff now.'

'You are old. You need a strong pair of lungs during this crazy pandemic.'

'Age is inconsequential in the paradigm I inhabit. Death is immune to disease.'

'Oh yes, of course. I forgot you are dead. What's that like?'

'Death? It's alright. It's just a shift in perspective.'

The next morning, Puppy told his grandmother that he would leave the village and go live in Gooday Nagar. He wrote a few emails and made a few calls and in less than a week he got a job at the city's best PR firm 'Perspectives (Un)limited' with the 'spec' part of its name designed to look like a pair of spectacles. The tagline read 'From Disbelief to Belief'.

He took with him his grandmother's knowing smile and her blessings and the vuvuzela from the garage, and settled into a life of creativity, gain, and noise. Music had been as natural as good food in his family. His grandfather had been a trained tabla player which he had maintained as a serious hobby and had only accompanied the pure and the high at private *mehfils*. His father had received early khayal lessons which, although he quit after no more than a handful of years, equipped him to be a connoisseur of Hindustani classical music and the bugbear of the amateur performer in the local newspaper. His oldest brother had been handed a flute at a tender age as an aid to fight his asthma, and he had turned out to be a prodigy. He had pursued it with a dedication bordering on obsession and finished his Madhyam Purna level exams of the Gandharva Mahavidyala board. He took no further exams as he didn't want the structure of syllabi and certificates to interfere with the meditation of music. And he continued to learn, practise and explore music even as he gained great scholarship as a physicist at university. He refused to perform on stage or for money. When in the village, he played to himself, seated at the window in one of the many large rooms of the manor, overlooking green or brown fields depending on the age of the crop. And at university, he carried a small mat and his electric tanpura to the national park flanking his campus and sat by the lake and soothed the wild ears of nature with his flute. Word had it that the early bird dropped its worm, monkeys stopped their chattering and the deer and the leopards from the national park stood peacefully next to each other to listen to his haunting concerts.

Puppy's other brother, though not exactly gifted, had studied vocals for many years and made up with hard work what he lacked in raw talent. The household was woken by the sound of his hot-water gargling at the crack of dawn followed by his riyaz, where he dug into the low notes for a minimum of half an hour. ('Mine your voice from the navel to climb the heights of pitch—the lower you go, the higher you fly,' his guru had instructed him.) He then repeated, to perfection, predesigned taan patterns. He won many medals and trophies in every possible competition ranging from the 14 of November, Children's Day celebration at school, to the inter-district below-fourteen Youth Festival, to the Natya Sangeet competition held by the state government on the occasion of the anniversary of the State Formation Day. In the last competition, he won the first prize with his practised-to-perfection rendition of a song imploring the moon to weave a glowing cocoon with its beams around the singer's lover. The judge who handed him the prize waxed eloquent in his speech on how the young lad epitomised the triumph of perseverance over genius. He quit music after that to focus on his studies and gain a highly successful corporate career in engineering.

And then there was tone-deaf Puppy Kicker, for whom 'sa re ga ma pa dha ni' were consonants. The music tutor continued to visit for weekly lessons for fear of further reduction of his already meagre income, until one day when he asked Puppy to repeat his last lessons of Bhupali, the only raag he had been trying to teach him since the beginning. Puppy gave him a blank look.

'Why Puppy? Haven't you practised it?'

'Ummm … I have … I mean I do … but I'm not sure which song you mean, guruji. Is it the one about the drowning boat?'

The master let out a deep sigh and whispered under his breath '*Nayya mori daga maga doley… paar lagao sharan tihari*' and with great conviction uttered the following words aloud: 'Beta … any song you sing has the capacity to drown boats.'

With that ended Puppy Kicker's reluctant music journey, and his family's insistence that he learn.

And now, years later, he found himself warming to the vuvuzela—an instrument that lacked music with a vehemence that matched his own. It would be his weapon of non-conformity, his battering ram on the door of the ivory tower of snobbery. He would play his favourite songs on it—or at least sing them in his head as he blew into it. He would redeem his childhood with nostalgia struck by the nine tails of an off-key cat. He played on the vuvuzela the popular Hindi film songs he grew up with and ad jingles for family scooters that functioned as the building blocks of the nation, detergent powders that promised milky whiteness to whites and shine to coloured clothes, biscuits that combined taste and strength, and songs of national integration on Doordarshan. He particularly loved the one which said the same line over and over again in all Indian languages: that all voices mingled to form a river of notes that merged into the harmony of the ocean only to rise up as clouds and rain down as musical showers on the country united in diversity. The irony of a non-musical instrument damming the damned flow of melody washed away the fine line between revenge and justice and was oddly satisfying.

Today, Puppy played the tune of a much-loved teleseries bearing the stamp of the brothers RK—one's writing filmed to title cards with caricatures drawn by the other—and the *taana-na tana-nana naaaa* was a series of tortured brays.

After finishing his anti-riyaz, Puppy sat down to write his anonymous satire column for the newspaper.

Letter to the editor

Dear Sir,

With heavy heart I am writing about state of affairs in country. What and all is going on. So much agitation for what God only knows. So smoothly one after other *taka-taka-taka* government is passing bill like machine gun fire—even Udupi restaurant will not bring bill so smoothly. Sometimes saunf also is not fresh. Why opposition is making noise, I don't know. If we want opposition to run country we would vote for them only, no? Soldiers are dying on border and these peoples are making noise about potatoes and pumpkins it seems.

Sir, I am writing to your esteemed paper so that your kind self will bring to the attention of the nation the more pressing matter instead of all these *nansayns*: these cats. Sir, what are these animals thinking of themselves? As if gods! You think little fur ball's and take in home and heart and they are colonising worse than Britishers. Not even divide and rule. They are ignoring and doing as they please. They are demanding food whole day and when you give, they are not eating. They are urinating on beanbag! They are bringing rat inside house and leaving. Rat is screaming. Cat is dreaming. They are getting stuck above tree and shouting like some pralaya only happened! They are mixing with low caste tomcats and always giving birth under cupboard. What to do with so many kittens? Yesterday night my cat is sitting on my bladder. Little bit I am shifting means so much displeasure! It is hissing at me only, sir. Biting the hand that feeds it, I say! Day before yesterday it is bringing boyfriend to the house. In the backyard only they are doing everything. Oh God! If not me, at least for aged persons in house they must show respect, yes or no?

Sir, on behalf of all anguished citizens of this great country with ancient civilisation, I am requesting to make cat our national animal! As you must be aware best strategy is to make ally of powerful. That is the most important aspect in democracy. Majority means most numerous persons are taking all the decisions because if they cannot decide their own fate means who will? That is why I am thinking cat is best symbol. It is also very flexible and supple and self-sufficient: it can able to lick own private parts.

So sir, kindly put cat on all posters. And why our motto should be satyameva jayate? Truth alone shall prevail it seems. As if! Please change to 'Frankly my dear, I don't give dam!' It is suiting personality of cat.

Hope you will kindly do the needful. Thanking you.

Yours most obediently,

Proud Indian.

Editors who had formerly sneered at his polemical retorts about the country's state of affairs now eagerly sought his articles since he adopted this style. Links to his articles were widely shared on social media leading to a greater number of hits and increased ad-worth to the newspapers. Even when the paper decided to stop print and go entirely soft behind a paywall, Puppy Kicker's column was one of the main things that assured them dedicated subscriptions. Many readers wrote to the editor suggesting topics for the next satire piece. Since his political leanings were camouflaged in humour, aspersions on his mother's sexual morals or open threats to his non-existent sister's chastity or offers of one-way tickets to unsavoury fundamentalist countries were rare. With his vuvuzela and his popular column, Puppy Kicker was in fact living the dream as a writer and a musician—only on his terms. His parents' disdain for the way he lived his life only strengthened his conviction that he was self-made. This knowledge combined with the homebound solitude of the lockdown had given him a smugness that he carried around like an aura even when things eased and he had to go to the office once a week.

That was a work-from-home day, however, and he went out to buy fruit. It was his smugness that made him shrug when the fruit vendor asked him if he wanted his chikoo 'ready' or for 'tomorrow'. And that's how he came home with a kilo of unripe chikoo. He didn't have large aluminium tins with tens of kilos of rice, like back in the village, in which to bury and ripen fruit. He had switched to millets recently and didn't keep any rice in his apartment anyway. There were no old newspapers to wrap the chikoo in for warmth either as he had switched to e-newspapers months ago. That's when he noticed the calendar hanging on the kitchen door. At the turn of each year nearly half a dozen calendars made by various political parties were slipped under the door. They mostly ended up in the dustbin unopened but this time the maid had found it first and opened up the scroll, smoothed the roll marks and hung it up. Puppy looked at it and a smirking politician's countenance, with palms joined in humility, stared back at him. 'I thump, you thump, we all thump for a thumping majority.' *One can almost read the politician's thoughts like a speech bubble,* Puppy thought. 'I beg you with joined hands to make me the official muscle around here with prachannnnnnd bahumat,' this white-clad and capped gym-bro was silently mouthing from a sheet of paper marked with the regularity of finite time. *Not in a hundred years will I read numerals in the Naagari script without pausing to count in my head,* Puppy thought and ripped out February and March from the politician's dreams and wrapped his unripe chikoo in it.

The bell rang. It was the maid. She walked in looking flustered. 'Bhaiyya, that Monal didi. I don't like her one bit!' she muttered as she took off her mask and washed her hands and face at the kitchen sink.

'What did she do now, Usha bai?' Puppy didn't like to linger and talk with the maid. She was a chatterbox and always managed to irritate him with useless information. But it would be rude to ignore her outright. With infection cases skyrocketing, another lockdown seemed imminent. Usha bai, like tens of thousands of women eking out a living as housemaids in Gooday Nagar, was facing several more months of loss of livelihood. He had told her that if there indeed was a lockdown, he would pay her for the entire duration.

'I told Monal didi that you are giving me paid off during the lockdown. She said nothing. I know she won't pay me. She's so stingy! She makes me wash her underwear by hand to save on electricity for the washing machine. They have made an appeal on TV asking people to pay their maids during lockdown. Look at her arrogance! She doesn't even watch TV! She has a new man in her house every day. She hasn't put aside a cup and plate for me and insists I use her utensils for tea and snacks. But who wants to eat off the same plates as all those dirty men who visit her? You are so good bhaiyya, I have never seen any lady visiting you. It shows you are from a good family. But you know me, I never stick my nose in other people's affairs. Arre! You tore the calendar?'

'Yes, I needed it to ripen chikoo in. Why? Do you support this party?'

'Yes. They promised to give us a pair of sheep in the village. The other party promised a TV. I already have a TV. Bhaiyya, you must not throw the brandy quarter bottles away. They have narrow necks. They are perfect for storing mustard and cumin. It's easy to pour the seeds from them into hot oil for the phodni. I only taught Monal didi how to do it. I have been working in her house for ten years now. I know all her lafdas. Shall I make aloo bhindi for your lunch?' She didn't wait for Puppy to respond and took out the okra from the fridge and began washing it.

Puppy used the opportunity to walk out of the kitchen. Usha bai would be here for another hour. He wouldn't get any work done in that time owing to her constant interruptions. He opened his phone to check his messages and was surprised to see a notification on a dating app he had installed a few weeks back. He had forgotten all about it. He hadn't called himself a 'dreamer' or 'foodie' or 'avid-reader' or 'passionate' about something or the other or asked 'feminazis' to stay away. Instead, he had written, 'Thirty. PR professional. Antireligious but aware of my privileges. I like dogs, but I'm stuck with an unfortunate nickname that says otherwise. Try to do the right thing but there's always something to learn and unlearn every day. Open-minded, looking for interesting experiences. Consent is key.' He had considered putting in 'sapiosexual' but decided not to in the end.

It was one of those apps that allowed women to make the first move. He had been quite happy passively swiping through images of women in a radius of twenty kilometres and not having to do anything about it. He was surprised to find a message today. It was from a woman who called herself Maîtresse. Her profile picture was deceptive. She wore dark shades and bright red lipstick that distracted the gaze and upset the rest of the mental image of her face into a broken jigsaw. Her dark red hair peeped out from under a black scarf. 'Twenty-four. Not looking for anything serious. Need great communication. Impeccable personal hygiene is mandatory. *Fifty Shades of Grey* is awful but let's talk if you are BDSM curious.'

'Hello. A non-wannabe profile is a rarity. Felt we could talk. I think we are on the same page on consent.' the message read.

'Glad you think so. BDSM, huh? Would like to know more.' He texted her.

'It is not torture as is the popular perception. Nor is it an aberration. You might be surprised to know almost everyone has unarticulated desires of domination or being dominated which are mostly repressed in unhealthy ways. We acknowledge our innate desires that stem from deep-rooted, psychological conditioning and give them a release in mutually agreed upon/agreeable ways. Everything is pre-discussed. One is allowed to change their mind midway and consent and trust are the most important factors. In fact, consent is practised at a much higher level among the BDSM community than in the vanilla,' came the reply.

'Wow! It's a community?' he typed.

'It's very, very secretive but thriving. We are extremely selective about who we let in. Think you might be interested in giving it a shot?' came the reply.

'Ummm ... maybe. How does one go about it?'

'We must gauge where you stand on the spectrum. Would you be interested in taking a test? It's free and multiple choice and will take less than an hour. Let me state on the outset that I'm a Dom. If we must start a relationship, you will have to lean towards the Sub. We have to be mutually complementary.'

He hesitated for a moment before keying in, 'Ok. Send me the test'

'Here it is. Take it in your own time. No hurry.'

He received the link and was scrolling through it when the maid came out of the kitchen. 'Bhaiyya, I've made six rotis. The aloo bhindi and dal are on the kitchen counter. There's rice in the cooker. Have put everything else in the fridge. I will go now.'

'Hmm ...' he said absently. 'Have you eaten something?'

'I'm not hungry, bhaiyya. I just had some tea and biscuits. I wouldn't touch food in Monal didi's house. She is not—'

'Yes, okay, okay. Take care on the road. Wear your mask over your nose,' he cut her short as he ushered her out and shut the door behind her.

Maîtresse had logged out and he decided to eat lunch. He went into the kitchen to find Usha bai had mixed up the two boiled eggs he had left on the stove with the raw ones in the tray and put the eggs back in the fridge.

The next day was an office day, but he was simply in no mood to go to work and wanted to stay home and chat with Maîtresse. He had taken the test and it was firmly established that he was submissive and his new friend said she would be happy to enter into a relationship with him but had told him they mustn't rush things. Their communication needed to strengthen and trust had to evolve.

He pushed himself to go to office. The workday was unremarkable and routine. They were functioning with half the staff—the other half came in on days this team didn't. He had a meeting with a prospective client, a handmade soap and chocolate maker, whose business was doing well and who now wanted to scale it up into a fancy brand and perhaps even consider exporting her products. She sounded eager and willing to put herself in the firm's hands. After that, he had a session with the new intern he was supposed to mentor. The twenty-something, fresh graduate from one of Gooday Nagar's most expensive liberal arts colleges had a quiet, confident demeanour. He realised she must come from a rich family as not every unpaid intern drove a sedan to work. She listened to everything he said, took notes and asked intelligent questions. He was impressed enough to hand her the task of researching the soap and chocolate market on social media.

He was microwaving yesterday's lunch of bhindi, roti and the omelette he was forced to make when he cracked a fresh egg to see if it was the lost boiled one, when his phone beeped. It was a message from Maîtresse. He felt his pulse quicken.

'Do you like your job?' it read.

'I don't hate it. How about you? You still haven't told me what you do.' He responded.

'I'm trying out a few things. Still haven't chosen a serious career path. Why do you do yours if it doesn't satisfy you?'

'For the dough, my dear, female dear.'

'Haha ... you are funny. I will let you get back to work.'

'I'll message you later tonight.'

Back home, he sat down and wrote her the following message:

'What's a concubine?' I remember asking my grandfather. 'Mistress,' he said simply. I was reading an Agatha Christie novel set in Egypt. That definition of "mistress" confused me. To my ten-year-old mind it only meant the feminine of master—a woman who wielded power. But the context seemed to suggest otherwise. I wonder when the meaning of the word changed from that of being the one in control to the one who submits to control. I read a Tamil play in translation recently where the heroine is addressed as "my mistress" by her maid. She is also the "mistress" of the hero where she is his sexual partner and he supports her financially—and she wields considerable power too. It's an interesting culmination of meanings. Was reminded of this since you call yourself Maîtresse, which I know is French for mistress.

Her reply came an hour later: 'What you shared is fascinating. I'm going to let that sink in. But I'm afraid linguistics and etymology aren't exactly my areas. I'm more interested in the psychological aspects of power equations in sexual relations. But since you enjoy writing, I want you to write an essay on your fantasies of submission. I want you to know you are in a safe space with me. So feel free to write as eloquently as you like, without the fear of being judged. I need to know your thoughts so we can plan the details of our first session.

Puppy Kicker was nervous and excited at once. He had had a few serious girlfriends and several casual hook-ups back in university but none of them were sexually satisfying. *Is it because I was required to repress my desire to be dominated in them?* he wondered. This conversation he was having with Maîtresse seemed hopeful and rife with the possibility of release. He hadn't been this turned on since his teens when hormones dictated images to the mind rather than vice versa. After tossing and turning in bed for an hour, he flung the sheets off and sat down at his computer to write that essay.

He started with an early memory: how as a young boy he loved to be caught out in the game of blind man's buff.

When others teased the designated 'it', but managed to escape without getting touched, he would deliberately put himself within arm's reach of the 'it' and allow himself to be touched and made into the 'it'. Blindfolded and groping around to touch the other players, he had felt a strange ecstasy. He loved the thought of being seen by everyone while being unable to see them back. He dwelt on the memory and analysed it with terms of popular psychology that he had gleaned from the internet and general conversations.

And then he imagined a scene in which he was alone with Maîtresse in a private space and conjured up images of how he would like to be dominated and wrote about it in detail. It was two in the morning when he finished and emailed it to her from his anonymous account. He was so turned on he had to masturbate twice in order to fall asleep. He even messaged her to tell her that.

The next two days he worked from home. But he couldn't focus on anything. He checked his messages every ten minutes to see if there was something from Maîtresse. There wasn't. But the day he was supposed to head to the office, he got the following reply from her:

'Thank you for the long piece on your fantasies. It is clear that you take your writing seriously. Your thoughts are lucid and the prose is limpid. I particularly liked your use of metaphors. Keep it up. Talking of your fantasies, you are clearly an exhibitionist. You are not exactly a fan of pain but are eager to have your partner control you psychologically. That's good. I can easily imagine ways of enacting them in a mutually pleasing manner. As for your masturbation—since we have not entered into a relationship yet—you are allowed to do it now, but once we make a pact, you will be required to seek my permission for any kind of release. And if I don't give it, you must withold. And you will address me as ma'am.

Rather than further his erotic disposition of the last few days, her response to his email stung him in a way he could not explain. He showered quickly using his untrimmed pubes as a loofa to work up a lather, dressed in what he could lay his hands on and headed to work.

The intern had done an excellent job of the task he had given her and had drawn a plan to promote the homemade chocolate and soaps on social media—complete with a tagline, an emotionally woke storyboard of acceptance for an ad film and SEO strategy. Puppy was pleased with it and asked her to join him for coffee. As she made them their espressos on the coffee machine, she hummed something under her breath. 'Da—da-dada, daa—daa-dada …' It caught Puppy's attention. 'What's that you are humming?'

'Ummm? I don't know sir. Just an earworm. *Doe, a deer, a female deer.* Not sure why that got into my head.'

Puppy was stunned. He gaped at her.

'Is everything okay, sir?'

'Yes, yes … sorry. I've been distracted a bit. Sorry, I'm also terrible with names. What did you say your name was?'

'Maithili, sir. Maithili Rao.'

'Maithili? Oh … er … um … I really like what you are doing with the project. You are very proactive.'

'Thank you, sir.'

He decided to walk the ten kilometres home rather than call an Uber like always. For once he was glad he was wearing a mask. It hid half his face and he needn't worry about his expressions giving his thoughts away to strangers on the road.

The first two kilometres, he burned with shame. But it cooled down to a simmering embarrassment mixed with chagrin turning into regret as he turned a corner. That's when he saw the strangest sight he had seen in a while. A cauliflower. The vegetable by itself was not strange, but the way it was arranged—discarded on the low-lying branch of a tree inside the premises of an apartment complex—was what caught his eye. He stood there gazing at it for many minutes. And then, he made a decision. He walked the rest of the way home as if in a dream.

'Thanks for your response. I admit I was eager to be sexually submissive to you. But I'm afraid I'm unhappy about something. Livid, in fact. You may be a Dom, but you had no business commenting on my writing with that patronising tone. I'm not comfortable with this anymore and wish to discontinue this conversation.' He sent her the message, blocked her from his email and uninstalled the app from his phone.

That night, as he slept fitfully, he was cut into medium-sized florets. He tossed in a wok and turned in sauce. He was covered in corn starch and soy and ginger and garlic and finely chopped spring onion and green chillies. His bed was made of sliced capsicum. He was the hunger. He was the hungry. The bastard child of a cuisine's cousin. He was the desire for *phoren ka maal*; a palliative for a global palette on a desi palate. He was birthed again and again in a vendor's cart by a busy road, in a food truck on the beach, in a pure-veg Chinese restaurant in central Gooday Nagar, as South Indian khana in Birmingham and Brisbane. He was neither here nor there … No wait, he was here! Here! Here! Waiter, over here! Bring me some paprika for this. I said medium spicy, not as bland as your mum. Don't you know whose son I am??? He cannot breathe. Is it Covid?

He woke up late the next morning feeling exhausted. He read on his newsfeed that a full lockdown had been announced in Gooday Nagar. He grabbed his vuvuzela from the shelf, flung it to the ground and stomped on it. It broke unceremoniously. He picked up the phone and called his older brother, Vithu. It was still night in the country of which his brother was a naturalised citizen. His brother, roused from deep sleep, sounded groggy and worried.

'Puppy? Are you okay?'

'Dada, sorry I woke you up. But I want to get out of here. Think I can get a job there?'

'It might be difficult with your impractical degree and no PhD even. But I'm sure we can find something for you. But why are you calling suddenly like this? What happened?'

'I don't want to be gobhi manchurian.'

'Gob— er … Puppy, I must go back to bed. Have an early day at work tomorrow. But we will talk soon. And I will help you get here. Just relax.'

'Who's it?' Puppy heard his father's voice on the other side. Vithu had turned off his mobile phone and Puppy had called him on the landline he kept for emergencies. Roused by the ringing phone so late in the night, their father had come in dreading bad news from the other room.

'It's Puppy,' Puppy heard Vithu's voice responding to his father. 'He is as crazy as ever but I think he has finally seen sense.'

'Should we call your grandmother in the village? She might know what's going on.'

'She is fine. I spoke to her earlier today. She told me Puppy would call.'

I wandered lonely as a shroud
that gloats and sighs o'er tales and bills,
when all at once I said aloud,
'Cauliflower? How horrible!'

The traffic beside it moved, but it
sat there as if in meditation.
A poet had to admit defeat
at this fall of the gobhi's station.
I gazed and gazed and felt a fury
like I was about to turn manchuri.

7

Ladies of Lore

Paru was ten years old, agog, and roused from her afternoon nap. Her neighbour, who Paru had, in turn, roused from her nap, took no more than half a dozen seconds to regain her composure when Paru told her that her grandmother had died.

'Paru, wait. Do you have incense sticks at home?'

'I don't think so, aunty. Mummy might have scented candles. Why?'

'Candles won't do. We are not setting the table for a romantic dinner. Have some respect.'

'She only just died, aunty. She isn't even cold yet. It will be a while before she starts smelling.'

'It's not for that. You are too young to know all this. But you have already seen death. Might as well tell you. Corpses fart. And you vegetarians eat so much dal. Wait here. I might have a box of agarbattis in the puja room.'

When Paru came back home with a group of neighbours, Nisha had already made several phone calls and more people were on their way. The only doctor in Gooday Nagar who agreed to come, braving death by Covid, to certify Nisha's mother as dead, was a distant relative.

Someone had placed a pair of marigold garlands on Aai's body. Someone else had stuffed cotton wool in her nostrils. Someone had hidden the sight of setting rigor mortis by covering her up to the neck with a sheet. A handful of incense sticks, stuck in a glass of rice, stood emanating thick rose-scented smoke beside the remains of Nisha's mother who was now being referred to as 'it'.

As they were brahmins, the cremation would be quick. They wouldn't have to wait for every relative from Sangli to Seattle to arrive. Travel had been rendered difficult owing to the pandemic anyway, and other castes were learning to perform hasty funerals too. So, there was no need to rent a refrigerating glass coffin from the municipal hospital.

Only the overweight and the ones who had had knee replacement surgeries sat on chairs. Everyone else sat cross-legged on a dhurrie on the floor.

'How old was she?' someone asked.

'Sixty-nine last September.'

'Virgo?'

Someone sniggered at the back. There were a few stifled chuckles. Nisha ignored them.

'No. Libra'

'Ah ... the sensuous sign,' someone whispered not realising it was audible. One look from Nisha made the speaker wish she hadn't said it.

'*Punya-cha maran*,' was the first utterance of praise for the dead. 'Death fit for a saint this is. Grace in death is accorded only to a lucky few. She did not suffer a minute more than was necessary. Was never bedridden. Never had to use a bedpan. May God grant us such ends when our time comes.'

'Hmm ... mmm,' was the murmured agreement from everyone.

The only person visibly crying was a contemporary of the deceased. She lived in the apartment directly below theirs and hadn't heard a thing since 2010. She wiped her eyes with her dupatta and sniffled. 'I will miss her morning riyaaz. Her voice is a national loss …' She hugged herself as she made her lament.

Old-man Barret, who had acquired his name from the beret he wore at all times while walking the apartment lawns at odd hours, chimed in after seeing the woman hugging herself. 'Yes. It's terribly cold these days. That is what took her, I'm sure. However strong you are, the cold catches your bones after sixty winters. I'm tired of frequenting the bathroom myself.' He hadn't heard much since 2012 either.

'Yes,' nodded the deaf connoisseur of song. 'Me too. I wonder when it will end. It is all the government's doing.'

Seeing the others go quiet and pay special attention to the obscure patterns on the dhurrie, the duo decided they must extend the lament further.

'Did she have arthritis? I do. The doctor said it's a rare variety.'

'One in a million. A gem.'

'Can't agree more.'

'Swell woman she was.'

'… swelling in the joints … terrible.'

The mourners struggled to keep a straight face through the inadvertent mirth in the banter of the deaf and looked imploringly at Nisha who took the cue.

'Aai … my aai. Why so soon?' she wailed and shed chubby tears. They all turned to her, patted her on the back and cried sympathetically with her.

The doctor had been sitting quietly in a corner by himself. Having discharged his professional duties, he wasn't obliged to stay. But he had stayed nonetheless. He motioned for Nisha to follow him into the bedroom.

'I'm sorry for your loss,' he said when they were alone.

Nisha nodded sombrely. 'I had no idea there was anything wrong with her heart,' she said.

'It wasn't that bad actually. It was a minor heart attack.'

'Minor? Then how did it kill her?'

'It didn't.'

'What do you mean?'

'You know perfectly well what I mean.'

'Doctor, my mother just died. I don't like your tone. What are you implying?'

'Recount to me the events of her death.'

'Well, I was in the other room logged on to work. I had a video conference. Paru was taking a nap. She wakes up early to study these days and feels sleepy in the afternoons. Aai was sitting beside her, on her bed, and listening to a recording of her own performance on the new tablet I got her. She was using headphones as she didn't want to disturb Paru. I suddenly heard Paru exclaim. She came running to me and said aai had collapsed. I rushed to her and she was clutching her chest. Her voice was feeble and she complained of a wringing feeling in her left arm. I lay her down, undid her blouse and massaged her chest. But her breath was growing faint. I thought she was trying to say something. I put my ears to her lips and heard her ask for Gangajal. I think she realised her time had come and wanted the libation of the Ganga to cleanse her of her sins.' Nisha paused there for a second before continuing. 'I asked Paru to fetch the Gangajal from the puja room. I broke the seal of the copper pot and poured some into aai's mouth. There was a gurgling sound and it spilled out of her mouth. Aai tried raising her head, but I realised she needed help drinking, and gently held her down and poured some more. This time it went down quickly. Aai writhed a little but suddenly stopped moving. I didn't know what to do. I was in shock. I hugged Paru and sat there for a long time. I would have sat like that forever if Paru hadn't pulled away after a while and suggested that we call people. I saw aai's open, unseeing eyes. It was horrible. I closed them with my hands and started calling people.'

'Well …' said the doctor. 'She might have survived the heart attack had she not choked on the Gangajal.'

Nisha stared.

'I won't tell anyone,' he smiled, 'if that's what you want.'

Something about his expression told Nisha he wasn't being very sympathetic. She wiped away her tears and looked at him sharply.

'Your wife is my brother-in-law's cousin.'

'So?'

'That practically makes me your sister.'

'No, it doesn't.' He placed his hand on her shoulder. 'No one need know.'

She shrugged his hand off. 'Fuck off!'

She walked out, trying to convert the red rage on her face to grief.

'What happened?' One of the many assembled neighbours asked her once she resumed her place.

'The doctor demanded extra money.'

'How terrible! Has he no grace?'

The doctor walked out of the room to the collective glare of indignant mourners. He hung his head and left without saying goodbye.

'Have you called your sister?' Someone asked after a long silence.

'Yes. She has set out. But she will need a health test and clearance certificate to cross the state border into Gooday Nagar. She has contacts, so I am not too worried. But even then, it will be a while before she gets here.'

'Are you not going to wait for her before performing the cremation?'

'No.'

A priest known to be flexible and easy-going was summoned to perform the last rites. The rituals, already rendered threadbare by the pandemic, were further abridged upon Nisha's request. When she asked to be allowed to light her mother's pyre, there was no protest. These acts of religious reformation had been in vogue among urban folks for a while now and were not seen as aberrations anymore. Although not quite the norm when there was a son in the picture, a daughter submitting the body of a parent to flames when she had no, or only female, siblings was seen as an act of righteousness.

It was a cold evening and everyone went home after accompanying Nisha back from the cremation grounds. A neighbour brought rice and a pot of highly seasoned aamti and a thermos of Bournvita. Another neighbour promised to bring breakfast the next morning. When deaths rendered hearths unlightable for three days, neighbours made sure the next of kin were fed. Although Nisha was doing intermittent fasting, and had not eaten a single dinner in two years, the emotional toll of the day left her drained, and she welcomed the comfort of hot food. Nisha and Paru finished the rice and aamti in two helpings each. Nisha poured out a mug of Bournvita for Paru and fixed herself a drink. They huddled together in the large, four-poster bed that had been in the family for several generations.

'Mummy, why did you hate aaji so much?'

'I didn't hate her.'

'She said you did.'

Nisha looked at her daughter with an expression of sadness and concern. But she knew it was not Paru's fault. Her daughter spent more time with her grandmother than with her, and the old woman had filled her head with all kinds of nonsense. The child wasn't confronting her. She was merely asking for her side of the story.

'It is not like that Paru. Your aaji wasn't an easy person to be with. We fought, yes. But I did not hate her. You will understand when you grow up. Ummm ... actually you may not. You and I are best friends, aren't we?' Nisha smiled.

'Yes, mummy.'

Nisha's mind wandered back to the time she had come home after a long day at the office. There had been numbers, ideas, backstabbing, strategy, deadlines, planning and casual sexism weighing on her. It hadn't been a difficult day. Just more of every day. It was around 10 p.m. when Nisha turned the key in the door of their apartment and softly walked in, not wanting to wake baby Paru. Aai should have been at the dinner table waiting with cold food and a snide remark. But Nisha walked in to find aai sitting on the couch with one of her nipples stuffed in Paru's mouth. Upon seeing Nisha, a flustered aai tried to cover her exposed breast with her saree.

'She wouldn't stop crying for you. So I thought I would comfort her,' she began explaining. Nisha snatched the baby from her arms, and Paru promptly started crying. 'You simply miss having your tits sucked,' she hissed at her over the din and slammed her bedroom door in her mother's face.

Aai was crying hotly by then. 'Don't talk to me like that, you whore! You think I don't know who Paru's father is?' she screamed at the closed door.

'You do, do you?' came the reply from within 'And do you know who is mine?'

That was years ago. She wished there was someone to talk to and distract her from these uncomfortable memories of her mother.

Paru was asleep when Nina arrived. Nisha was sitting on the armchair in the corner of the drawing room, beside the handmade lampshade, staring into space. They hugged without comment. Nina set her bags down.

'Naresh and the boys?' Nisha asked, more as a formality that anything else.

'Naresh is travelling for work. Aman has his piano lessons, and Ahan is just recovering from a fever. His immunity is down, and I didn't want him to risk Covid infection.' Nisha nodded. Both of them knew it was a polite fib.

'Drink?' Nisha asked her younger sister.

'Hell yes! With hot water please. I feel a bit of an itch in my throat. It's cold.'

The Hindu sisters sat down with a bottle of Christian Brothers. After two pegs, Nina put her glass down and gave Nisha a mischievous smile. 'I hope you made sure she was dead before you cremated her.'

Nisha's look went from horror to mirth in a second. They burst out laughing but quickly covered their mouths and shook with noiseless giggles. Laughter wasn't allowed in a house visited by death for thirteen days.

When the fountain of laughter subsided, Nisha sighed. This sudden gust of irreverence felt good. She couldn't remember when they went from being close sisters to formal friends—from pulling each other's pigtails to exchanging hollow pleasantries.

'Have you told Prashant?' Nina asked, as if on cue.

'Don't see why I should. There has been nothing between us for years now.'

'Ummm ... akka, may I ask why you didn't get a divorce?'

'Dread of paperwork. Neither of us wants to get married again, besides.'

'What about Paru? Doesn't he want to meet her?'

Nisha held her sister in a long, steady gaze. 'You know she isn't his, don't you?'

Nina nodded. 'I had guessed as much. But didn't want to ask.'

Nisha was silent.

'So, this is something of a relief, huh?' Nina asked after a while.

'I don't know. Perhaps it is. Too early to say.'

Nina sighed.

'How are things with you and Naresh?' Nisha asked.

'Usual. Y'know ... you make your bed with someone, you lie in it.'

'You could ... well ... try telling the truth in bed ...'

They exchanged sad smiles at Nisha's meagre attempt at a joke in a humourless situation.

Nisha spoke again after a minute of uncomfortable silence. 'Kulkarni doctor made a pass at me today.'

'What??? Despite aai's death? How awful. Was he trying to make it look like he was offering sympathy?'

Nisha began to say something but changed her mind. 'Yes,' she said instead.

'The bastard,' Nina said without passion. Silence re-entered the conversation. Nina tried to refill Nisha's glass but she held her hand over it to keep her from pouring.

'I think I'm done,' Nisha said. 'I started before you came. There will be fresh condolence givers arriving tomorrow. I can't receive them with a hangover.'

'Oh yes. What is worse? Grief or the obligation of gratitude for sympathy?'

'The only consolation is that the pollution of death means we are not required to offer refreshments to the visitors.'

Nina nodded. There was more silence.

'She mentioned you more than usual the last few days,' Nisha said after a long pause.

'Don't start the whole premonition story now,' Nina said and rolled her eyes.

'No, no. No premonition. She just missed you. She was too proud to call you herself. But you do know you were always her favourite.'

'Do I know? That's all I was allowed to know!'

Aai was the last of a long line of thumri singers who, married to their music, needed the patronage of rich men to sustain their art. In this rather harmonious tradition, pain and pleasure were like the Aarohan and the Avarohan—the ascent and descent of notes—necessary and beautiful. But in the latter half of the last century, this rise and fall of musical notes had hit the boulder of a new morality resulting in an off-key crash. This passion was renamed profession and that brought with it a whole new system of jugaad and judgement—the need to make, unmake, remake and make do. Many gave up singing to seek the respectability of marriage and domestic drudgery. Some turned to singing and acting in films. Some sought the patronage of a new man—the State—and sang to grants and honours. It was an endeavour that was fraught with politics and philistine pins and needling. Aai's mother was one of the very few who had chosen to play with the ragged ropes of the old order. And when aai took over, she hung by a thread.

Nisha had never known her father. In her rare tender moments, aai told her that he had been a handsome man of refined tastes—and one who loved a good laugh. But Nisha suspected it to be a posthumous image: a wishful sketch of a stranger who paid for a song with a baby. Nina's father, on the other hand, came into their life when Nisha was about three years old and continued to be a presence for a good many year. He was soft-spoken and gentle. He was the CEO of one of those companies that liked to keep its employees happy by giving them two pints of beer and snacks on Fridays and taking high performers to all-expense paid holidays to Bali. He was a connoisseur of music and in love with the dusky, doe-eyed aai, but most importantly, he was brahmin.

Although he was kind to Nisha, aai felt obliged to please him by being partial to Nina. While he was 'baba' for Nina, aai only allowed Nisha to address him as 'kaka'. And while he never asked for an account of their expenses, aai made it sound like Nisha's clothes and education were bought with the leftover change from Nina's upbringing. The only thing that prevented Nisha from growing bitter through all this was her sister. Sweet, sensitive Nina who resented their mother's overt doting more than anyone else.

It was when aai was pregnant with Nina that they had turned vegetarian. One Sunday, they had fresh mutton delivered home and when aai opened the lid of the box the meat shook with strong tremors—like it thought it was still sheep. Aai was horrified and gave the meat away to the servant. When she recounted the incident to kaka, he told her that he wanted his child to be raised satvik like himself, and they immediately became vegetarian. They even began calling themselves brahmin. Kaka later told the girls the story of the brave Maratha warrior Tanhaji whose corpse continued to swing its many swords after his head was cut off in a battle with the Mughals. Nisha was not sure why this story was entwined with the mutton incident in her mind.

Nina wanted to study music but was discouraged by aai. And tone-deaf Nisha gave it up after a few sargam lessons. Aai did her riyaz regularly, however, and the girls were allowed to be bored of it—and alternatively, detest it.

Thanks to baba/kaka, the girls did not lack for creature comforts while growing up. They went to good schools and received worthwhile educations. Baba arranged Nina's marriage to the son of one of his senior employees, another respectable brahmin. But when baba died suddenly a month before the wedding, the groom's family, rather than return the hefty dowry, very generously offered to go ahead with the wedding on the condition that Nina cut her mother out of her life. Baba's legitimate family had prevented Nina from inheriting any of his property and faced with an uncertain financial future, Nisha had pushed Nina into accepting her prospective in-law's terms and leaving the wobbly nest for good. Although aai was secretly happy for Nina's secure life, she outwardly blamed Nisha for her estrangement with her beloved Nina.

Kaka had left them a house and Nisha supported aai and herself with her job in a bank. There, she met and married Prashant, ten years her senior. Prashant was a good man but nothing more. He had come to live with Nisha and aai. While aai was relieved to have a man about the house, she never let an opportunity pass where she could rub it in Prashant's face that he was a ghar jamai—a live-in son-in-law—spineless for breaking the honourable tradition of taking his bride to live with his parents. Despite his good salary, which he generously spent on the household, and treating Nisha well, to aai, he could never be as good as Nina's legend of a husband.

Prashant was quiet and passionless. He never responded to aai's taunts. But although Nisha always sided with him, he did not give her credit as an ally either. He simply didn't want the tug to be there, and Nisha, who only knew her mother as a woman o'war, couldn't imagine peace. So, when Prashant left, she didn't stop him. She was just eager to resume her loud fights with her sweet-voiced, but terminally bitter, aai.

The only person for whom Nisha had felt any passion was her lover with whom she had become entangled for a short while soon after Prashant left. They knew the affair couldn't go on for ever, all along. When it was time to end it, Nisha told him she would love his children as her own and be kind to the slip of a girl who was going to be his wife. She hugged him one last time and wept liberally on his chest. He wept with her but there was no question of breaking off his impending arranged marriage with a girl from his own caste for Nisha, twelve years his senior and still legally married to another man.

Nisha had washed her face, dusted powder on her cheeks, lined her reddened eyes with kohl, and draped the cheap red nylon saree he had bought her and prepared to attend his wedding.

'You are going dressed like that?' Aai asked her. 'You might hide your shame better with silk.'

'Shame? If you had any yourself, I wouldn't be born!'

When Nisha discovered she was pregnant, Prashant, in his usual wordless way had come back to stay with them for a month—giving her pregnancy the respectability of a failed reconciliation with the legitimate man. He braved aai's venom with the same silence with which he accepted Nisha's gratitude before leaving for good.

And then Nisha had gone on to take an online course in German followed by a one-year weekend class PG diploma in the language, and got a job translating technical manuals in an international company. The job paid her four times as much as her previous bank job, had flexible hours and a two-days-a-week work-from-home option. With that, she managed to keep her mother's mouth muffled in silken finery and buy her daughter a happier childhood than her own.

She named her Parvathy, the daughter of the mountains. She would be tall and strong and beautiful. And she grew up so quickly. It was as if she was a character in a plot-ruled story where things happened every second line. All good things, thankfully.

It felt like only yesterday that she had that conversation with her about careers.

'You know my friend Monika? Her daughter is doing an MS from the US. What is it?'

'It's a degree that gets you jobs and things, mummy.'

'What do they do?'

'Everything they are told.'

'Pays well?'

'Yup'

'How much?'

'Forty-eight lakhs.'

'A year?'

'If they survive it, yes.'

'In white?'

'No. They stand them up like burlesque dancers and flip wads of cash on them—one banknote at a time.'

'The world has come a long way since I went to college.'

'Yup.'

What a delightful, intelligent and witty young woman Parvathy had grown up to be. Nisha saved and invested wisely. She prided herself on giving her daughter a lifestyle where careers are for meaning and motion and inheritance is for surety and sustenance forming the bedrock of art and articulation. Parvathy had a bachelor's degree in something popular, a master's degree in something whimsical, and a PhD in something useless. And she threw it all away to pursue music, in which she was very successful. She had raw talent and a little training was all she needed to launch herself on the fusion stage.

Nisha, who had wished safety upon her in the matters of career, love and reproduction, was nonetheless happy that her daughter followed her heart. Parvathy travelled the world and she travelled light. Every journey, she said, was about packing her voice and her two ChapSticks—one scented, one tinted. She never married and dipped into mankind only for offspring and never heartbreak. And Nisha grew to be an old woman full of nothing. Not even regret. That nothingness proved to be an asset at deathtime.

Nisha drifted out of her reveries to find Nina talking about something.

'Initially, even I was sceptical. There is so much new-age eyewash out there. But I couldn't find fault with this idea. I mean, it had no religious connotations, no fancy jargon. All it said was breathe. Focus on your breath as breathing is the only action that is both voluntary and involuntary. You cannot control the beating of your heart. On the other hand, you cannot lift your hand without willing it. Whereas you continue to breathe while you sleep. But you can also regulate the length and depth of your breath wilfully. And that is how it is the bridge between the spiritual and the physical world. You needn't do anything, chant nothing, seek nothing. Just sit there. Close your eyes. And focus on your breath. Sense it, feel it, know it. An hour of that and you feel lighter, calmer. It has given me a lot of peace. You must try it too.'

'Hmm ...?' Nisha said.

Nina noticed Nisha was distracted. 'Akka, are you okay?'

'Yes, yes ... just tired. It's been a long day'

'It's nearly morning. Let's get some sleep'.

They went in and lay down on the twin beds. Nina didn't bother changing out of the clothes she had travelled in. She drove alone and had come dressed in baggy sweatpants and a loose t-shirt. She simply undid her bra from under her shirt and flung it on the nightstand.

'Akka ...' Nina whispered.

'Mmm?' Nisha said groggily.

'Sorry if it's a little too early to say this. But I think you must consider finding someone. You will be lonely. Aai is not there to ruin it for you, besides.' Nisha didn't respond for a long time. Nina thought she was asleep and turned on her side to drift off when Nisha finally spoke.

'I'm not lonely. There's Paru.'

Nina sat up suddenly. 'Akka, stop talking like that. You sound like you are beginning to believe your own lies.' Nisha didn't reply. Nina came over to her bed and hugged her from behind—something she hadn't done since they were children. Nisha pulled Nina's arm closer. They lay like that for a long time before Nina spoke again.

'Akka, why did you abort her?'

Nisha said nothing. She finally began sobbing.

8

The Visitors

(A Strange Murder Non-Mystery)

It is surprising how our move here was so effortless, both mentally and logistically. It is also surprising how taking this fact in our stride is not only an offhand quality but a requirement of the residents of the castle—of which there are many. It probably stems from the unquestioning way in which a twelfth-century English castle with all the moss and mist of history and dislocated geography came to stand in Gooday Nagar, and how the castle happened to be the ancestral home of one, such as me, for whom old money can only mean finding a tattered and devalued banknote inside a long-forgotten book.

I took my boyfriend to the castle to meet my parents. We were seeking refuge and not a large, song-and-dance wedding. I am South Indian. We don't dance at our weddings. We have several hour-long ceremonies before a smoky fire leaving the bride and groom sufficiently asphyxiated to keep them from doing it on their wedding night. And we have squabbles between the bride's and groom's parties. It is certainly no party. I took him to the natal abode simply because eloping is no longer as romantic as it used to be in this horribly unrecognisable world and it seemed like the only place where we could live without extensive paperwork.

It was a lived-in castle and there were always visitors occupying several of the dozens of rooms. And they were living well. They did leisurely things like going for walks in the woods, birdwatching, journal-keeping, chess-playing, and falling in and out of love with each other. Some also wrote letters the old-fashioned way. I even remember seeing a golf bag in the corner of the courtyard by the potted plant and the marble bust of a curly-haired man. I also saw someone in knickerbockers and someone else in a monocle. No one knew who cooked for them or cleaned their rooms or washed their clothes. The servants were invisible.

It was a community of visitors. And the hosts were nowhere to be seen. My own boyfriend kept escaping with the Filipino woman every time I mentioned my plan of dressing him in the Maharashtrian, zari-style dhoti left behind by my ex.

And then there was the writer. He had come to the castle as a nobody and become a writer of repute while visiting there. He was bald now but the wispy crescent on his scalp suggested he had been a redhead. He was pale and fat. One day, he had gone up to the turret to look at the horizon for inspiration when he saw three men walking towards the castle through the woods. They wore Lincoln green and looked merry. They were clearly robbers, with robbing on their minds, and would rob the visitors of castle and home. But rather than go down and warn the others, he was inspired to write a novel. He sat there in the turret, writing. The words flowed like water from a secret spring in the desert and he wrote and wrote without pausing to eat or sleep or pee or sigh or stretch or comment on the weather or cry out from exasperation or walk the dog or water the plants or file his taxes or learn a new language or a musical instrument or overthrow the government or get open-heart surgery or look for discounts on groceries or polish his boots or write poetry. He wrote prose. He wrote and wrote until he had a 750-page manuscript that was rejected eighteen times before being published by a small publisher that went on to gain fame and fortune over his prize-winning novel. He finally came down from the turret celebrated, reviled, thrice married and divorced an equal number of times, savagely disparaged before being wished well in the memoir of one of his ex-wives, and clutching a half-written letter to a new woman who had expressed her doubts over his advances in which he waxed lyrical about how she may just be the one who would cure him of his image as an unfaithful lover. Since then, he has written ten or so articles in editorials and journals of every kind on how rejection didn't deter him.

When I met him later that evening, over the six-course meal that we mostly ate in silence, I asked him what had happened to the robbers. He pointed at the brightly dressed men at the far end of the long table. They had stayed on as visitors in the castle, just like all of us. They had shed their Lincoln green for clothes of every colour of the spectrum—that is, each of their outfits contained patches of every colour. After giving up their former vocation, they had turned into jolly, gregarious men who were everyone's best friends. But it hadn't been a simple transition.

Each robber had taken his own, never-easy, entirely unique, route to discovering peace and meaning as a butterfly. The first robber, let's call him 'A' (because that's what he called himself as he did not believe in qualitative nomenclature and insisted names did strictly what they were meant to do, which is to identify and not create images), had gone out of the castle briefly to study law and become a judge. He had gained a reputation as being fair and just. He had upheld the law and delivered judgements that were both legal and ethical with a firm head and a soft heart. He was the champion of the weak and the downtrodden. Criminals and wrongdoers shook like leaves in his presence, gangsters and murderers feared his very shadow, and goons and thugs peed in their pants at the mention of his name. He lived a life of smug glory that warmed his heart from within, like the glow of a paper lampshade. But all that changed one day when he stumbled on the stairs of his beloved temple of justice. The stumble wasn't metaphoric. It was physical. He tripped on a small protrusion on the ground that he had failed to notice, and fell flat on his face. His assistants ran to his aid, helped him to his feet and eased him down on the ground while they checked for broken bones. There weren't any. He was more shaken than hurt. But he was also curious. 'What there?' he said. His assistants were stunned by this sudden drop in eloquence from the master of oration and checked him for concussion. He brushed them away and repeated his question. 'What was it that caused the fall of one so sure-footed—morally and physically—as myself?' This time they knew what he was saying. One of them examined the ground and said, 'It looks like a protrusion to me, my lord.'

He was irritated. 'How many times must I tell you that the days of people lording over each other are long gone? We now live in a democratic republic where everyone is equal before, and after, the law. Do not call me "my lord". But if you must show me respect—which I insist must be free of deference—do so as a fellow human being. I am just like you, albeit with a few extra law degrees and more polished mannerisms and a greater enterprise for a just world. But I am no highborn. I started off as a common robber myself. I believe in reformative, and not punitive, justice. Just call me sir. Anyway, I know it is a protrusion, you moron! I want specifics. What is it that is protruding from the ground?'

The assistants rushed to examine the ground again. 'My lord,' one of them said, 'please forgive my continued address of you in words you disapprove of. But it is my belief that while assumed greatness by birth and suchlike are wrong in this time and space in history, real greatness is achieved. And you, my lord, have done so by the sweat of your brow and the burnt midnight oil, and that must be acknowledged. I addressed my school teacher as "sir". He was scum. But you, my lord, will remain my lord as an inspiration. Now, that protrusion seems to me like a piece of stone that is embedded deep. It may be a fault in the masonry of the building. I could have it levelled.'

'No,' said Justice 'A' as he glugged down the water from a tumbler that another assistant had brought him. 'I want it examined. There can be no action before the case is fully examined.'

The assistants rushed back to the protrusion and began kicking at it to loosen it. One of them fractured his toe in his enthusiasm to dislodge the thing. The protrusion did not budge. Someone brought a pen to dig around it. It revealed a centimetre or so of stone before the pen broke. They paused to rename the town New Pembrokeshire before continuing the operation. They brought a garden fork and tried to uproot the stone. That loosened the soil only deep enough to show that the stone was too large for a simple fork. A pickaxe was brought and earth was shovelled out by the bucketful. The stone turned out to be the statue of a lion—or a tiger or a dragon. It was hard to tell. And it was not just a single statue but attached to a larger one. A bulldozer was brought next. It took seven days of relentless digging to excavate the mystery stone. In the meanwhile, news of the digging reached far and wide, and people came in hordes to watch the spectacle. They came in tractors and lorries, in cars and buses, on motorcycles and scooters riding four to one, and on bicycles and on foot. They set up food carts and souvenir shops and magic shows for children while they waited for the revelation. It was only when a Ferris wheel was installed that the earthmovers completed their job to reveal a humongous stone chair: a throne of epic proportions! It had a hundred steps leading to the seat. The banisters on the sides had the bust of one or the other majestic animal on each end. The backrest had an enormous serpent looming over it to form a canopy with its many heads. The carving on the stone showed no delicacy. It was meant to, and did, inspire awe. It was grand and spectacular.

'A' stood transfixed before it. This was the throne of the mythical king Trikramaditya the Boundless. The king who inhabited the lore of the land as the epitome of justice was no matter of myth after all. And it was from this very place that he had grandly upheld the law when time was called yore. 'A' was moved beyond words. He adjourned the day's hearings and went home. His shoulders sagged and his eyes were downcast. Back home, over several glasses of an amber-coloured liquid of much antiquity and hence expense, he mulled over the implications of the find. All the name and fame he had gained, all the reputation of being the best judge of the land, was simply owing to the fact that he had stood on King Trikramaditya's throne. The wisdom of 'A's head and the quotable quality of his words had in fact radiated into him from the throne. None of it had been his and 'A' had no true claim over his achievements.

First, 'A' wept at the loss of glory. But then, he came out of it cleansed and free. He embraced his inner nobodyness and felt lighter than ever. The next morning, amidst great waves of disbelief, he resigned from his position stating 'personal reasons'. Leaving a great big muddy hole where his court had stood, which caused water logging during the monsoons, and only a huge Ferris wheel to tell the tale of the monumental dig, he packed the one suitcase he had arrived with and returned to the castle to live out his life as nothing but 'A'. And there he sat at the far end of the banquet table downing glass after glass of dry wine and telling a funny story to anyone within earshot.

I headed back to our room on the second floor overlooking the courtyard garden with a fountain in the middle. The building had been renovated for modern comforts. There were ensuite bathrooms in each of the bedrooms with a washstand, toilet and shower pod. There was central heating and soft electric lighting. There was no TV room as vulgarity was strictly disallowed. There were some billiards tables and chess boards with ivory pieces, however. And then there was the library. A room with wood-panelling, thick carpets, shelves of hardbound books, and tables on which stood banker's lamps with green shades and brass fittings. I normally stopped by to browse through the poetry section before bed but it had been a long day full of strange stories, and I needed a shower and sleep. I asked for some hot chocolate in the usual manner, which was to lean through the kitchen door and call out casually, 'Please send a cup of hot chocolate to my room. No sugar. Thanks,' to no one in particular. I could never spot anyone there, but I knew the chocolate would fetch up in my room in a nice stoneware mug on a wicker tray.

I undressed and stepped into the shower pod, turned the knob and stood aside in a corner waiting for the cold water to be flushed out of the pipe before the hot water poured down, and I could step into the jet. I stood under the stream and it felt divine. I imagined myself modelling for a luxury bathroom fixture company and airbrushed away the flaws on my naked skin and struck a sexy pose. I rubbed soap on myself and worked up a lather. Damn! I had made the same mistake I always did despite enough mental notes to exhaust a whole wad of virtual Post-its. I had turned the water off to soap myself, and now, I couldn't turn the stainless-steel knob back on with my slippery hands. I tried again and again, working myself into a panic. Although Gooday Nagar was a sweltering city, the castle itself stood in a bubble of temperate coolness which, like everything else about the castle, was unexplainable. The heat in the pod vanished and I shivered as the soap dried on my body. I finally had to step out of the bathroom, rub my hands on a towel and turn the knob before I could get the water to start again.

My boyfriend, who had returned in the meanwhile from wherever he had been, was now snug in the bed, reading a murder mystery. He took no notice of me as I walked out of the bathroom. I had finally washed the soap off and came out wrapped in a towel. I seemed to have caught a chill and wanted desperately to warm myself upon him. I slid under the blanket and held him. He resisted at first. We hadn't been making love since the squabble over the lights. He had discovered his pubes were greying and had insisted on keeping the lights off when he undressed. My lecture on the vanity of youth and the need for intimacy and love to be free and ageless only heightened his indignance, and he had refused to touch me since. But today, after much coaxing and stroking, he responded owing to what must have been sheer instinct. I didn't complain. We went through the whole thing passionlessly and finished in ten minutes, including foreplay. Sufficiently warmed, I turned around and dozed off—but not before I heard his half-asleep suggestion of an open marriage. I responded to that with a snore. 'Well, we need to be married before we talk of opening it,' he said and laughed at his own joke. 'When are we meeting these parents of yours anyway?' He waited a whole minute for a response before realising there was none forthcoming and went to sleep.

The sun was sky-high when I woke up the next morning—a regular day, as that is where the sun usually hung out. My boyfriend must have woken up and gone out much earlier. His part of the bed was neatly made. There was a tray of breakfast waiting for me. Two pieces of toast, a chip of butter, a small sachet of jam, two runny eggs, mushrooms, a slice of brie, a cup of muesli and fruity yoghurt, a glass of orange juice, and a mug of black coffee with two sugar cubes on the side. I sighed. Why couldn't we have some upma or poha or idli-chutney for a change? But I suppose when in a castle one must act and eat castley—or what we imagine castley to be. I gobbled up my breakfast without pausing to taste it, had a quick wash and headed down.

The castle seemed deserted. But I somehow didn't feel alone. Sometimes it is easier to let one's guard down in a crowd where one is assured of apathy. But when ostensibly alone, one is not entirely sure of their solitude. It is almost like we develop a new sense in which we become aware when light bouncing off of us reaches a retina. I turned around to find one of the former robbers looking keenly at me. 'Phew! You gave me a fright!' I said. 'I apologise. It was not intentional,' he said. He was dressed in his usual bright colours. 'Where are the others?' I asked. 'They are away shopping in the bazaars of Gooday Nagar. One cannot have enough of the exotic local finery,' he said with a flourish that I couldn't quite tell if it was colonial hangover or South Bombay-style campiness. I had been wanting to hear his story after 'A's strange tale yesterday. But I had imagined it would happen over supper like the previous narration. But since there was no one about and I didn't have any plans for the day, I settled down to listen to his story which he seemed inclined to share.

Let's call him 'B'—not because that's his name, but it comes after A and is easy to remember. There is also another reason, but I won't disclose it just yet. 'B' like 'A' had once decided to leave the delusional neverendingness of comfort in the castle and gone out into the world. He had become an HR executive in a multinational company. He was a team player and had great eye for detail. With his positive mindset and never-say-no attitude he rose through the ranks and became the top HR manager of the entire operation in Gooday Nagar. He had a big salary and a huge office with an efficient secretary and a great view of the sea if he ignored the shanty town right under his building—and the fact that Gooday Nagar was landlocked. But he stayed humble and confident and spent most of his time on the floor, motivating the executives—although he could not say what it was exactly that they did. It had something to do with the management or processing of knowledge or data or some such (or was it finance or programming?). Anyway, he conducted team-building activities and employed the positive-reinforcement method to get them to give their best.

One Friday, he organised an office party to celebrate the achievement of a milestone in sales (or was it stocks?) and after some singing and dancing and games and confetti strewing, everyone hit the beer. The first crate was glugged down in no time and never one to miss an opportunity to cheer everyone along, 'B' went to the copy room to fetch the second crate. In his hurry to bring it fast enough so as not to allow a break in the revelry, he slipped on spilled beer and hit his head on the photocopier. He must have lost consciousness because when he came to, it was pitch dark and he seemed to be alone. The executives, he gathered, had continued the party without him—probably even stepped over his prone body to fetch themselves beer after beer—and gone home leaving him behind when it was all over. 'B' was dazed and hungover and a little confused. He let himself out and wandered the streets. As if the realisation of being secretly despised wasn't enough, he got mugged. The thieves took his wallet, phone, wristwatch, and even his shoes and hit him in the same spot on his head where he had hit himself a few hours earlier. 'B' walked around Gooday Nagar bruised and barefoot with his clothes in tatters. He slept on a park bench and by the time he was roused by the noises of the waking city, he had forgotten who, and where, he was.

'B' was hungry. He saw a sweet shop and walked in, and before the shopkeeper could shoo away this ragged and injured straggler, 'B' grabbed a barfi and put it in his mouth. 'Hey! Hey! Who are you! Bloody beggar stealing my sweets. I'll teach you a lesson!' the shopkeeper screamed and lunged at him. 'B' tried to dodge him and missed a step, and the two fell down in a heap on the pavement. Unknown to the shopkeeper, an electric wire in his old shop had come loose a few days ago and touched another wire that very moment causing sparks to fly. The combustible decorations the shopkeeper had not removed since Diwali caught fire and spread in seconds engulfing his whole shop in a frenzied blaze. The shopkeeper was saved because he was outside grappling with 'B'. If not for 'B', the shopkeeper would have burned with his shop. 'B' stood up, dusted himself and not knowing what to say, merely smiled at the shopkeeper and walked away. The shopkeeper stood, watching 'B', struggling to comprehend the spike in life-changing events of the last few seconds.

'B' wandered on. Before long, news that the curse of a holy man destroyed the business of a sweet shop owner for denying him a piece of sweet had reached the next sweet shop. In his amnesia, the barfi was the only thing 'B' recognised as food. He went in and grabbed a piece again. But this shopkeeper allowed him to have his barfi without protest. 'B' smiled as he ate. Just then, the shopkeeper's assistant called him to the phone. The shopkeeper had won the lottery! That was the birth of 'B' as Barfi Baba, the blesser of the benevolent and the bugbear of the bad.

He became an overnight legend as a holy man. He was welcomed with great deference everywhere he went, and could walk into any shop of his choice and eat as many barfis as he liked. He only had to smile at the shop owners and that was all the blessing they needed. Their businesses thrived, their daughters married well, they added storeys to their houses, and their sons passed their exams.

Barfi Baba did not have to wander the streets long after that. They built him a monastery with all luxuries imaginable. He sat on a pink cushion on a high seat of burnished brass that shone like gold, and looked at his devotees. He did not have to say a word. He was not a speech monk. He was a smile monk. They brought him mountains of barfi on decorated trays and sought his blessings, which he was always generous with. And they left large sums of money in donation, which members of his staff put away. He smiled through all the adulation neither demanding nor rejecting it. Months and years passed.

His fame spread far and wide as did his girth owing to the steady diet of refined sugar. His monastery had a sophisticated administrative system where men with degrees in management from fancy universities ran the barfi-blessing enterprise worth millions. They even had an HR department. There were durbars for him with devotees in attendance. And to remain true to the original story, he was driven around to sweet shops on festive days for onsite blessings. They also planned tours for him so his glory reached the farthest corners of the land. He was oblivious to all this and simply continued to smile and allowed himself to be led around.

On one such tour the local devotees decided 'B' should have a procession on an elephant. It was to be a grand scene with great pomp for piety. Thousands gathered. They brought a magnificent elephant with his tusks encased in brass, his head covered in a beautifully embroidered caparison. Bells and garlands hung on his neck and there was a big, decorated howdah for the Barfi Baba to ride in. The elephant knelt down upon the mahout's command and, with a step ladder, 'B' was helped up into the howdah. The procession began. There were neat matrices of men and women, dressed in synchronised clothing, in front and behind the elephant. Two brass bands—one playing *Jhalak Dikhlaja Ek Bar Ajajajaja-aaaanja* and the other *Huttidare Kannada Naadal Huttabeku*—led the procession in a competitive cacophony. They were followed by a team of married women dressed in silk saris balancing steel pots filled with water on their heads and a coconut on top. They wore red for auspiciousness, green to symbolise fertility—which is always a good thing for a woman—and yellow because it went well with red and green. Behind them came a group of teenage girls dancing with sticks clacking away rhythmically. Then came men in brightly coloured turbans shouting his hails. More people followed flinging flowers at the elephant. Barfi Baba sat grinning plumply through all this.

And then, with no warning, came a huge clap of thunder. It was completely unexpected as it was not the season for rains. The music stopped suddenly and people looked around scared and confused as the skies burst open. When they realised their silken finery was being ruined, the people ran helter-skelter. The crowd dispersed in a matter of seconds and sought shelter under shop awnings along the street. The mahout turned around and said something indecipherable to Barfi Baba then jumped off the pachyderm and touched the ground with a parachute landing fall. He rose to his feet with a quick jump and bolted into the darkened streets. Barfi Baba was left alone in the pralaya-like deluge—the ultimate flood that marks the end of an eon before the rise of the next. The elephant, however, did not seem to mind the rain. It had not been taken to the river for a wash in a while, and it missed water and was enjoying itself. It walked on with the helpless and soaked-to-the-bone Barfi Baba on its back. Without a mahout, it was its own master. It decided to leave the town and walk into the forest. It walked and walked for what seemed like hours as the rain kept falling in sheets. And then Barfi Baba had a strong sugar withdrawal. He had not been far from a barfi since he had been organically ordained, and his kidneys were shot. This brief lull in sugar supply made him lightheaded that—owing to a brief lexical mix-up—caused light to enter his head and it all came back to him: who he was, where he was. Robber, HR manager, holy man, head of a cult ... everything flashed before his eyes like a mad, psychedelic dream.

'B' had had enough of the barfis and the smiling and the life of luxury that denied him opinions on anything and everything. He wanted good, healthy, savoury food. He wanted salads and potatoes with herbs and unsweetened porridge with almond milk. He wanted to love and hate things—and say as much. He was homesick for his old life. But his nostalgia overshot the recent past and landed in the castle. He no longer wanted to be an HR manager because he saw that as just another version of the barfi life—sweet, boring and hazardous. He gathered all his will and jumped off the mischievous elephant. He did not know the parachute landing fall and therefore broke his ankle. But that did not deter him. He ran with no sense of direction into the driving rain. He ran like a madman, dragging his ankle. He ran and ran until he made it back to the castle, which remained dry despite officially being a part of the Gooday Nagar County. And there he remained.

He was over the trauma now and a slight limp was all he had to show for his ordeals with glory. He was content and chirpy.

Although I had got used to strangeness as the norm in the castle, my head was reeling under the rambling narrative of the last story, and I needed to lie down. But as if it wasn't enough to feel like I had been swung around in a whirlpool of implausibility, I found my mother waiting for me in my room. The mother I had hoped to meet every day since I had arrived in the castle weeks (or was it months? years?) ago. There she sat casually looking through my clothes. Owing to the new reality of this place, I couldn't remember the actual number of years since I had last seen my mother. Was it a decade ago? Was it more recent than that? But her calm and casual demeanour at spotting me seemed to suggest that I had seen her only yesterday. She looked changed though. She was willowy, tall and ramrod straight. Her lush, grey curls were gathered up in a cupola above her head and she was dressed in a calf-length, pastel green skirt and blouse cut from the same cloth. She had a choker of large white pearls around her throat. Her face was a mask of boredom and disapproval. She was a far cry from the homely, but comely, sari-clad woman I had known her to be all my life: short and round-faced with plump forearms, exhibiting a variety of smiles ranging from childlike to witchlike to sardonic depending on her several moods in a single day. But it was her all right. I didn't know what to believe anymore.

'Are these your clothes? Poor child …' was her opening to a conversation with her only daughter after many years of separation. 'Such bright colours … dowdy …so vulgar … common …'

'Am-amma …' I stuttered.

'Call me mother.'

'Moth— uh … But you bore me!'

'Amuse yourself elsewhere child … I am not obliged to entertain you.'

'Entertai—? What? What are you saying? What happened to you? Where have you been? I have been looking for you for months … years … What is this castle? What happened to our home? Where is daddy? Who are all these people?'

'Shhh … calm down.' Her voice sounded like a whisper. 'So many questions! It's so common.'

'Mother, I wanted you to meet my boyfriend. We have been waiting for you and daddy to meet him. We hope to get married. We need your blessings. Um … he is not of our religion, but—'

'Religion? Oh dear, oh dear! Do you have to make everything so vulgar, my poor changeling? We don't discuss things like religion here.' She ceremoniously waved her hand before her nose like she had smelled something bad. 'I know your boyfriend. He is a sweet boy. Rather common, but one doesn't go to prison for being common, does one? Not anymore in any case. Of course, you have our blessings. But marriage? In this day and age? Really, child?'

She had never called me child. Not even when I was one. And I am a grown woman now. I sat down with a thump on the bed. My head was spinning.

'Do you want my smelling salts?' she asked sympathetically. At that, I fainted.

When I came to, she was gone. Was that all a dream? But the faint whiff of her perfume—an expensive petrichor that was dabbed, not sprayed, on pulse points with a glass needle—suggested otherwise. As did the letter she had left on my desk weighed down by her gold-rimmed lorgnette. The letter was written on personalised stationary that had a gold insignia of a dragon that appeared to be lighting a cigarette, which I guessed was the castle coat of arms.

'My sweet child,' it began. 'I fear I may have failed you as a mother by not teaching you to not ask questions. Or that reality is simply the gestalt of your senses at any given time and all memory is corruption of the only truth we may know, which is ephemeral. We may choose to accept and therefore be free. Or, we may keep questioning and lose ourselves in the labyrinths of possibility and endure endless torture. This castle is our home whether or not you remember it. I am who I am and what I appear to be. The third robber is your father (let's call him 'C' because I know you have called the other two 'A' and 'B'—and order matters in small doses). You will hear his story eventually. Don't ask me if I left your father and married 'C'. I didn't. 'C' is your real father, your only father. Don't use memory as an argument. I have no patience for it. And if you remember him as something or someone else, it only shows how compromised your reality is. You don't need it. You and your boyfriend are no more, and no less, welcome here than everyone else—as you have known for some time—which is to mean you can belong and be beautiful in any way you find fit. You may get married if you like—whenever you like. You may leave too—if you like. But you will very likely come back like everyone else. There will be no questions asked. But you must also not ask questions that are unreasonable: you may ask what, you may even ask how (for which you may receive a response, but you are not entitled to one) but you must never ask why.' The sign off simply said 'Your mother'.

I don't know if it was the relentless attack on my reason or the brief break in consciousness (a drugged nap?) or that this experience of bizarreness had been so gradual and steady that the letter, rather than heighten my confusion, calmed me down. I felt a peace like I had not known in a long time. Time was not a straight line like I had imagined it to be. It was a closed loop that had been twisted around several times like the rubber band on a ponytail, and its far edges touched and retouched making a fine mesh and a great mess.

That night, my boyfriend didn't return to the room. I tried not to think too much about it. My mind was preoccupied by thoughts of 'C', my father. Did I even want to know about him anymore? Although he dressed colourfully to maintain solidarity with his former mates, he was the least gregarious of the three. In fact, he was what would have been called 'eccentric' in a world where memory was a building block of reality rather than a deterrent. I decided I would just watch him from a distance and speak only if I felt the need to. I switched the light off and slept soundly that night.

'C' followed a simple routine every morning: he walked up to the castle ramparts to a corner where they had installed a fire escape. He had bunged the stairs with large blocks of kindling and other combustible material. He had several buckets and pails arranged on the ground in no apparent order. He picked up one after the other and emptied the water from one to the other. Perhaps he is a water conservationist collecting dew and is gathering up the dawn's haul to use in a sustainable way, I thought. But no. He was simply transferring water from one bucket to the other at random. I didn't know how the water got there in the first place. And then, he grabbed a bucket with a handle entangled in a coil of rope and let it down over the rampart as if to draw water from the moat. But the rope was not attached to the bucket and it fell into the water below. He wasn't surprised in the least. He simply coiled the rope back up and put it away. He then fed crumbs to some birds before walking back to his room.

I knew I was allowed 'what' questions. So, I walked up to him as he sat sipping a cup of coffee at the picnic table in the garden. 'Good morning, father,' I said cordially expecting him to look askance at me for being addressed so. But he gave me a warm smile. 'Hello, my child,' he said. 'I was wondering if you might explain to me what you did on the ramparts this morning,' I said formally. 'I would be happy to. I am an applied philosopher. That should explain it. Let me know if that isn't clear enough.' It wasn't. I said so. I also said—despite mother's warning—that I remembered him to have been an accountant, the one job that pops into your head when you want to think of the most soulless, spirit-on-a-short-leash, dead-end occupation known to mankind in the modern world. I wish I hadn't. I received the same new-age, castle-hued answer. 'I was only as much an accountant as your imagination of it.' Sigh. Very well. 'What is an applied philosopher then?'

'My life is all about demonstrating the pointlessness of life in the larger scheme of things. But despite this ultimate lack of purpose, man's acts constitute the only meaning known to the one who lives it. We think we are in control of our lives—and there is value in thinking so—but luck comes into play more often than we like to imagine. Right from avoiding death by the most unlikely of things—which is rendered likely by its occurrence—to being able to do the things that bring us the most joy, everything depends on luck. You may calculate the probability of an event to the closest possible decimal with the factors known to you, but there are always more factors than you can comprehend that can bring everything crashing down. Yet we must occupy ourselves with life—routines, rigmaroles, boredom even.'

'That dropped bucket?' I asked.

'It may or may not have been an accident. If I am lucky, it will turn up back on the ramparts.'

'Has that happened?'

'Many times.'

'Who brings it up?'

'A bird, a beast, the elements, the hand of fate. I'm not interested to know. I seek no answers.'

'Have you studied philosophy?' I asked.

'I tried to. I ventured out and enrolled in courses. I read different schools ... Indian, Chinese, Continental ...'

'Those are cuisines.'

'Well, different kinds of philosophies are but cuisines of the mind. It's ultimately food for thought. There are theories and speculations. There are descriptions and prescriptions. Sometimes the descriptions don't fit everything and most times the prescriptions are wrong. Even if they aren't, they are hard to implement or they go horribly wrong because there is just no accounting for stupid or deliberate misinterpretation. Anyway, to read and to know true philosophy, one needs a deep understanding of mathematics. I don't have it. But I do know that the life instinct is pretty much all we have. And we must distract ourselves with things and activities for as long as we live. So I do what I do again and again to demonstrate this. I also throw in a reference to the economy of the world to whoever is willing to look at it that way—that it represents movement, accumulation, more movement, and a shift in the position of accumulation. All very pointless in the larger scheme of things, which doesn't exist. And that is how I am an applied philosopher.'

'But the fire escape is blocked with wood. Is it to tempt fate? Is it an experiment?'

'Oh that? No. That's just firewood for the boilers. The woodshed needed repairs, and I put it there while we waited for it to be fixed. It is fixed now, but I have been too lazy to move it.'

'And laziness is a virtue, I suppose?'

'Nonsense. There is no such thing as virtue.'

'And feeding the birds?'

'That is for kindness. That's part of it too. As I said, luck is a great factor in life. Because we have sentience, we must try to be the luck factor in others' lives by being kind.'

'So that it comes back to you?'

'No. Because it simply needs to be done.'

'Do you believe in God?' I asked.

'Don't ask stupid questions.'

'Yes, father.'

'I hear wedding bells are about to be rung. Have you thought of a date?' he asked kindly to make up for the harshness of his last remark.

'Not yet. Now, I'm not even sure if I want to ...' My voice trailed off.

'Ah,' he said, 'very well then.'

The part of the castle-people's minds that contained curiosity had been scrubbed clean. He didn't have anything more to say. He only smiled.

'You are quite a prophet you know.' I tried to tease him.

'Oh no! I'm anti-cult!' he said innocently.

'Nice to know you, father,' I said and kissed him on the forehead and left for my room.

My boyfriend didn't return to the room that night either.

As luck would have it, I was the one to discover the body in the library the next morning. I had gone in at dawn because I hadn't slept too well at night and, rather than stay in bed and swim between sleep and wakefulness, which always left me in a bad mood, I decided to wake up fully and tire myself so I could take a restful nap later. It was still too dark to go for a walk so I decided to read in the library.

I screamed in horror when the body of the Filipino woman fell on me when I opened the door to the poetry section that was housed in a separate, but tiny, room. I stood rooted to the spot and continued to scream until the others came running in their bedroom slippers, hastily tying the straps of their robes. There was no blood fortunately; no puncture to the form from the outside. I hate a mess. It must have been poison then—the woman's weapon. But don't victims of poisoning die calmly in their sleep or fall face down into their pudding depending on the speed of the poison administered? Why would anyone who had been poisoned go hide in the library to drop down on the door opener? That is reserved for stab victims.

Before I could express my doubts, my mother arrived and took charge. Her grey hair in curlers, dressed in a magenta silk robe and blue velvet slippers, she gave me a concerned look. 'Enough screaming now. It's not as if someone has died. Well, someone has, in a manner of speaking. But who doesn't? You would too, given half a chance. Don't judge the poor woman,' she said looking rather school headmistressishly at everyone gathered, and forcing us to lower our gaze. 'What a bother,' she continued. 'Well, we must have all this cleared up before breakfast. Poor woman. But there's no need to wonder why and that sort of thing. That would be so vulgar. What is done is done. Oh, do please carry on with your knitting, won't you, Miss Marble? There is no need to be so dramatic about it.' Her last remark was aimed at the little elderly lady in the corner armchair who was in the act of putting her knitting down to meditate on the murder. I don't know how she had materialised there. I thought I was the only one in the library. But that woman had a certain stealth to her and a knack for making herself so insignificant that she was invisible despite her outdated English costumes.

'Very well, dear,' she said and made as if to gather the wool back into her lap. Mother was barking instructions at the servants—no amount of rubber necking gave me a glimpse of them though—to call the doctor, priest, crematorium. No coroner, however. They had gone extinct after the Corona virus outbreak.

'Oh, I seem to have dropped my ball of pink wool. How clumsy of me. Would you pick it up for me, dear, if you'd be so kind? My arthritis, you see …' Miss Marble asked smiling sheepishly. As I bent down to pick it, she whispered sharply into my ears. 'You must always go for the jilting man, my dear, and not the other woman. Revenge must lead to closure and not drag on as a Greek tragedy. Prolonged pain only leads to endless melancholy. It is boring. You must live many stories in one lifetime and not wallow in the same old tale again and again.' I straightened up sharply but my jaw remained on the floor as I gaped at her.

'Oh dear. I really must stop pairing pink with grey. It is so out of fashion now. But I cannot help it. I seem to live on in another time,' she said aloud appearing flustered.

'It wasn't m— How did you know? I mean … What?' I stuttered.

'I know. I just do. At my age you will too. But don't worry, your secret is safe with me. I have reached a phase in life where I am more concerned about wool combinations and knitting patterns, and remembering to take my medicine, and not going the whole hog on the bread pudding to be bothered about who killed whom. Well, I do know who did it by force of habit, of course, but I cannot be arsed to do anything about it.'

I was more startled by the sudden dip in her propriety than the content of her speech. She winked at me.

'But tell me, what kind of wedding will it be? Will you wear a gown or a sari?' she asked and smiled sweetly.

'Er ... I'm not sure about it. Not sure about him, I mean, Miss Marble.'

'Oh dear,' she said and began knitting.

Supper was a sombre affair. That was only fair. After all, there had been a murder in the castle. I was sitting next to the writer again after many days, and he seemed in a thoughtful mood that day. 'Whodunnits don't work in Gooday Nagar,' he told me. 'Lives are a dime a dozen here. There are so many—too many—lives. But more importantly, the murderer's identity is never unknown. More often than not it is committed in consultation with the authorities who will show you how to clean your tracks and throw the law off. The law is, after all, just an old lady with a blindfold and a set of outdated weighing scales. You could set a legal thriller here with a friend or a relative of the victim fighting not just the criminal but the entire judicial system to get justice. It has to be dramatic, dialogue-ridden, a power struggle, a revolution, an entertainer. Never whodunnits,' he explained. I nodded. My boyfriend had returned from wherever he had been and was sitting as far away from me as possible. He was glaring at me whenever he caught my eye.

The food arrived just then. I was delightfully surprised to see that it was khichdi, curd-rice and lime pickle served on stainless steel plates with no cutlery. It had to be eaten with the fingers as soul food is meant to be eaten. For the first time since arriving in it, I felt comfortably engulfed by the castle.

9

A Writing Competition

'Inspired yet?' he asked when he saw her wistfully looking at the unceasing rain. She shot him an irritated look. But realising it was a sincere question she smiled.

'No,' she sighed. 'Watching the rain fall on the trees is all very well the first ten minutes. You pose for photos with a cup of tea gazing at nothing in particular, post the photos with a quote about love or life or something similarly vacuous and your equally jobless friends gush over it, and you begin to think you are a poet—'

'The last is a tragic risk,' he interrupted.

'Bitch rain! It is zero per cent inspiration, one hundred per cent precipitation.'

It was his turn to give her a crusty look.

'Do you regret getting together with a loony?' she asked with a smile.

'No,' he said fondly.

It had been two weeks since they arrived in that place—that was neither his nor hers—after nearly two years of a torrid internet romance, which began with the pandemic and, like it, held fast. Biological complications were worsened by the diplomatic ones between their respective countries, rendering thoroughfare difficult. So the moment they found a window open to a third country, they jumped through it and landed there. They left their previous lives behind to set out together on a journey of surprises.

The day before she left, her mother who had survived the virus sat her down in her Gooday Nagar apartment and offered her daughter support to a prospective lesbian liaison, despite her daughter's protestations that it was a man she was going to meet. But the mother insisted. She said she had seen death from close up and lived to tell the tale as a matter of random luck—others fitter and younger and with greater responsibilities than her, had been called away through no fault of theirs. She wanted to be a better mother to her grown daughter by turning more open-minded, and they had had a most awkward conversation.

'It's a man. And I am happy about him.'

'I thought ... you know ... I thought it was a euphemism.'

'What is? The man or happiness?'

'Both when claimed together.'

His family, on the other hand, had only cautioned him against over-indulging on curry and naan-bread—and to not make a personal thing of colonial guilt.

Their first meeting was full of film-like wonder: delicious, shyly tactile and poignant. They settled into their bed-and-breakfast apartment atop a hill and had been rained-in ever since. These were unseasonal thunderstorms of an incorrigibly changed world, with leaders who had only recently met in a country whose climate suited talks. Planning was beginning to be an obsolete idea in this new world. Yet the couple had planned because that is what they knew how to do—though it was mostly by luck that they got this far. Being shut indoors in a strange country wasn't bad because they had one another. They told themselves they were expats, and not tourists, so being deprived of the country's sights did not bother them. When romance settled into blissful domesticity, their minds demanded entertainment. And although they both had subscriptions to video streaming platforms, the internet in the place was shaky, and they had to live like people did a few decades ago: slowly.

'Horror?' she asked. 'Why horror? You want us to do Shelley just because we are stuck in the rain? Write a twenty-first century Frankenstein? Why not a nice romance or something?'

Neither of them had studied literature in college. She had done business something or the other and he studied ... umm ... international relations or some such new-fangled American invention. Whatever his degree was in, it was certainly not medicine or biology, going by the way he answered her question about the new variant named after yet another Greek letter. 'It is virile and dodgy and when it sees the vaccine, it moves like this to avoid it.' He pantomimed a Hollywood actor weaving his way through a laser beam security system.

She hadn't asked him why he thought they should take up writing to pass the time. It was their shared love for the quaintness of a bygone world that had brought them together when she had 'liked' a photo of him in a T-Shirt with the legend 'Analogue is Warmer' and a picture of a cassette. So sitting by the fire after the day's hunt, to tell each other stories, was perfectly suited for the glorious primordial instinct they both fantasised about.

'Because it is too late for that,' he said. 'Any projection of romance upon the future is a lie.'

'But isn't living through the great horror of the current reality horrifying enough? People losing those closest to them—people they thought they could not live without and then having to do the impossible. No one knows who is next in this carnage. How does one write stories to scare now that we are all cowering in our own hides anyway?'

Didn't she look cute when she spoke like that? He was tempted to take her in his arms—with her consent of course—and do the things to her that they had discussed, and agreed, would be pleasurable to both of them in a strictly recreational way and not imply a skewed power dynamic. But she was obviously waiting for an answer, and he was obliged to give one.

'That is the challenge,' he said. 'The project of horror can no longer be safe thrills—like those simulations in malls where they put glasses on to make you think you are walking on a rope dangling over a gorge only for you to collapse with relief when you take the glasses off. Now, horror must be aimed at acclimatising us to form calluses on our minds.'

Owing to his lack of training in literature, he had read far and wide, driven by pleasure alone and had formed some hifalutin thoughts unmitigated by curriculum and professorial interventions. But she wouldn't be left behind on deep-sounding observations.

'You are right. But the idea of a monster of one's own making running amok and angry—indignant and vengeful at being created—is too easy a metaphor.' Her communications professor had been a Comparative Literature PhD on his first job. She had been the only student who kept him from growing cynical and disillusioned about the appreciation for finer things such as literature in a business college.

'Baby, in fact, I think all metaphors on horror have outlived their purpose. Everything one writes in that genre has to be a blunt statement—all narrative methods have been rendered superfluous and all writing has to be an observation of subjectivities growing narrower and narrower.'

By now their lexical mating dance had left them sufficiently incapable of further conversation, and they sought to attend to more pressing primary instincts.

Later that day, having sat with their respective laptops for hours in separate rooms, they regrouped to share what they had written. She cleared her throat and began first. 'It's nothing special ... disjointed thoughts really. "The prayers' prayers clashed and clanged—"'

'No poems,' he interrupted her.

'Why?' She had, in recent times, taken to writing her thoughts on fashionably melancholic topics vertically with line-breaks and was hoping to go on stage with it.

'That's cheating. You can claim abstraction of any nonsense lacking in rhyme or reason.'

'Rhyme is for oldies.'

'And reason is obsolete.'

If she was offended, she didn't show it.

'Well then I will need time to write a new piece,' she said.

The lunch khichdi was extra spicy that day. And she was impatient with him. 'You cannot go around renaming things just because you cannot pronounce their original names. What the hell is a kedgeree? It's khee-cha-dee ... say khee-cha-dee? Pass me the woh-tah please.'

'It's delicious,' he said handing her the water bottle but not willing to take her cue for a quarrel. It would be his turn to make supper. They were nearly out of supplies and he was wondering how in the world he was to fashion a meal out of two cucumbers and half a portion of tofu.

They sat down again after a short while and she read hers first. It was a short, reflective piece:

'MS died, someone messaged me today. It took me a while to remember him. We went to school together. Although "went together" is just an expression, as I cycled to school and he travelled by bus from his village to mine, which had the only English medium school in the area. Every time I looked at him, his uniform crumpled from jostling for a seat with people and farm produce and chickens and goats, I remember feeling grateful for living in the same village as the school. I had terrible motion sickness and shuddered at the thought of throwing up every day just to get an education. He told me that you didn't feel giddy if you rode on the luggage carrier on the roof. But they stopped the practice after a schoolboy was knocked off the bus by a low branch of a banyan tree and crushed to death by a sand truck. We weren't friends. But since we sat in the same class for ten years, some sort of familiarity had crept in. And since our initials were close together, we had adjacent roll numbers and were seated next to each other during exams. I knew his birthday. I remember because he once told me that he had more wisdom since he had a four-day head start over me. I told him off when he tried to copy my answers on a test. I am currently giving my memory a sideways glance for holding on to the most random anecdotes. I don't think the meagre biology lessons our underpaid teachers taught, prepared us for the possibility of a viral apocalypse decades later. I might have wished him good luck on school leaving day, after which he receded into the realm of obscure memories. If we had gone on to live and die of nothing but time, I probably wouldn't have thought of him again. But Covid caught him, and here I am thinking of him for the first time since 1999. I feel no grief. Just a strange wistfulness at the precariousness of dreams. Goodbye MS. You do have a head start after all.'

He sat back in stunned silence.

'Well?' she asked.

'I wasn't expecting this. It is not horror. But it is the acceptance that comes after getting callused. Mine is dark in comparison.'

It took some coaxing to get him to read his. It was shorter than hers.

'There's something bigger than the sum of all lives put together: the gestalt which adapts prey to resemble predator, and live things to blend with their backgrounds—moths that look like owls, mantis that look like leaves, pigment cells in chameleon skin that sense the colour of the surroundings. That is the greater sentience that governs whole hives and ant colonies to act as one being—that which renders us cameos in our own stories. It is waiting and watching with glacial perseverance. We broke away from it when we began thinking of ourselves as individuals, and it seeks to avenge our audacity. It may be all-knowing, but it's certainly not all-loving. It proves its point by disproving karma. It punishes the meek and the lovely. It recalls the noble and lets the evil and the ugly be—they are its tools, the handyman's hands. It metamorphoses into the death instinct. It writes, in an unhurried hand, the destiny of the world with bat soup as ink.'

She looked at him with a mixture of horror and admiration. 'You win,' she said slowly.

'Baby, if I win, nobody does.'

They sat there contemplating the words that had been read aloud. The rain had stopped while she was reading her piece and an extra bright sun was steaming the earth. They couldn't tell if it was a brief interlude or the beginning of improved weather. Forecasts were hopeless. Someone started a brush cutter and it sounded like a moped struggling in the mud.

'I would rewrite the last bit,' she said after a while. 'The bat soup theory has been discarded.'

'You are right ... let me change that.' He thought for a minute and then tapped on his keyboard.

'With an unhurried hand, it knocks over a test tube. Better?'

'Much.'

They sat in silence.

'They are recommending booster doses,' he said looking out of the window.

'We must do what we can to ... uh ... be there for each other.' She smiled at him and it made him sad.

'Hmm ... shall we go for a walk?' he asked in an effort to change the subject.

'Yes. Let me get my mask.'

10

Alone at Last

Cake art had appeared on the horizon just before the end of civilisation as we know it. They had begun making cakes in shapes and colours unimaginable so far. They were perfect replicas of things one would never have associated with cake or anything edible: jewellery, vehicles, mattresses, kanjeevaram silks, snakes, the kind of people who keep pet snakes, a child's laughter, nostalgia, the infinite compassion of the world's richest.

This cakey mess (resembling a party thrown for a Global Southern, nouveau-riche brat leaving for America to get a management degree) may have been more correlation than cause for the last strike of the hammer of Shiva to fall on the anvil of modern society, but the appearance of the cakey mess, on the horizon like UFOs (which were probably just cake), ensured the symbolism was stark. The downward slide of society was attributed to the discovery of fondant and the reckless mining of mountains and rainforests for the precious shapeshifting mineral that destroyed the tribes that worshipped it.

When the end came it was not with the spectacle and special effects of a high-budget, apocalyptic film—giant waves tossing ships like so many leaves in the sea, the tide rushing in to submerge entire cities, great fires engulfing the skyline, corpses and people about to become corpses thrown around in the chaos, alarms ringing, bells clanging, horns blaring with the drivers dead behind the wheel. The end arrived as unceremoniously as a kitchen accident: a pot of hot stew that slipped from the hands and shattered on the floor leaving broken chinaware and boiling blobs all over the kitchen. Nothing more serious than a lost dinner and a bloody mess to clean—something annoying, but not unfixable. But a closer look shows that the pot landed on the cat. Knocking, if not burning, it dead, and the sprayed stew fell on the blender's faulty electrical connection causing a short circuit in the house's wiring and starting a fire that destroyed everyone, and everything, in its wake.

The cake in the oven being ruined and the evening's birthday party being cancelled is only one way of looking at a home gone up in smoke. This is what they would call it on a news show by a media house belonging to the oven company perhaps. Fortunately, the media house had burned down too—with everyone inside. Thus, one was spared 'perspectives' on truth.

And that is when I entered the new reality with only my senses to guide me and every story-making mechanism vanished from the world. Like a newborn baby without the faculty of judgement, I had to build a new system of information, knowledge, opinions and prejudices entirely on my own. It took me a while to realise I was the sole survivor of, if not the whole world, certainly, my immediate surroundings. I sat there stunned as if recovering from a blow to the head. Perhaps the blow had anesthetised me to whatever it is that had destroyed civilisation as I had known it. My knowledge of it was already fading when I came to my senses and I felt a strong urge to begin to know civilisation differently. I had memories; some vivid, some vague but they were not enough to give me the whole picture of the devastation. I knew my name and age and gender and that sort of thing. I remember there had been a terrible disease that had swept through the world with an impunity that outmatched that of humans. 'Human lives are being lost in numbers similar to those of animals in slaughterhouses across the world for the first time since industrialisation,' one news story had claimed. I didn't recall losing anyone I knew. Perhaps I was the one who had died and my spirit had fetched up in this strange place?

I remembered I had parents—their faces were fairly clear—and I had an estranged sibling whose name nor features I could recall, try as I may. I remembered I had an 'un-Googleable' ex, because he had a famous cousin behind whose surname he hid on the internet. But I think the shared last name may have been a coincidence and being related to him was probably one of the hundreds of lies he told me. But I didn't remember my ex's name—just the elaborate story around it. And I didn't remember where I was. I looked around me and found the place entirely unfamiliar. It was a small, but neat, house with a bedroom, a hall and a tiny kitchen. There was a bathroom with a shower, a toilet, a wash basin, and black floor and wall tiles that gave the bathroom a cave-like appearance, in spite of two powerful lightbulbs. There was a bed, a small desk with a wooden stool, and a bean bag as furniture. A meagre, but functional, collection of pots and pans, a single burner stove with a gas cylinder and a small fridge in the kitchen. The coconut shell ladle made me wonder if I was in Kerala although I wasn't quite sure what Kerala was. I looked out of the window. I appeared to be on the side of a hill of some sort. The slope below the house was so steep that it looked like a sheer drop. But there was no naked soil anywhere. Everything was covered in thick vegetation. Below was a valley which had some buildings and many trees. The window panes had stickers saying 'Keep Glass Closed Monkeys' in bold letters. Was it a warning of, or for, monkeys? I looked at the mirror in the bathroom to see if I was a monkey. I wasn't. I looked exactly as I had before the end of civilisation as I had known it. I suddenly felt very lonely. I could do with company—any company. Even monkeys. I opened the windows and peered out. There were no monkeys. Perhaps this was not the time they appeared. I kept the window open for a monkey if it chose to visit.

I felt hungry. I went into the kitchen to see if there was something I could eat. There wasn't anything except for a few mouldy biscuits and a bunch of bananas long past their prime. I picked them up and tossed them out of the window into the valley below.

Before I could sit down and wait for memory to find its way back into my mind and give me a few clues as to my whereabouts, I had to eat, for which I would have to go out and find food. I didn't know where or how but if the place I was in was similar in any way to the only world I had known, food could be bought. But did I have any money? I looked around and found a wallet with a few strange looking banknotes with writing in a language I did not recognise and a picture of someone or the other. I couldn't tell if it was a man or a woman. A monarch? Freedom fighter? First president? Who cares! The grumbling in my stomach was threatening a chorus, and I stuffed the wallet into the back pocket of my jeans and walked out.

The ground was slippery and moss-covered. The valley lay below me but when I looked up, I saw I was closer to the top of the hill than the bottom. I wasn't sure what I could find up there. But if not a café or a shop selling food, I could at least get a better view of the area, I thought. So, I decided to climb up rather than down.

I didn't have to go far. There were rough stone steps on the hillside and when there were no steps, the dirt was firm and easy to walk on in my trainers—the only pair of shoes I found in the house. Soon, I arrived on a landing and found a pukka road winding around the hill. I followed the road uphill. There were houses poking through the greenery on both sides of the road. Luxury villas so silent, I wondered if I was deaf. But I could hear the wind through the trees. Strangely, there was no screeching hawk overhead that one would expect to accompany a scene like this. I surprised myself with the expectation—for someone who had woken up with most of their memory erased as the sole survivor of some kind of cataclysmic event, I seemed to possess the most random cinematic fiddle-faddle. I was either in a rich tropical country or one in which rich expats spent the winters away from their adoptive temperate countries.

After walking for about half an hour, the road forked—one path lead downhill and the other further up over an adjacent hill. There, in the corner were several shops. But they were all shut. And there was no sign of human activity whatsoever. The shops themselves were not very big or fancy. Most of them were small sheds with corrugated metal roofs. Some had rolling shutters. The names on the metal were too rusted to read. I knocked on a couple not really expecting anything to open. The large trees beside the road had shed their leaves over the roofs of the shops. Wet by rain and dew, the leaf mass had turned into a mush on which mushroom grew with abandon. In a couple of places, the aerial roots of the nearby ficus had touched the roof and taken root from which small saplings were growing. It was clear that the shops were not shut for a holiday. They had been abandoned and it had been a while since the abandonment.

I was suddenly scared. I hadn't seen a single human being or animal or insect since I woke up from whatever it is that I had been under. It felt like I had been the sort of person who craved and enjoyed solitude. Perhaps that is what kept me from fretting over the loneliness too much in the past several hours. But having walked for what felt like miles, only to find abandoned shops with trees growing on their roofs, I realised that my solitude was not a choice, and I had no control over it. This thought sent a shiver down my spine. But I remembered I was there in search of food. I kicked the padlock on the rolling shutter of one of the shops. It was rusted and I sensed that it wouldn't put up much of a resistance. I found a heavy rock and brought it down with force. The padlock shattered with one blow. I hauled the shutters up with all my might.

Inside was a rectangular room without windows. Thankfully, the open shutter let in daylight. I peered inside cautiously, half expecting bats to fly out or a rat to jump on me. But there was no sign of any form of life in the shop. I stepped in gingerly. There was a small wooden counter, behind which were three or four shelves with dust-covered tins and jars and packets of various sizes. Just as I started to move towards the shelves, something fell on me! I covered my mouth, stifling a shriek, and ran out of the shop. When I realised that nothing chased me, I stopped to turn back and look. The place seemed as innocently abandoned as before. I went back inside slowly. Whatever it was, it wasn't heavy or sharp, so I wasn't hurt. I looked down—it was a piece of cardboard about three-feet wide. I flipped it around and saw the words 'Stay Home. Stay

Safe' stencilled neatly on it in bold, black letters. Suddenly, I wanted to be home. I grabbed some cans and jars from the shelf without waiting to check the contents and started to walk out when I heard it. It was faint at first and then it grew louder. The sound of a vehicle ascending the hilly road!

At first, I felt relief. There were people around me after all. Thank heavens I wasn't as alone as I had imagined. I started to run to hail the vehicle when something at the back of my mind told me I must be cautious. I hadn't seen or heard a single soul in the hours I had been awake. What if the people I met were not good people? I stepped back into the shop, hid behind a shelf and peered out. The sound grew louder until I could see its source. It was a bus. Its engine was straining over the steep slope. When it went past the shop slowly, my heart nearly stopped and a chill descended on my skin like I had been touched by a hand that had been lying at the bottom of a lake for days. There was no one in the bus! Not even a driver.

The bus slowly wound its way up the road. As soon as it went round the bend and was lost to sight, I shot out of the shop and ran as fast as my legs could in the direction I had come. I kept running with my heart thudding in my mouth until I was back in the house. I ran in, shut the door behind me, put down the things I had brought, and sat down and wept.

A good cleansing cry cleared out the haze of fear from my mind. But clarity brought with it uncomfortable questions: Where was I? Where was everybody else? What was I supposed to do now? But before that, I had to eat. Two of the five cans were mouldy. I threw them out. Out of the remaining three, two contained sardines and one contained pineapple slices. Thanks to the vacuum seal, they hadn't gone bad. The stove in the kitchen worked. I warmed the sardines and ate them from the pan. I kept the pineapple for breakfast the next day. I didn't want to go out for food for as long as I could help it. I washed the pan and put it away, out of what could only be called force of habit. It was dark by then and I suddenly remembered the open windows. No monkey had come in, but I was worried mosquitos would have, though I heard no bloodthirsty buzz. I peered into the dark. No owls or bats, not even crickets stirred the air outside. Did nothing else live? But rather than put my mind at ease, the lack of any kind of pest or predator made me fearful. I closed and bolted the windows, shutting the dead night out. It wasn't cold. Far from it. But I shivered nonetheless. I found some blankets in a cupboard. I curled up on the bed, covered myself in the blankets from head to toe and fell asleep.

Wakefulness brought with it all the previous day's bewilderment and fears. Having had a chance to soak in the loneliness, I was sad. I wish I hadn't woken up. Despite the thickness of the vegetation outside, there was no birdsong. I opened the windows and the sun streamed in. I sat on the bed for what was perhaps hours adding 'stunned' to the silence around me. I was shaken out of my trance when hunger started gnawing at my insides. I ate the pineapple slices from the previous evening's haul. I knew my satiation was only temporary. I would have to go out and hunt for more food. The thought of hunting made me chuckle. Was I going to restart civilisation in my jeans and t-shirt and trainers and glasses? What if my glasses broke? Where would I get a replacement? How would I manage with my blurred vision? I must keep my glasses safe. My own laughter was the only animal sound I had heard in a long time. I felt hungry for more. I tried to laugh again but this time it sounded forced. I decided to speak instead. 'Hello! Hello! Can you hear me?' I said softly. And then, louder, 'Check one, two. Check one, two.' That felt good. I felt encouraged. 'How are you? Very well, thank you. And you? It is good to be alive. What is for lunch today? I don't know. Must check the larder. I'm sure I can slap something together.' I made small talk with myself for a few minutes before building up the courage to go out again.

This time, I chose the downhill path. If a phantom bus could drive up the hill, there was no reason why it couldn't find its way to the valley. But I wasn't ready to go back to a place where I had had a death of a fright yesterday.

The descent was slow and slippery. There were concrete steps here and there but they were covered in moss, and I avoided them as much as I could. Another random memory came floating to me of reading somewhere that the tangible marker of the beginnings of community was a healed femur (or was it tibia?). For the primitive human in the wild, a broken bone meant immobility; inability to hunt and find nourishment, inability to run and save oneself from a larger predator. It meant certain death. The fact that it had healed meant someone stayed back to look after the one with the broken bone—to feed and protect them during the time it took for the bone to heal. That is the beginning of fellow-feeling, of love as something more than instinct … a feeling of greater sentience. That was the foundation of community. And here I was, all alone in the world with no one to help me if I broke a leg— and with only the accursed ability to think of a future, even when its futility wasn't beyond my perception. I had the language and the articulation, and most importantly, the burden of anxiety from having lived through the death throes of civilisation as we knew it. And now, there is no more we. There is only I.

As I walked, lost in such pointless thoughts, I slipped on a mossy rock and landed heavily on my buttocks. If coincidence had its way, I would have broken a femur (or tibia). But I was unhurt apart from a sore bum. The seat of my trousers was stained a deep green by the crushed grass. But being all alone in the world freed one from the clutches of embarrassment, which took a minimum of two people to work.

I finally reached the main road on the ledge below, but I saw that the descent had not quite ended. But this time, it was a pukka road and I wasn't worried about losing my footing. Walking into the town in the valley was a surreal experience. It was a real ghost town. There were no ghosts—none you could see anyway. But the projection of my own fears hung in the air in ethereal forms like mist on a mountain. The buildings stood silently. An occasional hoarding, extolling people to stay home, that had withstood the onslaught of nature, reminded me of the great tragedy that I had survived. I wasn't sure why I had survived it but there was no time to think of all that right now. Bushes and creepers grew thickly making the buildings appear puny and powerless. Roots of strangler figs were already reaching onto some walls here and there. Soon, nature would take over and everything artificial would be crushed and buried.

I stood before a large building which was relatively untouched by hungry, vengeful vegetation. It had a glass front and I peered in to see aisles and aisles of provisions. This was a big supermarket. But it had no padlock on it. It must have used a more sophisticated electronic locking system. But sophisticated or not, brute force had never gone out of fashion. I grabbed a rock and hurled it at the glass door. Nothing happened. I grabbed an even bigger rock and threw it with greater force. The glass cracked in the shape of a spider's web but did not shatter. And this time the alarm came on. In the deathly silence of the dead world, it sounded more ear shattering than anything I remembered hearing. I froze. But a minute later, when I realised that the alarm hadn't in fact raised anything, I recovered from my fear induced paralysis. I found a fallen branch of a tree, and broke a stout stick and fashioned a hammer and a chisel. I worked at the centre of the web in the glass and after five minutes of banging, I managed to make a small hole. If sticks and stones could break the glass, how secure was it anyway? It had functioned entirely on the unverified promise of a robust security system when the place was populated by people. But now all it did was scream into the void at the top of its voice. The hole had weakened the glass and it wasn't too difficult to chip away until the gap widened enough for me to step through. The alarm stopped ten minutes later. The idea, perhaps, was that if there had been a break-in, the guards would be summoned and there was no need for the siren to keep blaring beyond ten minutes. While this would have not affected me, the alarm had still been annoying and it was a relief when it stopped.

Although convinced that there was nothing in there—nothing alive, in any case—I walked cautiously. The store had three floors. The top floor had clothes and shoes, the second floor had toys, stationery and kitchenware, and the ground floor had food and toiletries. The upper floors were dusty and desolate. Apart from the teddy bears and other soft toys appearing ghoulish in the context of a dead world, there wasn't anything too eerie there. I made a mental note of the things on these floors for later before going back downstairs. The vegetable counter was covered in a layer of compost. Perhaps the place had not been abandoned in one go. Perhaps a large quantity of vegetables had been brought before the place was shut down. Whatever remained rotted, of course. But it did not have the revolting vegetativeness of new rot but the musty lightness of a slow, but complete, decomposition. Had I been 'asleep' for months?

The dairy had gone off and one of the fridges was reeking foul. But the vacuum-packed and tinned goods seemed more or less unsullied—grains, flours, spices, salt, sugar, oils, jams, preserved fruit and vegetables. To my big surprise, the cold storage was working and the frozen meats were ... well ... frozen. But I couldn't bring myself to take anything from there. Was I vegetarian? No. I had eaten sardines last evening. Then, why would I not want to get lamb chops and sausages from the frozen section? I stood there in that dusty, loamy supermarket wondering, when a strange image floated before my eyes.

I was inside a vehicle of some sort: a rather open vehicle with just a roof and a floor and rods to hold on to but no body to speak of. An autorickshaw perhaps. It was stuck in traffic and I was looking outside. It was raining. Not three feet away from me was a butcher shop. Rusty cages imprisoned white chickens. They were huddled together dripping wet. A man in a dirty apron was dismembering a recently slaughtered sheep on a wooden block. Below, tethered to a pole, was a lamb. No more than a foot high, snowy white with a pink nose—the kind that would be featured in a video running in slow motion in a green field with butterflies and dandelions and instrumental music playing in the background. It was too young to eat grass. It stood there looking lost. I wondered what was passing through its mind. Did it know it was waiting its turn? Was that its mother on the table? Someone would have tender—innocent—melt-in-the-mouth lamb curry for dinner that night. I rushed home and wept.

I strained my memory to remember what my home had looked like or who else was in that auto with me. But nothing came. I walked away from the cold storage. I took a trolley from the supermarket and loaded it with food. I was about to wheel it back home when a thought occurred to me. This supermarket would be my source of food for a long time to come. It couldn't be filled with rot. I grabbed another trolley, lined it with carry bags to block the gaps, and started shovelling the composted plant matter into it with my bare hands. I filled it up and disposed of the rubbish in the only way I knew—taking it far away and piling it in a place that didn't matter to me. It took several rounds before all the spoilt food had been carted away. I grabbed a broom and swept out the place. I could have mopped it, but I was too tired by then. That would have to wait for another time. I found the water running in the bathroom. I took soap from the toiletry section and scrubbed my hands and face clean. I pushed my trolley of food out. I dragged over the broken branch from which I had taken a stick to break into the shop earlier and used it to block the hole in the glass. And then, I started the slow climb home pushing the trolley laden with enough food to last a week.

I was halfway up a steep slope—one of the many I would have to climb to get home—when I heard the sound of a vehicle coming in my direction. My heart started thudding in my ears. What should I do? If I let go of the trolley it would trundle down and crash in a gutter and waste a week's worth of food that I had worked so hard for. I couldn't find a rock fast enough to chock the wheels and run to safety. Also, there was nowhere to run to. I was on the tarmac with a sheer cliff face on one side and a deep gorge on the other. The vehicle was coming from below and I couldn't run in its direction. And I could never outrun it up the slope! I stood rooted to the spot.

The sound grew louder and louder until I turned and saw the vehicle. It was a car. An SUV. There was no one in it. It drove towards me. I stared at it in open-mouthed horror as it passed by so close I could stretch my arm and touch it. It went past me without event. It even blinked its indicator at the turn. I don't know how long I stood there looking in its direction. Finally, I reached into the trolley and got out a bottle of juice that I had brought along in the hope that it hadn't gone bad despite being over the expiration date and chugged it down.

I restarted my journey. Ten or so minutes later, I heard an engine again. This time I was less alarmed. I had no more adrenaline to spare. I didn't even stop pushing as an unmanned car went past from the other side—a hatchback going downhill. So, the vehicles were going around on their own. I was more surprised by my easy acceptance of this realisation than the realisation in itself. I didn't stop pushing until I reached home. Out of breath, a little shaken, but intact and with food.

I showered and changed into a fresh pair of clothes that I found in the cupboard. I made myself a simple khichdi with the things I had brought. It tasted delicious.

'Ahem,' I said aloud. 'Check one, two. Today, I wish to tell myself a secret.' A human voice, even if my own, was oddly comforting. 'It is just a theory but if I am wrong, no one is right. Literally no one. Because there is no one. The vehicles are running themselves. Have they developed intelligence? Have they not overcome their inertia of motion?'

Another image came floating from a long time ago. I was balanced on someone's knee and that someone was telling me a story. There was once a farmer who rode a cart pulled by his two faithful bulls every day from his home in the village to his farm ten miles away. After a hard day's work on the land, the farmer would return the same way and the bulls brought him back without needing him to make so much as a tug on the reins. The farmer liked to end his day with a little tipple and he would stop at the tavern for a jug of moonshine. The bulls would wait obediently for a quarter of an hour—that's how little time it took the farmer to drown his sorrows as there weren't many of them—before heading back home with the drunk farmer asleep at the yoke. One day, the farmer died and his grown son assumed his responsibilities. He went to work the same way—in the cart drawn by the same bulls and back the same way. But the son was a teetotaller and had no need to stop at the tavern. But no amount of coaxing or cursing would keep the bulls from stopping at the tavern on the way home. He had to sit in the cart looking like a fool until the bulls decided it was time to take their sober master home.

People had died, vanished from the world. But vehicles were running on the roads by force of habit. And I had somehow missed the spaceship or virus or whatever it was that took everyone away and was here to witness this bizarre scene. Were they going to come back for me? What's one life among billions? That's how worthless human life had become when the Earth was teeming with it. No reason for that to have changed in death or escape or whatever it was that had rid the Earth of it.

I am not sure how many days went by before I finally gathered the courage to do it. To get on a self-running vehicle, I mean. I had started to mark a calendar like a prisoner in a dungeon or a marooned sailor marking the trunk of a coconut tree with vertical lines for the days and slashed by a diagonal for each week. But I missed a few days in between, and I simply couldn't remember how many days I had missed because they all seemed the same. Was it the day I ate rajma before the day

I ate too much honey (because that is one food with infinite shelf life) and gave myself indigestion? Or the following day when I fasted? Or did I do all of that on the same day? It was hard to tell. And that messed up the calendar. Also, since I didn't have an exact date, day or year, for the time I woke up, all this marking had no reference point. I could have gone on counting with an approximation but after what could have been a couple of months of living like this, I stopped thinking of rescue, where other survivors would come in search of me and take me to where the party was. I lost hope that the marked days—a Robinson Crusoe-like account of my lonely ordeals—would mean something to somebody. Because there was nobody. There would be no history of my newfound existence.

But I did wonder about a future. My thoughts about it were coloured with a crippling fear of pain and a lonely death and the liberation and lightness of lack of responsibility and dependants—no child, no ageing parent, no pet, not even a houseplant, no hungry child on the street, no man selling homemade papad on the footpath to pay for his wife's cancer treatment, no frail woman who proudly resisted eating the leftover idli from the plates she washed in an eatery before going to the pharmacy next door and pushing a small coin on the counter and asking for something to ease the pain in her legs she knew was owing to malnutrition, no lost dog abandoned by humans for not being a cute puppy anymore, no bird injured by a kite wire. Why was I thinking in these terms? Had I witnessed these situations? If so, when? Where? Random images flashed before my eyes and I felt sudden relief at the deaths of all thinking, feeling beings. They are out of their misery now. My future, whatever it held, would not be burdened by the pain of guilt or helplessness.

All day I walked around the house. I sat and slept when I wished to. I had 'broken into' a library and lugged home a haul of books in the supermarket trolley. I picked indiscriminately, hungrily and without the worry of judgement: classics, poetry, crime fiction, espionage, thrillers, potboilers. But a few weeks into it, I found I couldn't read anymore. I hadn't forgotten how to read, I just didn't want to. Be it real, fiction, or fantasy, all stories were about people—or beings of some kind—interacting: loving, hating, talking, touching, seeing, fighting, killing each other. And the entertainment and experience of it was in relating to the sequences in some way. I had no one to do any of these things with. The lives of the characters in the books seemed frivolous. Poetry that worked entirely on the power of language and the ephemerality of words seemed pointless because words had started to seem vestigial to me of late. The only words I encountered were the ones I said aloud to myself when I felt like hearing a human sound. My thoughts were receding into the abstraction of instinct quite fast. The pleasure of reading lay in being part of the sphere of shared humanhood. I returned the books to the library.

I had started going into town just to walk around even when I didn't need food. I was less nervous now. Unmanned vehicles passed by once in a while, determinedly moving on to wherever they were headed. They didn't scare me anymore. One day, I stretched my courage by wandering beyond town to a hill nearby. I had grown stronger—all that walking and reduced eating had helped me shed kilos and my leg muscles felt harder. The climb wasn't too difficult.

The hill was covered by tall, thick trees and was densely shady and damp. It must have taken several hours of climbing when I arrived at the peak. I was sweaty and out of breath. I came upon a clearing where I saw a large statue. It was about ten or twelve-feet high and was of a person sitting cross-legged. The statue had suffered too much damage for me to know for sure if it was of a man or a woman; a ficus root wound tightly around the chest like a strange bra and the features had melted away. The left arm drooped to the side and the right one was truncated in the middle, and I didn't know if it was originally raised in blessing. It must have been an eastern god of some kind because western gods are inflexible from sitting on chairs very early in life and cannot sit cross-legged on pedestals or otherwise. So, I was in an eastern country after all. The weather and the vegetation had hinted at it but it had been impossible to know for sure. I reached out to the statue and it felt oddly hollow to the touch. I grabbed the intact arm and gave it a light tug and it broke away. It was indeed hollow and smelled rotten-sweet. I held the arm to my nose and sniffed. I recoiled, but not without having recognised the scent. It was fondant! The statue had been cake and had rotted from within. The outer fondant had stiffened forming a plaster of Paris-like shell. I stood there holding the arm awestruck by the situation.

Then, I don't know what made me do it, but I raised one end of the tubular arm of the statue to my eye like a telescope. To my great surprise, it worked like one and magnified the images I pointed it at. I looked at the side of the hill, the misty mountains in the distance, the different shades of green covering an undulating land for as far as the eye could see. I then raised it to the sky and noticed a strangely straight streak of white among the clouds. I started speaking aloud in my excitement. 'Could it be? Could it really???' Yes, the streak was still being drawn—sharp and straight by a jetliner. I could jump for joy! The planes were flying. 'Does it mean there were people elsewhere? Wait a minute ... What if the planes are flying themselves like the buses and cars?' I sat down at the feet of the fondant god wondering what I should do with this new information. That is when I heard another, more familiar, sound. A vehicle of some sort must be coming uphill. I pointed my fondant telescope down and looked through it. It was a bus straining its way over the small piece of snaky road that showed through dense forest below me. It had begun to grow dark. Although I had no animal nor human to fear on my way back, it wasn't easy terrain with risings and sheer drops and rocks all over the place which made walking in the dark rather dangerous. I could spend the night here by the statue but it was terribly windy and the sweat from my earlier ascent had cooled down and I felt chilly.

As I stood wondering what to do, the bus emerged from the forest and, surprisingly,came to a stop close to where I stood. On a whim, I went up to it and got in. The bus waited there for five minutes before reversing and heading back downhill toward the town. It was surreal. If I closed my eyes and pretended there was a driver and other people in the bus, it felt like a most natural thing. But when I opened my eyes, I was back in the world of which I seemed to be the sole human inhabitant, riding a bus that drove itself. I kept looking out of the window throughout the journey like I would have before I had woken up. I actually enjoyed the ride back home.

I spent the next few weeks riding buses up and down the town I had come to make my home. It was fantastic and dreamlike. My new life since the awakening had taught me that control was a fantasy and going with the flow was all a human was capable of, and riding the self-driving bus taught me how to enjoy. One of the risky things about being on the bus was that I had no way of stopping it. I had to get on and off when and where it chose to come to a halt. If it was a short stop, and I did not get off in time, I was stuck on the bus until the next stop and that would come anywhere between a mile or ten. My sojourns invariably involved a lot of walking if I was dropped off in strange places. I would get up in the morning, make a breakfast of anything edible in the house, wear comfortable clothes and walking shoes (I had found a suitable pair in the supermarket after sifting through boxes of high heels and stilettos with or without sequins), fill a bottle of water from the tap (I never understood where the water came from—perhaps a water supply plant somewhere was working on pure inertia too), and set out in search of my first bus of the day.

On the second day of bussing, I tried grabbing the steering wheel and directing the vehicle. Its response made me realise how powerless I was. It was like a mouse wrestling an elephant. The mouse heaving and the elephant not even aware of its presence. The wheel moved on its own like I didn't exist. After about five minutes of trying, I gave up. I was clearly not the external force that would break the inertia of this body in motion.

I felt like a trapeze artist swinging from bus to bus with brief interludes on the ground where I developed an instinct for the bus timings and made mental maps back home from the places they took me. I occasionally went to the supermarket to restock supplies. The supermarket was as I had found it the first time I entered, except the goods were gradually diminishing, of course, with no question of replenishing. I cleaned the place when I could—it was an extension of my home, after all. And along with the awareness of the finiteness of resources, I noticed that tree roots were entering the store through the hole I had made in the glass. It wouldn't be long before the strong, muscular roots grabbed the glass, ripped it open, snaked across the floor and grew over the aisles, and strangled and crushed the whole place like a leisurely, but determined, boa constrictor. The place wouldn't sustain me for too long, and I had to find another home—perhaps several homes. I had gone to the hill of the cake god many times and seen planes in the sky and longed to find the airport. If the planes operated unmanned, just like the buses, perhaps I could get on one and go somewhere farther than a bus would take me. I wasn't sure why I was fascinated with the idea of going far.

The mystery of my appearance in this place and this house remained unsolved but I had grown attached to it. If there is one lesson to be learnt from turning up fully grown with little more than language, toilet training and random non sequiturs as memory, it is that attachment is useless, if not harmful. And yet, I had come to feel close to the place that afforded me an escape from the bewilderment in the form of sleep. It was a hard decision leaving my safe place to head into the unknown, but I had to do it. I packed some clothes in a rucksack, threw in two packets of beans, a packet of salt, a bottle of water, a pot, a spoon and a box of matches, wore my walking shoes and left from there forever.

I found the bus down the hill. It had just come to a halt and, if routines were anything to go by, would stop there a good five minutes. I sat by the left window and looked out. This bus would go only as far as the next town. I had been there on one of my journeys. The town was as overtaken by nature as the one I lived in. In fact, the roofs of the supermarkets there had caved in ruining everything inside. I hadn't bothered spending much time there. This time, I walked through the town and found another bus at the other end. I realised that the town I lived in had a higher altitude as the bus kept going downhill.

It made me dizzy and I threw up my breakfast chickpea soup. This bus was a long-distance coach, and it showed no sign of stopping. Finally, when it did come to a stop, after about four hours of constant journeying, beside the ruins of what seemed like a café, I knew it was only a rest stop. I quickly got out and peed in the bushes and got back on for fear of being stranded in a place with no food. I was right about the stop. When the bus was convinced that all the travellers had had their breaks and reboarded, it resumed its journey. The landscape was monotonously green. The speed increased when we finally hit stable ground. It's funny I should think of myself and the bus as 'we'. Perhaps the machine had achieved beinghood by this projection of my mind.

I must have dozed off when the ride got smoother on the straight road because I was jolted out of my sleep when the bus came to a stop. I looked outside; it was dark. But I could see the outlines of buildings. We must be in some kind of town or city. The bus was probably going further but I was tired and hungry. I got off.

I found myself in an upper-class neighbourhood with beautiful detached houses surrounded by thick, overgrown vegetation that might have once been prim and colourful gardens. Each compound now looked like a little forest. The pavement around the houses was littered with fallen leaves, but the streets still retained the neatness of planned architecture. If I had any doubts about this town being deserted, they were quelled by this sight of it. I went to the first house, climbed over the low wall—obviously the rich here didn't feel the need to have high walls to keep away the gaze of the riffraff. They might have had guards to do that. Perhaps no one poor came here. Who knows? I stretched my arms out in front of me to push my way through the tangled creepers and branches to reach the door. It was solid wood and didn't budge at a kick. I walked around the house and found a low glass window. Unlike the supermarket door, this one was shattered with an improvised battering ram of a bougainvillea branch. I stuck my hand in, taking care not to cut myself on the jagged glass, and felt around for a latch. It was easy to find. I opened the window wide and climbed through. The house was dark. I felt my way around the wall and found a light switch. It was indeed a lovely house with carpets and chandeliers and bookshelves and framed photos. Soft pastel colours against shades of beige. Everything was covered in dust, of course, but I liked the general feel of it. I found my way to the kitchen, dusted the stove, and cooked the beans I had brought with me and ate hungrily from the pot. I found a nice big bed, pulled the dusty sheet off, curled up on the uncovered mattress and fell instantly asleep.

The next day, I explored the house. It had two floors, four bedrooms—two on each floor—all with ensuite bathrooms, a balcony overlooking what had become of the garden, and a large hall downstairs next to the kitchen. There was a shed in the backyard and a garage big enough for two cars. The garage was open and empty—the cars must have left. The house would be very comfortable with some cleaning. But I decided I didn't want to settle down. I was feeling restless. I had to find that airport. I don't know how close to, or far away from, it I had moved, but I couldn't stop until I found it. A few days rest and recovery from the last journey and I would set out again.

And as it happened, moving became a necessity rather than a choice because there was no food to be had in the neighbourhood. There were no supermarkets anywhere. Perhaps the people in these houses had their things delivered to them. I washed my clothes and added a jacket I found in the house to my wardrobe and left on the third day after my bean stock was nearly finished.

I walked the first day and rested in a school building at night. I caught a bus the next day and came to a town where I found shelter in what looked like a prayer hall. The day after that I caught another bus and fetched up in a city. There were large, stately buildings that looked like they had belonged to a government or bureaucracy. Thousands of memos must have been shot back and forth here; many policy decisions that made the lives and caused the deaths of thousands. How did it matter anymore? But it was all rather intimidating to even think about.

I walked on. The streets were wide and orderly—and entirely deserted of course. There was something oddly unsettling about them. But also calming. It felt like there had been some kind of riot here. The telltale signs had been swept away, but it had an aura about it that said people had danced in these streets in a combination of desperation and triumph; a dance of liberation as the last resort just before it all ended. I walked on not knowing where I was headed. I stopped before a palatial-looking house that had seen better days. I had been living in upper-class houses and apartments at will, but I had never stepped into a mansion of the had-been gods so far. Even though I knew there was no one to stop me from going in, I felt strangely conscious walking through its grounds.

To my great surprise, the door creaked open when I pushed it. I walked into a huge hall. The film of dust on everything did not conceal the illness of its begottenness: crystal chandeliers, large murals painted on the walls, and opulent silken upholstery on wooden furniture that had taken great bites off a rainforest. I walked past all this into a courtyard. There was an empty, rectangular pit in the middle: a swimming pool! I had visions of people dancing boisterously and jumping into the pool fully clad. Now, it was a picture of fallen might. I spied a small alcove past the pool in the garden that somehow did not fit into the picture of decrepitude that was the rest of the building. I stepped into it cautiously. It was much bigger than I had thought, and it looked clean and recently mopped. Then I smelled it. Spicy, coconutty and peppery—the unmistakable aroma of korma! I found it in a steaming pot on the only table in the room. Without bothering to wash my hands, I found a spoon in the drawer and scooped some of the thick brown stew and ate it. It was the tastiest thing I had ever eaten. Ever since I had woken up in any case. It is probably something I had eaten and loved before the awakening. There was a great familiarity about it. I had been living on watered down honey the past two days and I was extremely hungry, moreover. Without bothering to wonder how there was real food in this house, when all I had survived on was improvised bean soup, I sat down to bury myself in that unmarked gravy.

I was so busy wolfing it down that I did not notice him enter the room. It's only when I took a break from shovelling the korma into my mouth to swallow a particularly big mouthful that I looked up and saw him standing there looking intently at me.

'Jay!' I exclaimed the moment I swallowed. And he in turn came close and bent down as if to kiss me but bit me hard on the ear.

'Ow!!!' I screamed and fought him off. As if being alone in the world wasn't bad enough, I had to be alone with a psychopath. I broke away from him and started to run when he called out rather apologetically.

'Sorry. Didn't mean to hurt you. I was worried you were cake.'

'Cake??? Do people made of cake eat korma?' I screamed more shocked than hurt.

'You are right. I'm sorry. Checking for cake has become something of a habit. It's not a risk one can take. But how do you know my name?'

'Oh … I'm … er not sure,' I faltered. That's when it struck me that I had called out his name. Was he someone I knew? There was no point trying to remember because nothing of my past—if I could call it that—had come back. My faith-like certainty based on unreliable bits of memory upon which I had been building my understanding of the current world told me he wasn't someone I had known closely—a brother, a friend, a lover. He might have been someone who had probably never moved anywhere significant beyond my peripheral vision. Like a fellow student in a crowded class that one takes for easy credits. But while I couldn't recollect a sibling's name, this guy's name was on the tip of my tongue!

'I honestly don't know. Do you remember me? I woke up a few months ago in a town uphill, a couple of days' bus journey from here. I don't remember much. I came down on a whim. I was hungry,' I explained. 'What about you?'

Jay sat on a chair, and I dragged another one over to where he sat.

'I don't remember anything either. I seem to recall that I was on a scooter on a narrow country lane. I had to stop because a cow, tethered with a long rope to a lamppost on one side of the road, had decided to graze on a bush on the other side and had stretched the rope waist-high across the road like a barrier. There were about four or five people on scooters and cars stuck like me. We had to wait until the cow's owner came and pulled it away.'

'Couldn't you have done it yourself? Pull it away, I mean.'

'The cow had a determined look on its face that discouraged interference,' he explained.

'Hmmm … that's understandable,' I said. 'And then?'

'That's what I don't know. There was a flash of some kind and everything went blank. When I came to my senses, I was all alone on that road. The cow, my fellow commuters and their vehicles had all vanished. A rope lay stretched on the road like a roadkill snake. I remember I was clean shaven when I stopped there, but when I came to I had a long beard and the hair on my head had mushroomed into a frizzy cloud. I didn't know what to do. There was a scooter nearby. I thought it was mine and got on it. But when I tried to kickstart it, it wouldn't budge. Then, a minute later it started on its own. I thought I was driving, but in fact the scooter wouldn't react to my control. I had no choice but to sit on it until it stopped on its own accord.'

That sounded very familiar. But I didn't interrupt him.

'I don't want to go into the whole bewilderment and confusion and fear and grief and everything mixed together before acceptance struck and I started living through all this because I'm sure you have gone through something similar too. I tried knocking on the door of a house. Everything was desolate. The knocker broke in my hand and I found that it was cake. I ate it. The house was cake too. The whole town was cake. The first month I lived on cake alone. Then I got sick and constipated and fat and listless. I craved savoury food. I also worried I might get diabetes and with no doctors or hospitals or anyone with any knowledge of medicine … I was worried about suffering—not so much death because I felt I had already lived through death and it wasn't all that bad. But the thought of pain and prolonged suffering was scary. There was nothing else in that town to eat. So, I left.'

I was thrilled to hear the sound of a human voice that wasn't mine. I just sat there listening intently.

'I couldn't find a bus or a car and walked for miles. The next day, I came upon a river with a boat that had its engine running. On a whim I jumped in. It was all very well for the first couple of hours. I was sailing downriver and I loved the feeling. But then the boat started to disintegrate beneath me. The boat was cake too. It turned into a slushy mess like a Parle-G biscuit dunked for a second too long in a glass of tea. I swam ashore and found myself in a village where I met a man ...'

'Met a man??? There are others?'

'Of course there are others. The man I met had met a man who had met a man ... Apparently, one per cent of the world's original population has woken up. And we are scattered all over the world. The man I met was not a settler. He had decided to travel ever since he woke up and a day or two after helping me ashore, and making sure I was well, he left and went on his way.'

'I'm glad he was a good man and helped you,' I said.

'Apparently, now there is no other way to be than good. At first, I was afraid when I saw a man in the woods after months of believing I was the only person left on the planet. But I soon realised there is nothing to fear. When one can go a whole lifetime not seeing another human, there is no need to hurt another person, if you are lucky enough to run into one. There is nothing to be gained by hurting anyone. If anything, they might know something you don't—how to do things, how to find food or heal ailments or just what's going on in general. Information is too dear to lose, and every man alive knows something no one else does.'

'Is that why you were unafraid when you saw me?' I asked.

'I was only worried you might be cake,' he said with a smile. 'Did you like the korma?'

'It was delicious! Can I have some more?'

'I'm afraid there is no more meat in it. You ate it all. But there is more in the fridge. I can thaw it and cook it separately and add it to the gravy.'

'What! I ate meat?' I asked gagging.

'Why? Are you vegetarian?'

'I don't know what I was. But I cannot get myself to eat meat anymore.'

'You do realise the meat in the cold storages across the world is just that—meat. No more animals are being killed because there are no more animals. And all frozen meat doesn't resemble anything alive.'

What he said was right. Perhaps I could lay the images of slaughter to rest.

It must have been a couple of months since we started living together that I asked Jay why the other people left in the world weren't interested in finding others and rebuilding a community.

'Do you want to rebuild a community?' he asked me.

'No,' I said.

'That's what most people feel. But if they do, it will not be deliberate, I can tell you this.'

'Jay, if you break a femur, I will nurse you back to health,' I said on impulse. He just looked at me and smiled.

After travelling together for weeks we finally found the airport. We were living in the airport for several days before a plane arrived. We hadn't discussed it, but the reason we made a home of the airport was perhaps because we had wordlessly decided to get on a plane. It was risky. What if the plane ended its inertia mid-flight and crashed? What if it took us to a place where there was no food? What if it took us back to civilisation as we'd known it and we would be required to give up the joyous nothing we had and go back to reproducing and dead-end jobs and taxes and anxiety? The physical intimacy that Jay and I had come to have was for warmth and affection and orgasm. It was to fuel our shared lives in a lonely world. We were certain we did not want to reproduce, and feared that the new place we went to might not allow us the freedom to choose. But we couldn't be complacent. We had to move and we had to know. If the plane crashed, it could lead to another 'awakening' for all we knew. We could try coming back to our dimension if we ended up in another. Either way, we had to keep going.

We walked through the gates and saw the plane. It looked back at us with its glass eye like a giant bird of prey. I ran into a fancy clothes shop and grabbed whatever I could: coats, trousers, scarves, underwear, gloves, shorts, we didn't know what we would need in the place we fetched up. Also, there was no one to put a limit to the luggage we could carry. 'We could end up in a very hot place and decide to give up wearing clothes,' Jay said and laughed, but did not stop me.

He found a ladder with wheels and we pushed it with all our might to the door and climbed to board the plane. Just before we got in, Jay leaned over and gently bit the door of the aircraft. I wasn't sure what to make of his wince.

'Well?' I asked.

'Not cake,' he said sounding relieved.

We sat in business class—something that neither of us found familiar. We fastened our seat belts and the engine revved. Soon we were cruising over the sea. I hadn't realised we were this close to the sea all along. Had we been on an island? A peninsula perhaps? And where were we heading? It could be an hour-long flight or fourteen. Would we land safely or crash?

Jay seemed to be mulling over the same questions. 'I think we are going to Gooday Nagar,' he said.

'Where is that?' I asked.

'I don't know,' he said.

Further talk seemed futile. We just looked out of the window. It was a bright morning. As we relaxed, I dug into my bag to check the clothes I had brought. Jay must have seen a quizzical expression on my face and asked me what it was.

'When all this is over, will you show me how to knot a tie?' I asked him pulling a necktie out of the bundle of clothes.

'Yes,' he said.

Acknowledgements

Several of the stories in this collection were written in the beautiful Welsh seaside town of Aberystwyth where I spent the summer of 2022 as the recipient of the Charles Wallace India Trust Fellowship in writing and translation, at Literature Across Frontiers and University of Wales Trinity Saint David. I owe much to Alexandra Büchler and Elin Haf Gruffydd Jones who facilitated my residency and were the kindest of supervisors and hosts one could ask for. They also—along with Ned Thomas—decided homelessness was too exotic an experience of British culture to be had on my first visit, and took me and Rhys in when a certain miscalculation blew away the roof over our heads towards the end of our stay. My love and gratitude to them.

I feel a warm glow to think of how the compulsive punner, Peter Banks, and his wonderful wife, Caroline, who I had met over the internet, drove all the way from Yorkshire to Ceredigion bearing gifts of beer, books, and cheese and turned our virtual friendship into a real one that I continue to cherish. When I asked Caroline if she loved Peter for his sense of humour or in spite of it, she said, with a mischievous grin, that it was the former. That prompted me to think of the line 'when we make our bed with someone, we *lie* in it', which went into one of the stories.

I want to thank the nameless Turkish gentleman I met at the bus stop in Dolgellau. When a sudden bout of sickness forced me to cut short my journey to Portmeirion and get off the bus in that unfamiliar town, he ran up to me and helped me even before I had regained the strength to ask for help. I hope he is well, wherever he is. Life is impossible without the kindness of strangers. I am grateful for this realisation.

I want to mention here Sir Tony Robinson who stood on Terrace Road one bright morning doing thingamajig in archaeology. My writing sensibility owes a great deal to British comedies of which he is a big part, and I thought he might be one celebrity I could fawn over and not be the worse for it. I introduced myself and said 'We watch *Blackadder* all the time'. Sir Tony smiled. 'And archaeology,' Rhys added—whatever that meant. Sir Tony smiled some more.

I chuckle at the memory of the elderly gentleman I ran into on the promenade one afternoon. He told me his life story about being born 'illegitimate', adopted, and then discovering his half-siblings later in life and lifting them out of poverty. But that's not what I chuckle at. He then asked me very sweetly if I missed 'mummy and daddy back home'. I was thirty-eight.

Those four months were gentle on the heart and great for creativity for which I thank the people of Aberystwyth (except that woman in Tesco who refused to sell me a bottle of cider without ID). Diolch yn fawr.

And of course, Rhys Hughes, to whom this book is dedicated: I'll consider myself accomplished if I can achieve half your excellence in prose (I am the better poet). My life now, almost entirely, consists of marvelling at our mutual musehood and the amazing coincidences that brought us together. When all this is over, will you show me how to knot a tie?

– Maithreyi Karnoor